CONSPIRACY

IAIN GALE

Quercus

First published in Great Britain in 2016 by Heron Books
This edition published in 2017 by

Quercus Editions Ltd
Carmelite House
50 Victoria Embankment
London EC4Y 0DZ

An Hachette UK company

A CIP catalogue record for this book is available
from the British Library

PB ISBN 978 1 84866 487 6
EBOOK ISBN 978 1 78429 222 5

10 9 8 7 6 5 4 3 2 1

Typeset by CC Book Production

Printed and bound in Great Britain by Clays Ltd, St Ives plc

For

Susan Watt

CONSPIRACY

Iain Gale, art critic, journalist and author, comes from a military family and has always been fascinated by military history. He is an active member of the Scottish Committee of the Society of Authors and the Friends of Waterloo Committee. He is the Editor of Scotland in Trust, the magazine for the National Trust of Scotland, and founded the Caledonian magazine. He lives in Edinburgh.

Also by Iain Gale

James Keane series

KEANE'S COMPANY
KEANE'S CHALLENGE
KEANE'S CHARGE

Jack Steel series

MAN OF HONOUR
RULES OF WAR
BROTHERS IN ARMS

Peter Lamb series

BLACK JACKALS
JACKALS' REVENGE

ALAMEIN

FOUR DAYS IN JUNE
A novel of Waterloo

1

The bright orange flames leapt high above the smoking ramparts and lit the sky over the city and castle of Badajoz, casting a glow over the weary faces of the attackers. Two distant explosions and a chorus of screams tore through the Spanish night, and mingled with the crackle of musket fire almost drowning out the words of an unseen British soldier, as he yelled a dying curse against the French. One man had heard it, however, and mouthing a passing blessing for the soldier's soul, echoed its sentiments in his own mind.

Sitting on an empty powder barrel, apparently oblivious to the symphony of agony around him, his back resting against the dry earth wall of a narrow trench, James Keane rubbed thoughtfully at the stubble on his chin and pulled out his gold pocket watch, snapping open the lid and scanning the clock face in the firelight. It was four minutes after three o'clock in the morning. Five hours had passed since their latest attack had begun and Keane still had no idea as to its success.

Somewhere close by, to his rear, a solitary horse whinnied in its death throes, and from far below his position in the siege lines, where the darkness shrouded the killing ground of the ditches, the groans and cries of scores of wounded and dying reached up to make the living shudder. Along the trench the black forms of red-coated soldiers moved in purposeful silence, but Keane remained where he was. He sat listening, conscious only of the task in hand and of his own men sitting, standing and lying close by. All of them staring, listening waiting. It seemed to Keane momentarily that they had been transported from the daylight world into some other place, some forgotten corner of hell. A place where chaos ruled and where the great ragged, gaping jaws of the breach they had blown in the city's blackened, burning ramparts swallowed up column after column of attacking redcoats. This was bloody Badajoz, the meat-grinder of Wellington's army, its every stone tainted with British blood and the unmistakable stench of death.

Since Keane and his men had been waiting here, over the past five hours, successive messengers from the storming party had relayed news, good and bad. But none of it had yet given him the information he needed. General Picton's 3rd Division of Viscount Wellington's Peninsular army had been assaulting the ramparts of the castle, and during the same time, on the other, west, side of the town, the 4th and Light divisions had been beaten back time and again while Leith's 5th Division was escalading the bastion of San Vincente. It was with the 4th though that Keane had chosen to advance, against the huge Trinidad redoubt on the eastern side of the city. And it was in the shadow of this mighty bastion that he and his men now found themselves waiting for their moment.

Just half an hour ago, another courier had come down the line and told them that Picton's men had gained a foothold inside the town. But from the sound of the fighting and the stream of wounded who had somehow made it to the lines, Keane was not so sure. It was very clear to him that the battle was still going on, unabated. The French had made a good job of the defences here. They had used everything at their disposal to ensure that the city would not fall. They had constructed lethal obstacles, flooded the ditches and placed explosive mines along the ramparts. And there had been nothing for Wellington to do but storm the place head-on.

Keane turned to one of the men beside him, seeing his features now in the growing light of dawn. 'I wish I knew what the devil was going on, Archer. It's as much of a mess as I've ever seen this army get itself into. And, dammit, we're the ones who are meant to know, aren't we?'

It was true – James Keane and his men were the eyes and ears of Wellington's army. Observers, trained to go deep behind enemy lines and discover everything they could, from the dispositions of the French troops, their corps, divisions, brigades and regiments, to what their generals had ordered for dinner. But for once they were as much in the dark as anyone else.

Archer spoke. 'Damned if I know, sir. Perhaps we should just go ahead. Follow the storming party. If they've got into the town, we need to be with them before we lose our chance, and our quarry.'

'Yes, that's my worry. Finding the man before they do. We can't allow him to be killed.' Over the past few years Keane and his men had been given some strange tasks, but this, he thought, must be one of the most bizarre. They had been ordered to get into Badajoz, in the wake of the attack which they had been told must surely, eventually, succeed, but before the place was completely secure and armed with the most rudimentary of clues as to his location, to extricate alive

at all costs a French colonel who must then be returned to
Wellington's headquarters. The orders had come directly from
Wellington himself. The colonel, Keane had been told, had in
his possession important intelligence. That was all he needed
to know, for now. He sat still again for a moment, listening
with a trained ear to the noises now and any subtle differences.
There was a curious lull in the volume of the explosions. A
change which, while imperceptible to the untrained ear, to
Keane was quite clear in what it said. It signalled an opportunity. He turned to his right. 'Sarn't Ross. It's time. Now, man.'

He turned the other way and looked for the rest of his men.
'Come on, follow me.' Then, leaping up and sword in hand, he
ran towards where the attacking force had entered the breach
and, followed by his men close up, he led them forward.

The adrenalin was pumping now, and Keane was caught
up in the thrill of the moment. This was their time. This was
what they did. But it was more than just that. Yes, they had
been tasked with rescuing a French colonel. But here was a
chance. A chance for Keane to be back at the front line of a
battle. And it felt good. For the past three years he had largely
been denied real soldiering, and he missed it. That was a hard
thing to countenance, he knew, when one looked about the
charnel house of Badajoz. But it was most certainly the truth.

In the past three years he had led his men in search of code
books, chasing French spies and befriending ruthless guerrilla
captains. They had made a name for themselves as a unique
force operating deep behind enemy lines, often cut off, relying
on their ingenuity and all the guile they had. He had chosen
them for this and had made them what they were. Had plucked
them from the jails of Portugal, even from the hangman's

noose, and given each of them a second chance. And they had repaid him fourfold. They believed in him. Would, he knew, have died for him. Some of them had. And now new faces had come in their place. And they too would follow him. Not from the threat of the cat like the rest of the army. But because they all trusted him. He hoped that now, here, leading them into God knew what, that trust would not be tested.

Looking quickly to his rear, Keane counted off nine forms, crouched and running in the darkness.

He led them down the snaking line of the British trenches, past the sleeping sentries and the dying heroes, and then without a word but raising his hand to point, altered his course over the counter scarp into the ditch in front of the curtain wall. Although the dawn was rising, the darkness was still sufficient to allow them to pass unchallenged by the British, who, exhausted stood and lay around them. He had timed it within a whisker. There was a moment when the battle would be won and the town taken, but before the enemy had time to escape in their euphoria and before the looting began. He hoped that he had judged it right. Later, and it would be too late. Earlier, and he would be leading his men into the heart of the battle. And that was expressly what he had been told not to do.

Archer, ever quick on the uptake, whispered to him, 'Isn't this just what Major Grant said not to do, sir?'

'Yes, Archer. That's quite correct. And that's precisely why I'm doing it.'

Archer smiled. It was only what he would have expected from his officer. Keane had never been one to go by the book. Hunch, guesswork and gut instinct were his way of soldiering. And they hadn't failed him yet. Keane was a gambler at heart, but sometimes, as any gambler will tell you, it helps to bend the cards or load the dice. And Keane had been known to do both.

He turned to Archer again. 'You know why we're here as well as I do. Like it or not, we've got to rescue a bloody Frenchman. There's good reason for it. That's for certain. But don't tell any of these buggers.' He nodded towards one of the British redcoats standing en garde as they passed by. 'As far as they're concerned, the only good Frenchman is a dead one. Why confuse them?'

As they turned into the traverse of the trench, ahead of them Keane saw two figures standing in their way with their backs to them, blocking their path. Both wore blue boat cloaks.

Hearing Keane's men approach, one of the figures turned and Keane saw that beneath his cloak he wore the scarlet uniform of a British officer. The other man turned and was similarly dressed and both carried their swords unsheathed, the blades catching the dawn light. Looking at the figure on the left, Keane caught his sharp, birdlike features, and within seconds he had recognized the man as Fitzroy Somerset, Wellington's military secretary, a familiar face from Keane's frequent visits to headquarters.

The man, who had been staring at Keane, spoke. 'Keane? It is Captain Keane, isn't it?'

'Yes, sir. James Keane.'

'Of course, Keane. This is Captain Richard Clarke of the 3rd Guards.' He turned to his companion, 'Richard, this is the fellow I was talking about. The spy chap. Damn good at it too. What the devil are you doing here, Keane? I thought your place was among the observing officers. Not here in the front line.'

'I'm here at the orders of the peer, sir.'

'Well I'm here to discover what the devil's going on. You're quite welcome to join us.'

'It would seem prudent, sir.'

At that moment from all around them men began to cheer, as along the communications trench that led from the rear of the position a column of men moved forward. Led by a lieutenant and a captain and two drummer boys beating out the attack, they marched without packs, their muskets held with bayonets fixed at the 'present'. Behind the officers came six pioneers, all armed with axes.

The officers of the attack column acknowledged the cheers as they passed.

One of Keane's new men, a light-fingered Geordie named Batty, turned to Ross. 'Is that the forlorn hope, sarge? I don't envy them.'

Keane replied for the sergeant. 'That's no forlorn hope, Batty. That's the leading column of the rest of the army. We've got inside, lad. And now we intend to keep the place. It's up to this lot to make sure we do.'

Somerset nodded. 'You're right. It would seem that we have gained a hold in the redoubt. It's now or never, Keane. Are you with me?'

Keane smiled. 'All the way, sir.'

As the attack column disappeared into the breach, Somerset and Clarke led the way to follow them and with them went Keane and his men. They moved fast across the causeway and into the breach where the rubble lay as if some giant infant had thrown it around in a tantrum. Emerging through the wall, they shuffled together and crossed in single file the plank which had been laid across the trench beyond. Keane wondered at how the men of the original storming party had ever managed to get past this point. It must have been hell, he thought, to go in single file under constant fire from the battlements. But the French were gone from here now and all was silent, save for the groans of the wounded, with the measure of the continuing tumult of battle coming from the city which lay before them.

They were almost across the plank when Keane looked round and caught his sergeant, Ross, a brawny Scot, gazing down into the ditch below them. He followed the man's stare and saw what seemed for a moment to be a thick, dark liquid, a river perhaps, but within seconds he realized that it was in fact a mass of writhing bodies. Men who had fallen or been blown off the narrow causeway beyond the curtain wall and had fallen into the ditch. Men who had tumbled off ladders set to mount the walls, onto the blades of the wickedly sharp *chevaux de frise* below, spikes embedded in tree trunks left by the French to line the ditches into which any attackers were bound to jump or fall. For a moment he was transfixed, rooted to the spot by this ghastly vision of human agony. As he stared the mass took proper human forms and he began to see contorted faces and the full horror of their condition.

Ross swore. 'Christ almighty, sir, look what the French have done to our boys. It's bloody hell, sir. Look at them.'

But Keane didn't look. He walked forward, determined to get into the city and get the job done. This was no place for regret and no place for sentiment. They were in, but at what expense? he wondered. Keane had never seen such wholesale slaughter.

There was another huge explosion a little distance ahead of them. Keane and the others cowered instinctively and shielded their eyes as the ground rocked. Looking up, his ears ringing, he searched for the attacking column they had been following, but saw instead only smoke and flame. There were Somerset and Clarke, standing together and similarly shaken. But of the column there was no sign. Then, slowly, figures began to emerge from the smoke. A horrifying procession of wounded and dying, some of them on fire and shrieking, others blackened and charred, sightless or holding bloody stumps of arms. Even as the city seemed about to fall at last, the French had blown a mine and the column had caught the impact. The survivors pushed past him and his men, stumbling blindly on to get back to the lines. Keane tried to stop them, but it was in vain and he could only look helplessly as too many of them missed the narrow plank bridge and fell to join their dying comrades in the ditch. Ross managed to catch hold of one of them, a drummer boy who had lost a hand. The boy looked at Keane, his blackened face a mask of terror and shock. 'The captain. He was talking to me. Then he was gone. Just gone.'

Surely, thought Keane, the French must stop now. Stop the killing. Now they must realize that Badajoz had fallen, that further fighting was foolish. Ross handed the boy to a redcoat, part of another column that had crossed the causeway and was pushing on towards the city, and told him to take him back and help the others.

Keane turned back. Spoke to the men directly to his rear: 'Silver, Martin, all of you, stay close. This place isn't ours yet. We may have taken the city, but the French are still in there. Remember our task.'

They were climbing now, Somerset leading the way, up the huge pile of debris that filled the breach. Treading on the fallen stones, he realized that he was also, with every second step, walking on softer stuff, the bodies of the attacking redcoats which had somehow, in successive explosions, been incorporated into the rubble.

Then, reaching the top of the stones, they began to descend, making their way down the storming ladders, which had been placed to take them down into the ditch before the fortress.

He had caught the stench now. The sweet, foul smell of death. And the lower they got into the ditch, the more unbearable it became. For three terrible weeks the British had besieged Badajoz. Three of the bloodiest weeks that the army had ever seen. Looking behind he saw a thin line of men following him up the rock pile, his men. Ahead of him the battle still raged, but now they knew that the forlorn hope had broken through and the British were pouring into the city.

Silver, one of his most trusted men, who had come through the last three years astonishingly unscathed, Silver shook his head. 'God knows what the lads'll be about, sir. They'll slaughter every Frenchman they see. Who knows what else. They've no love for the dagos. You remember what the Portuguese did at Coimbra? I've never known a battle like it.'

The previous day Keane had heard the tally. Almost three thousand dead. And that had been before this bloody night. Of the 27,000 men who had attacked it, he reckoned that almost one in five must surely be killed or maimed.

'Yes, they've done it for Wellington. But who's to stop them now?'

Keane worried more about what their 'brave lads' might do. He knew the British soldier. Knew him well. Most of them had 'listed for drink. His own band of mavericks was made up mostly of criminals he had plucked from the jails of Lisbon some three years ago.

But Keane's men were not bad men. Not evil. He had seen

evil in the eyes of men before. In his own regiment, the 27th Inniskilling Fusiliers, a corporal who had managed to break every rule in the book and had invented some of his own, until the truth had caught up with him. Every regiment had such men.

Keane knew that at the heart of all regiments in the British army lay a cadre of hardened criminals and he knew that it was these men who would command in the streets of Badajoz and that all the gold lace and swagger of the officers would count for nothing.

Passing through the second breach and what had once been a gate, they found themselves within the walls. Parties of red-coats were everywhere, some under command of an officer, others with an NCO. Some with no command. Many were wounded. Several seemed drunk.

They were in the San Vincente fort, a place they hadn't tried before. And here at last it seemed that they had met with success. As they pushed on, it was clear that ahead of them Leith's men were now pouring into the city from their own assault on the opposite side, and he guessed that in the north too the other divisions of the army would be pushing through the breaches where for days they had been mown down in their hundreds.

Somerset stopped and turned to Keane. 'Before we reach the French, I don't know what your purpose here is, Keane. What are your directions?'

'I need to find a certain colonel on the French staff, sir. That's all I know. I'm told that he might be in the governor's house.' He reached into his coat. 'I have a sketch map.'

Somerset waved it aside. 'Indeed. Well, I'm sure that the peer knows his purpose.

'In fact you're in luck. I'm better than any map. I know this place well, you know, from earlier days. I intend to find the French commander, General Philipon, and it's my betting that he too will be in the governor's house. Shall we go?'

Keane needed no further prompting and trotted on behind Somerset, followed by his men, as they went deeper into the enemy stronghold.

The buildings showed the evidence of a month of relentless British bombardment. Some had gone entirely, others stood roofless or with part of the walls blown away, others were still smoking from the most recent shelling and everywhere lay bodies. And among it all men were wandering or standing in groups.

Instantly, however, and bewilderingly, they suddenly found themselves at a point where those around them changed from British redcoats to the French. Keane stopped but noted that Somerset had not, seemingly undeterred by the presence of the enemy. And the French appeared to be ignoring him. It occurred to Keane that this must be the reason for the two officers wearing cloaks and he was thankful for once that he and his men wore the brown of their corps, the Guides, rather than British scarlet.

Keane turned to Silver. 'Follow me but don't speak. They're done for and they know it, but best not to give them the chance. Just follow. Pass the word.'

Silver nodded and whispered Keane's command to the next man. They hurried after Somerset and Clarke and soon found themselves in a wide square, the Place de Saint-Jean, at the end of which stood an imposing neo-classical building, enclosed with an iron fence.

Somerset called back, 'There that's it. That's the governor's house,' and leading the way, he walked towards it. There was no sign of any enemy presence around the building, nor any sentries posted on the gates which lay open, and Keane now realized that they had not encountered any French soldiers for several streets. Somerset walked to the main doors and pushed.

They swung open to reveal a large marble entrance hall with a check floor, hung with chandeliers and lined with portraits. It seemed to him for a moment that he had by some miracle walked into a ball. For the room was filled with women, well-dressed women in fine silk dresses, all of them in some degree of agitation. There were eighteen women in all: ten, two very young, in fine clothes and dripping with jewellery, who were perhaps the wives of French officers; the others, less well dressed, probably their servants. Seeing Somerset enter, one of them shrieked.

Ignoring her, the aide de camp waved his hand and gave a bow. 'Don't be afraid, ladies. We are British officers.'

There was another shriek and Keane realized that most of the women were, of course, French. Instantly he announced himself in French, and hearing their native tongue the ladies seemed to relax a little. Somerset smiled at him before turning to the ladies and himself addressing them in perfect French:

'I'm looking for the commander, General Philipon.'

'He is no longer here, sir. He has gone.'

'Well, he can't have gone far. We have the city surrounded. I have come here to accept his surrender. Where has he gone?'

None of the women spoke, until one of them, a tall hand-some woman in a bright green silk dress, came forward.

'Of course he's gone.' She looked at the others. 'What's the use? We might as well tell him. He's gone to the fort of San Cristobal.'

'And left you here? All of you? Alone?'

'He said we would be safe. Safe with the British.'

'I'm sure of that, madame. But there are others in this town. We shall leave you a guard.'

'Captain Keane?'

'Sir?'

'Post four of your men to remain here with the ladies until we return.'

'Ladies, Captain Keane's men will look after you. Isn't that so, Keane?'

'Yes, sir, of course. Sarn't Ross, take three men and guard the ladies. We're off to find Colonel Hulot.'

One of the women, a small blonde close to the front of their group, gave a little cry of surprise.

Somerset turned to her, 'Madame? Something is wrong?'

'This is my husband. Colonel Hulot is my husband.'

'Then be assured, madame, that Captain Keane will bear him safe to you here while I accept the surrender of the city from the governor.'

Keane looked at him. 'Accept his surrender, sir?'

'Yes, Keane. Didn't you guess that was my purpose in coming here? I intend to put an end to all this. General Philipon would be a fool to refuse. He's run his course. I'd value your company, Keane. Come, Major Clarke – if we are to parley we need to find ourselves a drummer.'

The two men left the house and Keane hesitated a moment before joining them.

He addressed the women in French. 'Ladies, you have

nothing to fear. My men will protect you. Sergeant Ross is in command. You are free to do as you wish, but you must stay inside.'

Madame Hulot approached him, 'Captain, you were sent to take my husband?'

'Yes. But not as a prisoner, madame. He has information we need and which we believe he intends us to have.'

'You say he is a traitor?'

'No, not a traitor. But he does have important information that will help the future of France.'

She nodded. 'I see. He is a true Frenchman, sir, a truly loyal son of France.'

Keane looked at her and saw a passion in her eyes, mixed with fear. So that was it, he thought. The colonel's great secret. Not all Frenchmen were Bonapartists. There were still some, thank God, like Captain Hulot and his pretty wife, who believed in the old order or perhaps, like others who after years of striving for Bonaparte's empire, were simply now disillusioned. Keane realized at once why he had not been given more information on Hulot. This was merely the latest in a series of actions intended to sow disunity in the French command by finding royalist collaborators on the staff of every one of Napoleon's marshals. The idea had come from St James's, from the Prince Regent himself apparently, via his spokesman at Wellington's headquarters, an odious man named Cavanagh, Colonel Rupert Cavanagh. Keane, along with not a few others, disliked him intensely. The problem was that Cavanagh held influence at court and had the ear of the prince. He knew well that Cavanagh's intention was ultimately to discredit Wellington and it was for this reason that he continued to advance hare-brained schemes. Thankfully most of them had been put to rest. But occasionally even Wellington had to kowtow to London, and this was one of those moments. In fact the idea, thought Keane, was not so bad. But he was damned if he would let Cavanagh take the credit for it. He looked again at Madame Hulot.

'As you say, madame. And there is always honour in following our true beliefs.'

Keane was interrupted by a din from the doorway. Somerset had returned, and with him a drummer boy who was beating a tattoo. 'Come along Keane. We've no time to lose.'

Keane summoned the men who were not remaining and together they left the house. Immediately they were out, Ross secured the doors.

Somerset led them northwards through the streets where already the victorious redcoats were beginning to break into shops. Keane paid them no heed but hurried on behind Somerset, who did indeed appear to know the way. At length they came to a causeway, littered with the bodies of the dead, French and British.

It was now six o'clock in the morning and Somerset, advancing with Clarke and his drummer ahead of the others, stopped at the doors of the San Cristobal and called up to General Philipon to surrender. It happened quickly and remarkably, without fuss, given the appalling suffering which the French had inflicted in their stubbornness.

With a white handkerchief tied to a bayonet, held by a sergeant before him and his remaining staff officers and perhaps fifty men, General Philipon marched out to surrender. Keane was surprised at his age and, as he drew close to the man, his abundant grey hair. Somerset accepted the general's sword with customary grace and Keane approached him. 'I beg your pardon, general, but I would be most obliged if you could indicate to me Colonel Hulot.'

The general looked at Keane with weary eyes and pointed towards an officer behind him. 'There, captain, that's Hulot.'

Keane walked across to the colonel. 'Colonel Hulot?'

'Yes.'

'At last. I do confess, I thought I wouldn't find you, sir. James Keane. I come direct from Wellington.'

They made their way quickly back from the fort through the violent, darkened streets, lit with the orange light of the burning city. There was no other way to reach the British camp save to return through the shattered citadel. Keane was shocked that in just the past half an hour since they had come this way before, the situation had become ten times worse. Every street corner now witnessed some new outrage, some act of cruelty, and several times Keane was of a mind to stop and help. But he knew it was impossible and pointless, so glancing away he pushed ahead, mindful of the task in hand.

As they turned into the square where they had left Ross and the Frenchwomen, Keane was aware of a commotion coming from outside the house. Shouting and raised voices in English.

He turned to Hulot. 'That's coming from your house, colonel.' He quickened his pace, 'What the devil's going on?'

As they neared the door Keane saw that there was a mob of soldiers outside, redcoats, and after a few more paces heard the sound of splintering wood.

'Christ, they've got inside. Let's go.'

Keane, followed by his men and the others, ran to the doors, but already they had crashed open and several dozen redcoats were now in the hallway. Keane moved fast and together with his men, Hulot, Somerset and a dozen of the French prisoners, pushed through the crowd towards the women. He could see Sergeant Ross and the other men he had left forming a ragged line in front of the Frenchwomen and headed straight towards them.

'Ross, hold hard.'

Ross, seeing Keane, drew his line together and had them level their carbines so that they were pointed at the advancing redcoats, who stopped just as Keane reached them. They were led by a sergeant whose filthy tunic, like that of several of the others, bore green facings. All showed the signs of the battle, blood and soot mixed in equal measure on the washed-out brick red of their coats and across their grey overall trousers. While the sergeant still wore his stovepipe shako, others had adopted other headgear, a French shako, an officer's bicorne and, most bizarrely, a turban, and all were armed with a variety of weapons, ranging from muskets and bayonets to swords of all nations and an axe. The sergeant held a long curved light cavalry sabre with an ivory grip, clearly a prize taken from a dead Frenchman. He stared at Keane and then at the women, who were now screaming with terror.

Keane looked the man straight in the eye. 'Sergeant, you seem to have lost your way. The French here are already our prisoners.'

The man sneered and grinned at Keane. 'Well, that'd be a strange thing, sir, wouldn't it? And how do we know that you're not French yourself – you in yer shite-brown coat.'

The man spoke in an Irish brogue and reeked of alcohol. Rum, thought Keane, brandy most certainly and a copious quantity of wine. He replied, anxious to keep the situation in control, 'The name is Keane, Captain Keane to you, sergeant, and this shit-brown coat, as you call it, is my uniform. The uniform of His Majesty's Corps of Guides.'

To his right and left his ten men now stood on guard, their cavalry carbines having been lowered until they were pointing directly at the leading redcoats. From beyond the open doors came the sound of gunshots, mingled with the shouts of soldiers' shrieks and women's screams.

The army had been pushed harder in these last few days than he had ever seen. All the officers knew it. Knew that at any time keeping discipline was like sitting on a powder keg, just waiting for the spark to set it alight. And now, it seemed to Keane, someone had lit that fuse. And when the fuse burnt down, there would be only one result: mutiny.

He smiled at the sergeant. 'Sergeant, would you mind taking your men back out into the street. The ladies are becoming agitated.'

'Is that so, sir?' Again the man said the word in a sneer. 'Well, if that's them looking agitated, let's give them something to be agitated about. We'll agitate them right enough. Won't we, lads? We'll give them a proper seeing-too. And we'll have that gold and them sparklers off them first.'

The soldiers shouted their agreement and together the mob of redcoats took a step towards Keane and the women. The sergeant grinned again, and waving his looted sabre in the air looked back at his men before starting to move forward again. But then he stopped, his eyes still fixed on his men. For as the sergeant had glanced away, Keane too had stepped forward, and as he had done so his right hand had flashed to his left side and in an instant had drawn his own sword, a light cavalry model with a razor-sharp butcher's blade, which he now pressed, with the light touch of a fencer, to the man's throat. Keane spoke slowly, deliberately.

'You will take your men and you will leave this place now. Do not return, and consider yourself fortunate to take away your life.'

The sergeant was breathing heavily now, partly from fear of the blade at his throat and partly from fury. He managed to twist his face to stare at Keane, who held the blade close enough to draw a spot of blood. As he did so, however, one of the man's men moved forward and, raising the sword he held in his hand, aimed a clumsy, drunken blow at Silver. It was a bad mistake to make and the worst choice of adversary. With a single deft movement, Silver raised his carbine, swung it round and holding the heavy, brass-capped butt high, used it as a club against the redcoat, bringing it down with ferocious strength and splitting his head clean open. The man crumpled to the floor, spilling blood and brains, and Keane edged the point of his sword a millimetre closer to the sergeant's jugular. Three of the women screamed and one fainted, but was caught by her maid as she fell to the floor.

The redcoats froze, panic on their faces, uncertain of what to do. At length, one of them bent over the fallen man before looking up at the sergeant. 'He's dead, Sergeant O'Gara.'

The sergeant, trying not to move Keane's blade any closer to his throat, managed to mutter, 'You'll pay for this, whoever you are.'

Keane smiled and kept the blade where it was. 'Now, now, Sergeant O'Gara, don't get so agitated. You'll hurt yourself if you're not careful. Now call off your dogs before anyone else gets hurt.'

O'Gara mouthed the command and whispered the words, 'Right, boys, get out. They're not worth it.'

At last Keane relaxed the blade and O'Gara grabbed at his throat, rubbing it where the blade had touched. Keane kept the sword levelled and pointed at the dead redcoat. 'Now get out and take this pile of shit with you, and thank God it wasn't you.'

Two of the redcoats picked up the corpse and together they backed out of the room and into the madness of the street.

O'Gara stared hard at Keane's eyes. 'I know you, sir. And I'll see you again. Mind if I don't.'

Then he turned, and with his men was lost in the mass of redcoats who now filled the streets outside. Keane shouted, 'Shut those doors and bar them. Garland, Martin, get upstairs. Check the windows. Archer, Silver, you others, cover this floor. Check the doors. I want anyone you find in here with us.'

Colonel Hulot approached Keane, holding his wife, 'Thank you, captain. That was well done.'

'Thank you, sir. I'm only pleased that we arrived when we did. A few minutes later and it would have been very different.'

'Unthinkable.'

Keane looked across to where Somerset was reuniting General Philipon with his wife and two daughters. He smiled and, leaving the two most recent additions to his command on sentry at the door, went in search of Sergeant Ross.

Silver had done well to do what he had. Brute force was the only language that men such as O'Gara understood, and Silver had seen exactly where the situation had been leading. Keane would have expected nothing less from him, or from any of the men he now counted as not only his soldiers but his friends.

He climbed the staircase of the house and, standing at an open window looked down, into the street below. The place was alive with redcoats. But they were no longer soldiers. The army had lost its command and was transformed into no more than a mob. As he looked on, a group of redcoats broke down the door of a house, went inside and returned laden with bottles, two of which fell to smash on the cobbles. A third man emerged, dragging with him a young woman who was screaming and hitting him. He turned and slapped her face and she stopped and searched with desperate eyes for a saviour. But Keane could do nothing. He knew that to draw attention to themselves would only be to invite disaster. So he watched as the girl was dragged away by the redcoats and as two men, one in French uniform, the other a civilian, were bludgeoned to death in the gutter. Martin was at his side.

'I could shoot their leaders, sir, easily, if you tell me who they are. That might stop them.'

'Nothing's going to stop them, Will. And that would just turn them on us. You can't stop an army that's this much out of control. All you can do is hope that it burns itself out. They've taken enough in this place and now they're paying it back. And it doesn't matter to them who they're hurting – French, Portuguese, their own kind. They're all just as guilty in their eyes. Just as much to blame for what they've gone through. What they've seen. They need to get rid of their pain.'

'But, sir, look at what they're doing. There must be something we can do.'

'There's nothing that can be done, Will. All we can do is wait.'

But the rioting did not stop. It went on all night and into the following day. And the longer it continued, the more concerned Keane became that at some stage, sooner or later, Sergeant O'Gara would reappear, and he knew that next time it might not end so well.

2

Keane was out of sorts. Between them a bunch of French-women, a mob of mutinous redcoats and a staff officer over-anxious to cover himself in glory had ruined his rare chance of seeing real soldiering. Yes, they had found Hulot and succeeded in getting him out of the city, against the odds, and he should have been pleased. But that was far from the case.

Silver noticed his mood, 'Something up, sir?'

'You might say that, Silver. Yes, something's up. What do you reckon to this business?'

'Sir?'

'This work we do.'

'You say it yourself, sir. It's vital work, vital for victory. We take our orders from Nosey himself, sir, sorry, Lord Wellington, don't we? Must be important if it comes from him. That's how I feel about it, sir.'

'But don't you miss it? Real soldiering. The sort of thing we did, might have done, last night?'

'Don't know, sir. We see enough Frenchies, and I'd rather be with you and the lads dodging around than forced to stand stock still in a line and wait for a round-shot to blow off my head.'

Keane laughed. 'I dare say you're right. If it's odds you are looking at, they're on our side rather than the poor buggers in the front line. I just can't help thinking, is this really what I joined for?'

'Why did you join, sir? You've never told us that.'

Keane said nothing for a while and then, 'It's not simple, Silver. It has to do with family and duty and something someone did for me once. And a notion that was put in my head.'

They were standing, with the rest of the men a short distance away, outside the building in the fort of San Cristobal which Wellington had taken as his headquarters. In fact it was the same building to which General Philipon and his staff had fled the previous day and where Somerset had found them. But now it was filled with red-coated officers, and having turned over Colonel Hulot to his superiors, Keane waited to be summoned.

At length he was shown in. The tall room, the great hall of the fortress, was crowded with red-coated staff officers and a few Portuguese. Wellington was standing, looking grave, in conversation with a number of staff officers, two of whom Keane recognized as Sir Thomas Picton and Sir James Leith. Their conversation was animated and anxious. Another officer approached him from across the room.

'James, good to see you. I heard that you were in the thick of it last night.'

'Only obeying our orders, sir, nothing more.' Keane smiled.

The new officer was Major Colquhoun Grant, Keane's closest contact on the staff, Wellington's senior intelligence officer and his own direct superior. He smiled at Keane. 'Well, welcome back.'

'Thank you, sir.' He nodded across to Wellington. 'I imagine that they're discussing last night.'

'Yes, it's a bad business. Damned bad. I've never seen it worse. Not just one regiment, James, or even one brigade, but the whole army near as dammit. Only had the guards and the cavalry to control it. In the end we had to leave them to it. Nothing we could do.'

'At least we managed to get the general out and his staff. Not to mention their ladies.'

'Yes, and a few others, but God alone knows what happened to those left behind.'

Wellington had raised his voice now. It was not something that Keane had witnessed often. 'Well, God knows what will happen to the miscreants. We only just escaped with our lives.'

'Oh yes, Wellington has decided on that. There's nothing to be done with most of them. How can you flog or hang an entire army? He's going to hang a few to make an example, and have a few of the ringleaders beaten, if we can find them, and that will be that.'

'Apart from the misery of those who suffered.' Keane thought of the face of the Irish sergeant, filled with hatred. 'I could name you one man who needs to feel the end of the hangman's rope.'

'If you can name him, if he has any sense he won't have rested his heels for long.'

Keane nodded. 'I suppose you're right, sir. I imagine we'll lose a few men that way.'

'Oh, I dare say that some will run. But they'll be caught eventually by the provosts. Or die at the hands of the French more likely – or the guerrillas. No one likes a deserter, James.'

The door opened and Colonel Hulot entered, accompanied

by another British staff officer. Grant greeted him warmly. 'Colonel, I trust that you are recovered?

'Keane, I thought that it might benefit you to hear the colonel's intelligence directly from him, so we are all in agreement. Colonel?'

Colonel Hulot looked at Keane and began to speak. 'Captain, you will have realized, that I am no longer a follower of Bonaparte.'

It was strange to hear a Frenchman, an officer at that, talk of Napoleon as anything other than 'the emperor'.

Hulot continued. 'For too long he has ruled my country. He has sacrificed its sons on the altar of his ambition, and look where we are. His greed knows no limits. Spain will be the death of him. Already it is sucking away our lifeblood. I have seen some terrible things here, captain, Your Grace. Terrible things done to my men and terrible things done by them also, in the name of our glorious emperor.'

He paused. 'I cannot let it continue. That is why I have given myself to you. I am a royalist at heart. My family met their end at the guillotine. I myself fled to Switzerland, and when the time was right I returned and joined the army. I am a good soldier, and Bonaparte rewards good soldiers. So here I am. I want to live to see the king back on the throne of France.'

Wellington had extricated himself from his conversation and had been listening to the colonel. Now he nodded.

'And I am not alone.'

Keane was now interested. 'Sir?'

'There are others like me who would bring down the tyrant. They tried twice, once in 1800 and once 1804. But both times they failed. Now there are more of us and we must succeed.'

Keane spoke. 'You mean to start a plot against Napoleon?'

'Yes, but not just a plot, a military coup. This madness must end now.'

Wellington took over. 'What Colonel Hulot has told us, Keane, is that there is a movement in the French army which, if provided with enough support and under the right leadership, would be in a position to take power. If not immediately, at least to undermine the army from the inside while we attack it in battle.' He turned to the man on his left. 'Major Grant?'

'Yes, we've known about the existence of a few cells of counter-Bonapartist insurgency in the French army for some time now, but we've never had firm enough leads to penetrate them. Colonel Hulot is the vital link we have been waiting for.'

At last another figure stepped forward. Keane had been expecting this.

Colonel Cavanagh smiled at Hulot. 'Yes, this is all the most tremendous news. Well done, Captain Keane. It is precisely as I predicted, is it not, Your Grace? Here we have the evidence that the Prince Regent himself proposed: that the French soldiery have had enough of Bonaparte and are ready to rise against him. All that we need to do now is to go to their aid.'

Wellington looked at Cavanagh with barely disguised disdain, 'It may not be so cut and dried, colonel. Such things hang in the balance and we do not yet know the full extent of this anti-Bonapartism. I have no reason at all to doubt Colonel Hulot's intelligence, nor indeed his own sentiments. But surely we must first ascertain the depth of feeling in the army.'

'As you will, Your Grace, but if you want my opinion, and indeed that of my masters in London and the prince himself, we have no time to lose. We should strike at the centre of Napoleon's command in Spain while the iron is still hot.'

Grant spoke. 'So, colonel, what would you propose we do?'

'I would get a man in there. Inside the French army. Why, Captain Keane here would be just the man. Once inside he would be able to gauge the sentiment and then advise us on how best to exploit it.'

Wellington smiled. 'Yes, Cavanagh, that sounds like an admirable idea. Eh, Keane?'

Keane stared at Wellington. 'My lord, with all due respect, isn't it a little foolhardy? What chance might it have of success?'

'Oh, I should think at least fifty per cent, wouldn't you say so, Grant?'

'Yes, sir, about that, I should say.'

Cavanagh spoke, smiling at Keane. 'Captain Keane, it sounds almost as if you might be reluctant to take on such a role. Surely not? I have heard that you are fearless. Can you really be afraid?'

'Not afraid, colonel, merely sensible to the fact that there are calculated risks and those which might be simply unworkable.'

'And you are telling me that my plan, the Prince Regent's own plan, is not "workable". Are you quite sure that is what you intended to say, captain?'

'Not at all, sir. I approve of your plan. I am merely attempting to be prudent.'

Wellington spoke. 'Well then, it's decided. Captain Keane will infiltrate Marshal Marmont's staff at our earliest opportunity and will observe the extent of royalist sentiment therein, reporting back to us before we take further action.'

Grant nodded. 'That would seem appropriate, Your Grace.'

Keane stared at him. How on earth could Wellington and Grant, the two men in whom he had placed his trust these past three years, possibly be suggesting such a suicidal course of action based on a hare-brained plan put forward by an officer whom all three of them considered incompetent and merely the fop of the Prince Regent, who himself was merely indulging a whim to play at war? It was beyond comprehension. It was clear though that any protest would only incite Cavanagh again to cries of cowardice. Keane merely nodded and agreed in turn.

Cavanagh grinned. 'Splendid. I shall send word to the prince. He will be delighted. Good day, Your Grace, gentlemen.'

He turned, walked to the door and left the room. As soon as it had closed behind him Wellington shook his head and looked at Grant. 'Explain, Grant, if you would.'

Grant walked across to Keane. 'My dear James, I can see that you're wondering what the devil's going on and well you might. Have we, you are thinking, taken leave of our senses? The answer, I'm pleased to say, is no. What we might say to Colonel Cavanagh and what we might think are two entirely different things and we would no more send you into the French army than off to the moon.'

Keane sighed with relief. 'Then thank God, sir. I truly thought that you had lost your mind. It is surely the most ridiculous scheme. Certainly we must nurture any royalist spirit there might be, but to send in a British officer, any officer, would be suicide.'

Grant nodded. 'Yes, James, it is a ridiculous scheme, but don't become too complacent. We've another task for you.'

Keane sighed. This came as no great surprise to him. Both Wellington and Grant were old hands in coming up with extraordinary tasks for him, schemes that in effect often rivalled the absurdity of that which they had all three just dismissed.

'Really, sir? How very intriguing.'

Grant laughed. 'Don't be funny, James. We know you too well. You're wondering what new torture we've concocted for you. You thought that you had escaped the maddest plan in Christendom and find that you've dropped straight into the fire.'

'Yes, sir, you could put it that way.'

'I'll be plain then. We too have a plan by which we can harness the anti-Bonapartist feeling that is undoubtedly brewing in France.'

Wellington took over. 'My agents across Europe, Keane, and those who report to Lord Bute have been sending back intelligence for some time affirming that throughout the empire movements are stirring which intend to bring it down. It is our purpose to harness those forces.'

'This sounds uncannily like the scheme of which Colonel Cavanagh was just speaking.'

Wellington shook his head, 'No, no. You could not be more mistaken, Keane. It's quite different. Far more subtle.'

Grant explained. 'We want you to take two of your men and ride into enemy territory.'

Keane smiled. This was nothing new, merely the everyday round of being an observing officer.

'Then we want you to get yourselves captured.'

'Sir?'

'You heard aright. You must arrange it so that you are all taken prisoner by the French. You know that they know a great deal about you, James. There is a price on your head. Not, I'm happy to say dead or alive, as yet at least, but any man who brings you in as his prisoner will get 20,000 francs.'

Keane shrugged. 'I knew that there was a reward, but that's pretty good.'

'You're valuable to them, Keane. In fact you've become something of a legend.'

'And once we're captured, sir?'

'Then you somehow manage to make your way to Paris. It's my guess that you will be sent there in any case. There are people there who would kill to talk to you. In Paris, or before if you can manage it, you must escape.'

'Break my parole? That's hardly the honourable thing to do.'

Wellington spoke. 'You, Keane, know, better than many others, that this war is no longer about honour. It's a game of *sauve qui peut*. Yes, break your parole. You have my blessing, if that's what it takes.'

'Thank you, sir. And once we arrive in Paris?'

'You will make your way to our agent there who will provide you with a new identity, a safe address and money to finance your stay.'

'Our stay?'

'It is our intention that you should remain in Paris for some time. You will have two areas of operation. Firstly we need to know what Bonaparte is planning. It's clear that something's up. He has been for some months now. He seems to be mobilizing a large army and we need to know where exactly it's making for. Secondly though, we need you to find out the level of support for the anti-Bonaparte factions. We believe there are cells of Frenchmen who have it in their mind to rise up against him.'

'This does seem not unlike Colonel Cavanagh's plan with the army, sir. I really have to protest, Your Grace. I cannot leave my men. I am a soldier, sir. I must be here, on the ground, close to the fighting, with the army. Not hiding in the stinking back alleyways of a French city. Your Grace surely has other agents who are better suited to such a role. It is not in my nature. I am not a spy, sir. I am an officer.'

Wellington turned on him. 'You are exactly what I choose to make you, Captain Keane. And if I say you are a spy, then that is what you will be. In point of fact, that is what you have been these past three years. I have no concern with your trials of conscience over what might be honourable behaviour, nor with your attachment to your men. I require you to travel to Paris and undertake this mission. Should you succeed, I will be only to happy to discuss your prospects, promotion even. But for the present I must order you to put this plan into action, whatever you think of it. And it had better work.'

As Wellington turned away from them, Keane, regretting what he had said, spoke. 'I assure you, Your Grace, that I shall do everything in my power to ensure that it does.'

As Wellington ignored him and walked away from them, Grant carried on. 'It's true, James. It is different from Colonel Cavanagh's plan. And that's the point. This plan is far more ambitious. Far more daring.'

'More daring than putting a British officer into the French staff?'

'Well, yes and no. What we want you to do, once you've reconnoitred the situation, is to engage with each of the rebel leaders and assure them of our support. You will have access to sufficient gold to persuade them. We need to know contact details, locations, how large a force each of them can muster. How many arms they have and where we might deliver further equipment. Once we have all the intelligence we need, we'll pull you out.'

'I see. So the idea is to attack the empire from within as well as engaging it in pitched battles.'

'Precisely. If we can achieve something in the French capital, something truly spectacular that might confound Napoleon and make other potential rebels think seriously about an insurrection, then we will have succeeded. Also, and this is what the peer is concerned about, it's a chance to upstage Cavanagh's plan with the French army completely. Cavanagh's faction will look foolish. It is wholly his plan, not the prince's, and as soon as ours works the prince will claim it as his own, you mark my words.'

Keane began to see now and realized that their intention was well grounded. Quite apart from that, he knew that he had a duty to Wellington, and the commander in chief's talk of promotion had also not gone unnoticed. 'When do we start?'

'As soon as you can. I don't think you'll get anything more from Colonel Hulot. He's played his part, and he's decided to remain with us, with his wife. We think he might go down rather well in London.'

'Just as I might "go down" in Paris, do you think?'

'This is no time for joking, James. Besides, in his case, there will be no deception involved. Have you any idea who you'll take with you?'

'I had them in my mind as soon as you told me, sir. Archer and Silver.'

'Yes, of course, the grave robber and the housebreaker.'

Keane smiled. 'The doctor, sir. You will recall that Archer was a trainee doctor when he was caught.'

'As I said. Caught robbing graves, doctor or not. Nevertheless, a good choice. The doctor, as you call him, could quite easily pass as an officer and Silver might make a good servant for you both.' Grant placed an avuncular hand on Keane's shoulder.

'James, do take care, won't you? We should hate something to happen to you before you've even got to Paris.'

'I'll keep your advice in mind, sir. I'm sure that all will be fine.'

But as he turned and left the hall, Keane knew that he was lying. As hare-brained schemes went, this was surely one of the very best.

3

Keane had become used to surprises while serving as an exploring officer, but it had taken some time for the reality of the task to become clear to him. Now, four days after his meeting with Wellington and as he began to prepare to depart, he went over it again in his mind. Using Colonel Hulot's information Wellington and Grant had come up with a plan to end all plans. They intended to send Keane to Paris, right into the heart of Bonaparte's Imperial machine. Initially he would report back with intelligence about the emperor and his troops' movements. But what was really expected of him was to galvanize what appeared from the reports of Wellington's agents to be a growing movement against the empire. What they asked for and what they wanted were in fact different things. What they really wanted was an uprising, or a coup. Something that would strike a note for freedom. What they needed, Keane knew, was to impress the Prince Regent and to outwit his political and military henchmen. This was high-level internal politics played out on the international stage and Keane had just become, for the moment, the principal player. It was a daunting task and he dearly hoped that he might be its equal.

Since 1809 Keane had been learning his job the hard way. Trial and error were his only means and he had to rely solely on his wits and the talents of his men. No one had written the manual of how to be a good intelligence officer. All he knew was that he had to get information and get it while it was still of value.

He sat on a wooden biscuit box in his tent in the British lines on the north side of the city, in the shadow of the fort of San Cristobal, now Wellington's headquarters, and attempted to sew up a hole that had been torn in his tunic three nights before, during the fracas with the redcoats. The place still had the stench of death over it and no amount of gin or brandy seemed to be able to wash it away from his nostrils. It was always the way after a battle, but here at Badajoz, where so many had died in such a small, enclosed space, the stench seemed especially powerful. Keane cursed.

He was making a pig's ear of the sewing and he knew it. He turned to Garland. 'You any good at this sort of thing?'

The big man shook his head and showed Keane his huge, ham-like hands before laughing.

Keane tried again. 'Will?'

'I'm afraid I've never been very good with a needle and thread. My ma used to do it all, else give it to one of the maids.'

Silver piped up. 'Oh, here we go. Hark at Mister Martin. "One of the maids".'

Keane was well aware of Martin's origins. He had been compelled to enlist in the army after having had his way with one of the farm-maids and producing an unwanted heir. They all knew about it, but as far as Keane was concerned, in his unit, the past was not somewhere that was often visited. He preferred his men to focus on the present. Any regrets, any mistakes, and they all had enough of those, were best forgotten. It was an unwritten law.

He snapped, 'That's enough, Silver. We've all seen better days in some way. What about you . . . ow!'

He cursed himself for sticking the needle into his thumb. 'Damn, you wouldn't think a thumb could have such a quantity of blood in it.'

Silver spoke. 'I'm no good with a needle, sir, but you might try Gabriella.'

It was all the cue Keane had been waiting for. He held out his torn coat to Silver. 'Would you oblige me? There's a good fellow.'

Silver knew when he had been caught. Taking the coat he walked to find his wife. The two had been married under common law for three years, ever since Keane had rescued him from jail and Gabriella from the life of a prostitute in Lisbon. They doted on one another and she had followed him bravely through three years of campaigning in all weathers and against all perils.

Keane turned back to Archer. 'You see. I waited my time and exploited the opportunity when it came. Let that be a lesson to you in tactics.'

Archer laughed. 'Yes, sir. You played it well. And you've only a minor casualty.'

'Worth it for the fine job Gabriella will do on my coat. I need to speak to you. In confidence.'

'Sir?'

'I have orders from Major Grant.'

'A new assignment, sir?'

'A new assignment, and to be honest with you I'm

more than a little unhappy. It will mean splitting up the company.'

'Destroying the unit, sir? Surely not.'

'Not destroying it, Archer, but that is surely what will happen should we not return.'

'We, sir?'

'You and Silver and me.'

Archer said nothing. Keane continued, 'Of course I have to accept it. It's an order. But it doesn't go easy.'

For a few minutes both men were silent. He poked at the earth at his feet with a stick, creating pictures in the dust. A map of Spain with France beyond it and, along the line of a long road, the circle of Paris. He had agreed to obey the orders. Of course he had; Keane was a soldier, body and soul. Trained to obey orders and to do his duty. He lived by the code of honour of an officer, and while he might protest, there was nothing he could do that would persuade him to disobey a superior when given a direct order. Certainly in the past and he presumed in the present, he had managed to interpret certain orders creatively and to bend the rules. But this was clear-cut.

Yet in his heart he was torn between duty and instinct. While his head told him to obey, his heart said that he should not leave his men. They were a close-knit team. He had made them what they were, and to leave them and travel thousands of miles into France was in his mind to betray them, to leave them leaderless. He would have to have some assurance from Grant at least if not the peer that should he not return the men would be treated well and honoured for everything they had done under his command. It would be all too easy for them to be dispersed and forgotten. And that he could not allow to happen.

But he had another duty apart from that to his men. Wellington had done something extraordinary in the last three years. He had taken an army lacking in direction and of questionable morale and made it his own. And with that army he had beaten a French force more than five times its size. He had done so through brilliant strategy and tactics in the field and through the use of some extraordinary initiatives. He had compelled the people of Portugal to burn their own fields and abandon their villages and towns to the invader, and in doing so he had denied the enemy any source of supply. He had created his own logistical services and not least Keane's own service, the Corps of Guides with its role as the eyes and ears of the army. The army, like the whole of the Peninsula, owed much to Wellington, as did Keane himself. He had been plucked from his role as an infantry officer in a line regiment and given powers beyond his dreams. Of course at the same time, and much to his regret, he had left behind the life of that officer and the front-line action which it involved. But ultimately he had a duty to Wellington and it was this he knew which would prevail.

At last Archer could wait no longer. 'What is it, sir? Can you not tell us now?'

Keane looked up. 'Oh, it's a really good one this time. For your ears only, Archer, for the present at least. The peer wants us – the three of us – to get ourselves taken prisoner and then to escape our captors and somehow get into Paris. And once we're there he wants us to start a revolution. What do you think to that?'

Archer shook his head, but he was smiling. 'I think it's quite mad. Of course, sir. But it's no more mad than many of the things we've managed before, sir.'

Keane wasn't sure yet himself what he thought of their plan. He trusted Grant implicitly. He often thought that the man had become like a father to him. But did he, he asked himself, really believe that between them he and Archer could incite a rebellion that might help to topple the regime of the most powerful man in the world? And who were these shadowy figures, described by Colonel Hulot? He had only one name as yet. Grant had mentioned a man to him in Paris, Macpherson, and had promised him details of where he might be found.

He wondered about Hulot himself. Might he not, Keane wondered, just as easily be a Bonapartist agent, planted in Badajoz to infiltrate their own organization? Grant had hinted that even having checked the man's connections with the exiled Bourbons, he was not entirely sure of the colonel. Keane was sure that Grant would not make an error over such a thing, but such was the confusion now in this game of intelligence that he could no longer be totally certain.

The thought worried him and he wondered if there might be a way to establish Hulot's credibility. That was it. That was the answer, surely. If he were somehow to prove that Hulot was in fact a Bonapartist spy, then the colonel's information would be utterly discredited and the mission would have to be aborted. It was a long shot, but it was all that he had.

Archer spoke, interrupting his thoughts. 'Sir, don't you agree? We've always managed it before. All we have to do is believe we can do it. We can bluff our way through anything. Well, you can. I'd believe anything you told me, sir, and the Frenchies will too. You can lie with the best of them.'

Keane smiled at him. 'I'm not quite sure how I should take that, Archer, but I'll suppose it was a compliment.'

But what Archer had said made him think again, and it suddenly occurred to him that perhaps there was one simple way to ascertain whether Colonel Hulot was indeed, as the commander in chief was fond of saying, 'the genuine article'. Philipon had been only too ready to point the man out. It had all somehow been too easy. He decided that more proof were needed. It would be desperate, immoral even, but he had to be sure that his hunch was wrong.

Waiting until Gabriella had finished mending his tunic with her expert touch, Keane retrieved it and, slipping it on over his shirt, began to walk quickly from their bivouac, unseen by his men, and on up the hill towards the fort. Through the gate he entered the courtyard and walked across the cobbles to Wellington's headquarters building. The red-coated sentry from the 1st Guards, recognizing him from the previous day, saluted and made way. But Keane stopped short of the doorway. Instead he turned to the right and headed towards the living quarters where the French prisoners of rank were being held.

He had recalled Grant telling him that Colonel Hulot was to be taken that afternoon some miles to Elvas, to give some particular information about codes to George Scovell, and, knowing Scovell's propensity for exactitude, was playing a hunch that the Frenchman would not yet have been returned. Keane crossed an inner courtyard and came to the gate of the prisoners' quarters. The guard here too saluted and allowed him to pass. The prisoners had been placed in the city guard's rooms, which were around a yard in the centre of which stood a large ornamental fountain topped with a statue of a knight. He recognized two of the servant women from three nights before standing at the fountain using the water to scrub at some laundry. They looked up and one of them seemed to acknowledge him and turned to her companion, who gave him a smile. Keane went up to them and asked in French directions to Colonel Hulot's quarters. The smiling woman pointed towards the far wall, where a door lay open beneath a balcony. Thanking her, Keane walked across and knocked at the open door. A voice from within, a woman's voice, called, 'Come in.'

Madame Hulot was sitting in a chair looking out of the window down onto the land below and the road along which her husband was soon to return. She turned as Keane entered and rose from the chair, gathering about her the tapestry on which she had been at work and laying it on the circular table that stood in the centre of the room. She seemed surprised to see him.

'Captain . . . I'm sorry, I don't have your name.'

'Keane, madame, James Keane.'

'Captain Keane, how nice to see you. You were so kind to me, to all of us. My husband is eternally grateful.'

'Thank you, madame. It's about your husband that I have come to see you.'

'Really, about Colonel Hulot? On what account?'

'I'm very much afraid that I have some bad news.'

He turned and gently closed the door of the room. Turning back, he saw that she had sat down and was staring at him, ashen-faced. 'You have bad news, about my husband?'

'I'm afraid so. It would appear that there was an accident as he and his escort were returning from Elvas. A snake frightened the colonel's horse. He was thrown. It is most unfortunate.'

'He is hurt? Badly?'

'Worse than that, I'm afraid, madame. Your husband is dead.'

Madame Hulon stared at him for a moment in disbelief and

then looked away. Then, very quietly, she began to sob. Keane walked across and placed a hand on her shoulder. 'I'm so, so very sorry.'

She looked up at him, the tears coursing down her face. 'Did he die at once?'

'Instantly, I believe. He landed on his head. Hit it on a rock. He would have known nothing.'

'Why Jacques? Why now? Just when we thought we had managed to escape. To make a new life. A life with some hope. Why?'

'Yes, it is tragic. I am so sorry.'

'After all that he has been through. The war. So many battles. So many wounds. To end like this. Falling from his horse.'

'If it is any consolation, the information he has given us will be most useful in the war.' He chose his words with care to study her reaction. Thus far she had appeared to be genuine in her shock and grief.

'Oh, damn the war. What does it matter? He's dead.'

Keane said nothing. Madame Hulot continued to sob, her head bent. Quiet sobs that cut him to the soul. He had known grief, of course. When Morris had been killed and when he had lost the love of his life. But to see such grief moved Keane as little had before. He knew of course that it was needless, that Hulot was of course not dead at all, and that made it all the worse. That he was the source of this extraordinary sadness. But he knew that the need for reliable information was paramount. He was still not satisfied that Hulot was indeed on their side. He tried again.

'Madame, I am truly sorry. I was only trying to bring some sort of hope in the face of such tragedy.'

She turned and looked him in the eyes. 'Hope? What hope

have I now? You disgust me, all of you. You Englishmen, with your lack of emotion. Your bravery, your talk of winning. Can't you see, no one wins a war? Everyone loses. It doesn't matter whose side you are on. They're all the same.'

Keane smiled at her. 'Well, that is just what we were afraid of.'

'What? What do you mean?'

'We know the truth, madame. We know that the colonel was no more a royalist than you are, or Bonaparte himself. We know that you are both Bonapartists and that he was placed here in order to trick us and that the information he passed to us was false. What intrigues me is how you could think we would be deceived? The so-called information was known to us weeks ago and was proved quite false then by our own intelligence agents. How very, very stupid of you both. But I suppose he was only following orders. The poor fool. Perhaps it's just as well for him that he's dead. That's how he would have ended up. At the end of a rope.'

Madame Hulot looked at him for a few minutes with incredulity in her eyes. Then she spoke. 'Have you finished? I hope that you have, captain. For I do not wish to hear any more. I have never met anyone so utterly heartless. So very cruel. I had misjudged you. I thought you a friend. I thought you had come to tell me about Jacques because you had pity in your heart. But now I see that you do not even have a heart. You are so right, aren't you? So very correct. So sure of yourself. How wrong you are, how very, very wrong. Jacques was the most decent human being you will ever meet. Truthful, honest and with a deep love for life. I don't care what you do to me. Hang me if you like, as a spy. I have no life now. He was my life and I his. Now that is gone.'

Keane looked at her, all the time being careful to maintain the stern expression he had adopted.

She was shaking her head, still sobbing, but now an anger mixed with the tears. At length she spoke again. 'I don't know how you doubted him or how you decided that he was a spy. Did you kill him then? Was the story about the horse just a lie? Why did you do that? Why did you kill him? Can't you see that you got it wrong? Can't you admit it? You know very well that my husband was a royalist agent. You must know his true identity. He couldn't be further from Bonaparte; he was the son of one of King Louis' closest intimates. We escaped the guillotine and fled to Austria. It was there that he assumed his new identity. How stupid you have been and how wasteful of a life which would have been given so readily in the service of the king.'

She began to sob again. Deeper this time. Keane knew the sound of real despair. It was enough. He knelt down beside her.

'I'm sorry, madame.'

She turned away but he continued. 'Sorry, because I lied to you.'

She looked at him. 'Lied?'

'About the colonel. Your husband is not dead.'

Fury blazed in her eyes. 'Don't be cruel, sir. Don't be even more cruel than you have been. Don't give me false hope. How can I believe you?'

'I lied because I had to test you. I had to know if the colonel really was a royalist. I can see now that you are both genuine. I am so sorry to have put you through that.'

Madame Hulot stood up. Keane did not see her hand flash out, but he felt the pain cut through him as her hand made contact with his face.

'You bastard. You callous English bastard.'

Keane rubbed at his jaw. There had been real force behind the blow. 'I am truly sorry, madame. Please understand.'

She slapped him again, but when she raised her hand for a third time Keane blocked it, grabbing her wrist with a steely grip.

She tried to kick him, but he let go of her arm and she toppled backwards, almost unbalancing.

'Madame, I am sorry, please understand. Your husband is alive. Please believe me.'

She stood in the corner of the room, shaking with rage. 'Get out of here, you bastard. Get out.'

Keane backed towards the door, left and closed it behind himself. Turning, he began to walk into the courtyard where he saw a familiar figure coming towards him.

Colonel Hulot smiled. 'Ah, Captain Keane. I don't think I thanked you properly for saving my wife two nights ago. I am truly indebted to you.' He paused. 'What brings you here? Were you looking for me? I have been with your Major Scovell at Elvas. A most intelligent man. I hope that he found my information of some use. Perhaps I can help you with whatever it was you wanted?'

Keane smiled. 'No, thank you, colonel. Madame Hulot was able to tell me everything that I needed to know. I'm sure that she'll explain. Good day.'

Moving fast, Keane made his way back from San Cristobal through the redoubt to his bivouac.

There was now no alternative. He had been satisfied with Madame Hulot's response to his deception. Grant would undoubtedly be furious with him when Hulot informed him of his tactics, but it was too bad. At least now he had his answer. He believed Hulot to indeed be genuine and, having set himself the question and obtained an answer, he would have to play the game by his own rules. He would have to go along with Grant and Wellington's plan and have himself captured along with the other two. And then, Paris.

Silver was waiting among the tents.

'We wondered where you'd gone, sir. We've got a brew on and Martin's found some rabbits.'

Keane smiled. Martin, with his expert ability with a gun, was very adept at 'finding' rabbits. 'That is good news. But I've some of my own which will be less than welcome, I suspect.'

'What's that, sir? Word is we're off again.'

'The word is right. But not all of us, Silver.'

'That don't sound good, sir.'

'No, not good. Not good at all. But there's nothing for it.'

'Where are we going, sir? Those of us who are. With you, sir, is it?'

'Yes, Silver, you're coming with me, and Archer. The fact is we're off on a bit of an adventure.'

He called Archer and the others together in front of his tent, and as they gathered he cast his eye over them. His men.

Of the nine under his command, he had led six of them through three years of this bloody war. From the victories of Oporto and Bussaco through the barren mountains of the Serra Grande, to Almeida and Torres Vedras. Together they had witnessed sights he had never thought to see, nor wanted to again. They had bluffed, lied and forced their way into

French strongholds, played nursemaid to sadistic guerrillas, uncovered traitors and brought back to Wellington not only valuable intelligence but also secret codes, prisoners and above all the gold needed to pay the army.

The three new recruits aside, Keane knew every one of these men intimately now. Archer, the well-spoken Scottish doctor, forced into the army as punishment for grave-robbing; Horatio Silver, a London cat burglar, with his Portuguese wife, a brawler and teller of tall stories who had killed a Portuguese peasant in a bar fight and expected to be hanged for it; the expert shot and ladies' man Will Martin, chosen by Keane from his old regiment, the Inniskillings; the huge-fisted prize-fighter Garland; Jesus Heredia, the moody Portuguese dragoon; and not least his dependable sergeant Robert Ross, late of the Black Watch, rescued not from a jail, but from ignominy, having been reduced to the ranks and serving as a steward in the officers' mess.

Of the original band he had assembled in June 1809, he had lost just three along the way: his old friend Tom Morris, Israel Leech and Sam Gilpin. Those who remained were now truly his men. He had found three new men too and he hoped he had chosen wisely. Apart from John Batty, the thief from Newcastle, there was Carson, chosen to replace Leech. He was an explosives man, a liberal socialist adept with gunpowder and convicted of destroying a mill in Lancashire. Keane would have to keep a watch on him and be sure that he channelled his talents against the French. Finally there was Lanyon, a Cornish smuggler who had succeeded in concealing a huge quantity of brandy from the excise men of which only a tenth had ever been recovered.

In truth now, he thought, they were all his men. And he

was loathe to leave them, but as Martin's rabbits stewed on the fire, he told them of the plan.

When he had finished, Ross swore. 'Damn it. Sorry, sir, but it's a damn bad idea this. To split the men.'

Martin shook his head. 'No, sir. I won't let you go without me. Nor will Garland. Isn't that right, Sam?'

Garland nodded. 'Yes, sir. We can't stay here if you're off.'

'I'm afraid that's just what you'll have to do. And the rest of you. This is a job for three men. I can't say that I'm enamoured with the idea, both as a plan in itself and because it means splitting the unit, but there's no way out. I've tried everything. Sarn't Ross, you're in charge. You are now answerable directly to Major Grant. Understand?'

'Sir.'

'Good, that's that then. Now, where are those rabbits, Martin? I'm starved.'

They were ready the following morning, and as dawn broke over the citadel the three figures, all clad in blue officers' boat cloaks procured from Grant, rode out of the camp and made for the road that led from Badajoz out to the east, along the line of the Guadiana river. Their farewells the previous evening had been long and heightened by the emotion brought on by drink, and all three of them faced the new day in dampened spirits.

There was still no birdsong over the charnel house of Badajoz itself, as there had not been since the start of the siege. But as they drew away from the city, birds began to soar and dive in the sky above them. The chill air of the morning caught

Keane's face and brought home the reality of the situation. They had taken, on Grant's advice, the road east towards Toledo and Madrid. It was a good road, leading through Estremadura across the plains of the Tagus, over the river and through the mountains.

It was also the road that went the most direct route straight and deep into enemy territory. In Keane's mind now was the idea that they might make for the French fortified strong-hold of Almarez, and being taken in the area could explain their presence as being a reconnaissance force. Almarez was known to be a supply base for Soult's attacks against British garrisons and two exploring officers being in the area sounded feasible. It depended of course upon their being taken prisoner before they reached Almarez itself. The last thing that Keane intended to do was find himself riding up to the gates of the fort demanding to be made captive.

He reasoned that it might just work, and that at least solved the problem of their 'cover' story. But that was only the start, and when considering the mission as a whole, Keane was far from comfortable.

As an exploring officer in Spain and Portugal these past few years, he had been able to rely on the fact that wherever he might be behind French lines, at least the population would be friendly. He had nurtured relations with the local people. He had developed his knowledge of their languages and their customs. He had even learnt some of their dances. He had also, to his surprise, developed a liking for some of the local cooking and with the swarthy looks that came with spending days out in the field thought that he might now easily pass as one of them. At least to the French.

He knew also that the great majority of the Spanish and

Portuguese people, guerrillas and civilians alike, would shelter him and his men, hide them from the enemy and if necessary risk their own lives to come to their aid. Theirs was a country under the boot of oppressive enemy occupation and they had come to look on the British as their liberators. Now, however, Keane and the others were riding off into enemy territory. Into the heart of the empire where, whatever Colonel Hulot had told them, he was certain that most of the population were still avid Bonapartists. This was truly hostile territory, where they might be betrayed at any step or murdered in their sleep; where any civilian might turn on them.

He turned to Archer who rode alongside him with Silver behind. 'You do realize that we're in great danger, at least until we're in enemy hands?'

'Yes, sir, the thought had occurred to me. It's quite amusing really.'

'I fail to see the funny side of it. We really should make it our business to be captured as soon as we can. Whenever the opportunity presents itself. The problem is, we can't appear to be presenting ourselves for capture. That would arouse suspicions. We might make it seem as if we have lost our way, but I suspect that before the French find us, the guerrillas will do so. We could use their information and find ourselves a French column to shadow. That would make it easier to expose ourselves to capture.'

He looked at Archer for a moment. 'You know, you make quite a passable officer, Archer.'

For once, in an attempt to make themselves more conspicuous and not to be shot on sight as spies, but rather taken on parole, Keane had exchanged his brown, black-frogged uniform coat of the Corps of Guides for his old scarlet regimental tunic, that of the Inniskillings, with its brass buttons and yellow facings. Archer too was dressed in scarlet, the red tunic of an officer, this time with facings of dark blue, denoting a 'Royal' regiment of foot.

'Lucky that Major Grant found you that uniform, wasn't it? As a matter of fact, where did he find it?'

'I'm not sure, sir. Said it was surplus to needs.'

'Have you looked in the pocket? You might find the owner's name. Be good to know at least.'

Archer pushed open his cloak and reached inside the pocket of the scarlet tunic.

'It's rather hard to make it out, sir. Begins with C, I think. Yes, that's it. The tailor's name's quite clear, Dunmore and Locke, St James's.'

'That's a good tailor. You're lucky. See if you can read the name again.'

Archer squinted. 'I think it looks like Cavendish or maybe Cavanagh.'

Keane laughed. 'Well, I'll be damned. Grant's given you one of Colonel Cavanagh's coats. How's that for impertinence?'

They trotted on along the road through the growing heat of the dry day and as they came to a pass in the mountains Keane became aware that they were being observed. He spoke quietly. 'We're being watched. Did you notice?'

'No, can't say that I did, sir. Where from?'

'I'm not certain as yet, but I'm sure that we are. Let's hope that they're Spanish.'

They continued along the road, and the sides of the valley became gradually steeper and closer together. This, thought Keane, would make an excellent spot for an ambush.

At a bend in the pass, Keane saw that up ahead the road

had been blocked by a fallen tree and congratulated himself. It was the perfect spot. Almost instantly, from behind rocks on either side of the road, men appeared, guerrillas, armed with an assortment of muskets, along with swords and spears. Keane smiled. 'Thank God. For a moment I thought the French might have found us too soon.'

Two of the guerrillas stepped forward and spoke to Keane in Spanish. The one on the right was familiar. A heavy-set man with steely grey eyes, Keane recognized him as belonging to a group of the partisans that he had first run into three years ago.

'Coronel Morillo.' He spoke the words deliberately loud and was rewarded with a guffaw. From behind a large rock appeared a man whose face Keane knew at once.

Colonel Pablo Morillo was of medium height and had not changed in the past few years. His brown hair fell in a sweep over his tanned forehead and his eyes were just as black and piercing as Keane recalled them. His thick lips had the effect of making him appear as if he was forever pouting. His black bicorne with its tricolour Spanish cockade he wore fore and aft, and his uniform of a Spanish colonel looked as if it had seen better days but still bore the star of the Order of Charles III.

Morillo looked at Keane and shook his head. 'Captain Keane, James Keane. How are you, my friend?'

This was the man whom three years ago Keane had been told to shadow and to ensure that he came into Wellington's power. Morillo was more than a guerrilla leader; an ex-sailor and self-styled colonel, he was a warlord and a very rich and dangerous man. He had taken gold from the French and, rather than use it to buy arms, had kept a great deal for his own use. He would do almost anything for money or in the name of 'honour' and he was utterly ruthless to the point of cruelty. On their first meeting Keane had watched him torture a French prisoner to death and knew his methods well. His family had been slaughtered by the French early on in the war and Morillo hated them with a vengeance. It was reassuring that Morillo had found them. He for certain would know the whereabouts of the French columns and patrols. He would know where they would stand the best chance of being taken prisoner, though Keane wondered what on earth he would make of such a request.

Keane went to greet Morillo and the latter clapped him on the back. 'Good to see you, captain. You have been busy, I hear.'

'You do?'

'You are famous, James. A legend even.'

'You're some way from your country, coronel, aren't you?'

'I suppose I am, yes. If you count my country as Galicia. Not if you count my country as Spain, which I do.'

Morillo was as pompous as ever, thought Keane.

The Spaniard looked puzzled. 'I might ask you, James, what you are doing here and in such company? I would have thought you would travel with all your men or with just one. But to have two men with you? This is strange, no?'

'Perhaps it might seem so, but we have a purpose.'

'May I enquire as to what it might be?'

Keane laughed. 'Naturally you may enquire, but I'm afraid I can't comment.'

Morillo laughed too. 'I knew that would be the case.'

Keane shook his head. 'I am pleased that I found you.'

'That we found you, James.'

'It's of no matter, but I need your help.'

'I thought you might.'

'We need to find the French.'

'You've come to the right man. I know where they are, every unit in these parts. Who do you need to find? Which commander?'

'No commander. In fact no specific unit. Any French patrol will do, a squadron or a battalion.'

'I'm not sure I understand.'

'We need to have ourselves made prisoner.'

Morillo laughed again. 'Now you've really gone too far. You want to be taken prisoner by the French?'

Keane nodded. 'Yes, that's it.'

'They'll shoot you two as spies, and string up your sergeant.'

Keane shook his head. 'No, I don't think so. They know me, as you do, Morillo. As a legend. They are desperate to capture "*le capitain anglais*". Besides, I'm not in disguise; none of us are.'

'You're mad. Quite mad.'

'Quite possibly, but those are my orders.'

'Very well, we'll help you. But first let's eat. Follow us to the camp. I'm sure that we must have much to discuss. I want you to tell me everything, James.'

4

They rode fast, following Morillo and his men up the course of the river and then off to the north-west. They climbed steadily and, passing through the little village of La Cueva, turned east and found themselves high on a ridge of the Guadulpe mountains, looking to their right across the wide plains and leftwards towards the Tagus. After what Keane reckoned might have been twenty miles, they came to a halt and were ordered to dismount. Then leading the horses they passed in single file through what was no more than a crack between two huge sides of a rock face and emerged in a hidden valley, lush, green and filled with olive groves.

It was a natural fortress, cut off from the rest of the mountains by its own stone defences and unobserved by anyone riding past.

They dined well on spit-roasted sheep, olives, potatoes with garlic and onions, washed down with the robust red wine of Navarre. Over dinner Morillo made a simple offer of help.

'I myself will make sure that the French know you are close by.'

Keane was puzzled. 'How exactly, colonel, will you manage that? Are you in communication with Marshal Marmont?'

Morillo laughed. 'Better than that, my dear James. Much better. I have a double agent working for me in Almanaz – a Spaniard whom the French considered to be that rarest of things, a French sympathizer. How innocent they are. The man hates them so much that he has sacrificed his own reputation. Every day he risks his life and at any moment might be killed by his own people. There are very few of us who know his true sentiments. I have already sent a messenger with news of your presence in the area.'

Keane smiled, unsure as to whether he might not have been consulted on such a move. 'Go on, colonel.'

Morillo smiled. 'He might even now be passing on the information to his French masters. Of course he will be amply rewarded for his trouble.'

'Naturally.'

Keane could see now the nature of Morillo's help. 'In gold, presumably?'

Morillo nodded. 'Naturally as he is my employ, I expect to receive most of the French payment. And so everyone is happy.' The guerrilla leader laughed. 'You see, James, I have not changed at all. I always do things for the good of my country. I am a true patriot. Don't you agree?'

'I'm sure that there are many things that drive you, Morillo, but certainly one of them is gold. And if it's not Wellington's gold, then I suppose I must be grateful that it's French gold.'

'We all need to live, James. Gold is gold, wherever it comes from.'

*

They left the camp the following morning, having said farewell to Morillo, and, escorted by a party of his men, under Ramon Sanchez, rode back towards the west in the direction of Almanaz. It had been agreed that the guerrillas would follow at a suitably discreet distance and ensure that, in the event of something not going according to plan, Keane and his men could be taken to safety. But as Keane explained, the whole point of the exercise was to be taken prisoner and so the only thing that could go awry would be if the French opened fire. Otherwise the mission must be considered a success. Nevertheless, it was reassuring for Keane to have Sanchez and his men behind them.

Keane was explicit in his orders to Archer and Silver. 'When they see us make sure that you both act surprised and above all as if you intend to escape. They will want to take us alive. But you must put up as convincing a play as possible. Morillo has done his work, and the French know that I am in the country. Marmont will have doubled the numbers of his patrols. I'm sure that we shall have little trouble now.

Shadowed by the guerrillas at some distance, the trio rode along the ridgeway and entered the village of La Cueva. Morillo had told them that a house at the eastern end of the village was empty and would provide accommodation. It also seemed likely that this might be the place where they would be taken by the French. As they rode into the village Keane spotted the house on their right, just as Morillo had described it. He motioned them across and they dismounted and led the horses into the stables which stood below the house's bedrooms. Opening the door, Keane found a bottle of wine on the table with a loaf of bread and a cured sausage. With scarcely a word, the three men sat down and began to eat. It was curious, thought Keane, waiting like this, in the knowledge that at some point French soldiers were likely to burst in and take them.

He wondered where Sanchez and his men had positioned themselves and presumed that it must be somewhere in the high ground above the village, from where they would be able to observe what was going on.

There was a desperate hammering at the door and then it opened. Keane turned fast and placed his hand on his sword but was careful not to draw it. Archer did the same. But it was no French soldier who appeared in the doorway but a Spanish villager, a small man wrapped in a black cloak, his face a mask of fear.

'Señor, the French are here. They know you are in the village. You must go.'

This was a hard one to play. Keane hesitated. 'Are you sure?'

The Spaniard stared at him. 'Of course, sir. You must go, now. They will find you. Come with me.'

There was no alternative but to obey, and Keane and the others gathered up their weapons and cloaks and went after him, moving towards the stables.

At first Keane thought that if they were slow they might be taken. But the man was at their horses now, and there to Keane's horror stood another three peasants, leading their horses towards them along with their own. The villagers hoisted themselves into the saddle and looked at Keane and his men as they hesitated.

The leader spoke again. 'Quick, ride. You must come with us.'

There was nothing for it but to follow suit. At Keane's signal, his two men mounted up and with the villagers made for the street. They could hear a commotion at the other end of the village. Entering the street, Keane saw that the French had put a cordon of infantry around the town. The four villagers were riding for it and in Keane's mind there was only one course of action. Yelling to Archer and Silver to do the same, he rode directly for one of the French infantrymen who, seeing him, began to level his musket, but as Keane closed on him, gathering pace all the time, thought the better of it and stood aside at the last moment, allowing Keane to pass through. The others followed and Keane saw that the four Spaniards had done exactly the same and had cleared the cordon. From behind them several shots rang out and one of the Spaniards fell. This was just what Keane had hoped to avoid. He did not want to risk the lives of Archer or Silver, or indeed his own, in an exercise that had been meant to be bloodless.

They were all riding away from the village now, and after leaping a stone wall and a stream were away up in the hills that rose above the houses. He presumed that Sanchez's men had seen all that had happened but wondered how they would react. Their orders were to intervene only if Keane's life and those of his men were seriously at risk, and as they had now cleared the cordon with the loss of only the one Spaniard, he presumed that that would not apply. Slowing his horse he turned in the saddle and acknowledged the two villagers and then, looking beyond them, a hundred yards away saw a flash of steel and green uniforms as a patrol of French dragoons emerged from a field to their left. For a few seconds Keane pretended that he had not seen them, giving the dragoons just sufficient time to close by another fifty yards. Then he turned and began to ride again, first calling out a warning to the villagers. They turned and saw the dragoons, but it was too late. The French were upon them now and one of them tried to turn his horse and push it further up the slope. He managed to get twenty yards before two of the Frenchmen were on him. Keane saw him fall to a sabre blow and then rode towards the second and third villagers. As he did, two more dragoons reached them, one with only a pistol and the other an officer, who, with his sabre in one hand, had also drawn his pistol from its saddle holster.

The villagers raised their arms in surrender and the officer smiled at them and nodded. Then, raising their arms, the Frenchmen took careful aim at close range and squeezed their triggers. One ball hit the first villager in the forehead and exploded from the exit wound, blowing off the back of his skull, killing him instantly. The other took the second man below the heart and threw him backwards.

As the dragoons reloaded their pistols and replaced them in their holsters, the officer turned to Keane. 'Shall we go, Captain Keane?'

Keane looked at him. 'You know my name?'

'Everyone knows your name, captain, but few have seen your face. All that is about to change.'

Keane spoke quietly to the officer of the dragoons. 'Captain, may I enquire where we are to be taken?'

'Naturally. My apologies. You are very honoured, captain; you are being taken directly to Marshal Marmont. At his express orders. It won't take long.'

*

But it was not before Marmont that Keane, Archer and Silver found themselves initially. Keane had not been entirely convinced by Grant's assurance that in scarlet tunic he would at least not be hanged as a spy. The French, knowing who he was, would know very well that he *was* a spy, and that might be enough for them to execute rough justice upon all three of them. Napoleon's marshals, including notoriously that arch-spymaster Davout, were very single-minded on the issue of spies, and Davout had been quoted as saying that he had lost count of how many he had hanged during his campaign in the low countries. Might not Marmont be the same? The three men, each shadowed by a pair of dragoons and kept at the point of a carbine, made their way on horseback along the road that wound through the hillside where the laurel trees grew in thick groves. At last, having climbed with diffi-culty to the top of a ridge, Keane looked down and saw in the valley below a small town, its modest houses grouped around a fortress. Led on by the dragoons, they found themselves descending the hillside, through the trees and then across a stone bridge. From here the road climbed again, in a wide curve, leading to the gate into the town.

They passed through the gate and came to stop in the looming shadow of the castle. The officer turned to Keane. 'Dismount, please, captain, lieutenant. Your servant also.'

They did so, and immediately Keane and Archer found themselves surrounded by French officers, all of whom had a question to ask.

'How many men did you lose at Badajoz?'

'How is your morale?'

'Where is your army? Is it across the Tagus?'

'Do you know Wellington's plans?'

'What is Wellington like?'

'Is it true that Wellington has engaged with Marshal Soult?'

Keane's head began to swim with questions. He ignored all of them. Said nothing. The dragoon officer tried to calm the situation, with little effect.

At length a moustachioed French staff officer appeared, in the dark blue and gold uniform of an aide de camp to a general, topped off with white kid gloves and a gaudy sky-blue shako.

'Captain Keane?'

'Yes, that's right.'

'You are to come with me. Your friends can wait here for you.'

He led Keane past the gaggle of officers and through the castle gate into a building at the foot of the main tower.

The room was decorated sparsely, its walls covered with maps of Spain and Portugal. In its centre stood a large, leather-covered table, on which was spread another map of the area. Behind the table stood a French colonel.

'Captain Keane?'

'Yes.'

'Oh, I am pleased. We've been trying to find you for so very long. And now here you are, at last.'

The man spoke slowly and wore a smile, but the words were said in such a way that the pleasantry of their content sounded uniquely menacing. For one of the few times in his life, Keane felt genuine fear.

The general spoke again. 'Oh, I'm so sorry, captain. General de la Martinière, chief of staff to Marshal Marmont.'

Keane looked at him. Marmont's deputy was ugly in the extreme. He was bloated, his face a nasty shade of purple crowned by thinning hair with eyes that peered through folds of flesh. It was instantly clear that he had nothing but loathing for Keane.

'So you are the great English spy? I thought you might be more impressive, captain, more dynamic.' He sniffed and wiped his nose on his sleeve. 'The marshal, for some reason, wants to meet you. But before that happens, I have a few questions for you. Simple questions.'

Keane said nothing.

'We'll start with a very easy one. What is the size of Wellington's army?'

Again Keane said nothing.

'Tell me how many men Wellington has. I want to know everything. How many regiments, their names and numbers? How many English, Scottish, Portuguese? How many light infantry? How many accursed rifles? How many cavalry? Dragoons, hussars. And how many guns, their calibre? Horse or foot?'

Keane remained silent.

'I tell you, captain, I am not a man to be played with. I mean to get this information. I intend to have it and I will get it from you. Now, shall we try again? Let's start with the guns, shall we? How many nine-pounders?'

Keane did not open his mouth.

The purple of de la Martinière's complexion grew darker in intensity and his eyes became larger. When he spoke again it was almost in a shout. 'You will tell me now.' He brought his fist crashing down upon the table.

Keane remained silent, his gaze fixed on the colonel.

'Captain Keane, you should have no doubt that it is well within my power to have you taken out right now, and with your friend and your soldier servant, have you hanged as a spy.'

Keane spoke at last. 'I do not think that would be politic, colonel, do you? Considering that Marshal Marmont has asked to see me.'

De la Martinière's face became puce with rage. Now it was his turn to say nothing and Keane could see the rage boiling within him. Finally he managed to speak. 'You English are no better than dogs, in bed with those Spanish savages. You foul the very space you inhabit. It reviles me to have to stand in the same room as you.'

Keane shrugged. 'I'm terribly sorry. In that case perhaps I should leave.'

De la Martinière smashed his fist hard down on the table a second time and shouted at Keane, 'You will not leave this room, until you have answered all my questions. You will not.'

He was about to shout again when the door opened and the aide entered. 'Colonel, I'm sorry to disturb you. Marshal Marmont has asked to see the captain.'

'Yes, I'm aware of that.'

'At once, sir.'

De la Martinière looked down at his fists, both of which were now pushing down on the desk, supporting him. 'Very well then, go. Go, captain. But don't think that I have finished with you.'

The aide held the door open for Keane.

As he left the room, Keane looked back at the colonel. 'Oh, and just to make it quite clear, I'm not English; I'm Irish. Though we seem to have the same effect upon you.'

His Excellency the Duke of Ragusa, otherwise known as Marshal Auguste-Frédéric-Louis Viesse de Marmont, sat in his castle headquarters and smiled at the two British officers who had been brought before him.

Marmont, who had taken over from Marshal Massena after the disastrous debacle on the lines of Torres Vedras the previous year, had made his headquarters in a small Moorish castle and it was here that they had been brought by the dragoons. Never the type of commander to be content with the sort of rustic casserole enjoyed, or rather tolerated, by his men, Marmont did everything in style. On his arrival to relieve Massena he had brought with him from France his own kitchen staff of twelve cooks along with thirty valets and footmen whom he insisted should wear the full livery of his dukedom.

It was nothing of course on the Imperial travelling household. His old friend the emperor never embarked upon a campaign with less than sixty-five coaches of kitchen staff and equipment.

Keane was shown into Marmont's office, a high room in the Moorish style of the castle, its walls decorated with ceramic tiles in blue, white and turquoise. The late afternoon sunshine poured in through the open window with its heavy studded wooden shutters, flooding the room with light. Archer was already in the room, and Keane wondered if the two men had been speaking already and how good his officer impersonation had been. The aide had informed him that Silver had been placed in another room and was being cared for by one of the French sergeants.

Entering the room, Keane found Marmont standing in full dress uniform, in a pool of sunlight in the centre of the floor.

He smiled as Keane entered and gave a polite nod. It was extraordinary, but it seemed to Keane's eye that, with his aquiline Roman nose, slightly supercilious expression and high forehead, Marmont bore more than a passing resemblance to Wellington himself.

The marshal spoke. 'Gentlemen, may I say what an intense pleasure it is to meet you – particularly you, Captain Keane – at long last. You know you've been quite a thorn in our side these past few years. I have to say that in a sense I am deeply sorry for your capture. Sorry on your behalf, as now you have left your commander exposed. Who knows what will happen? I trust that my men were courteous with you?'

Keane nodded. 'The dragoons who took us prisoner were most polite. Although their officer did surprise me a little by having Spanish villagers shot in cold blood.'

Marmont sighed. 'It is the way with the men and many of the officers. They have seen too much savagery here. Life is cheap. You become . . . brutal.'

He paused and looked regretful. 'I am a great admirer of yours, captain. Your bravery and resourcefulness are exemplary.' He turned to Archer. 'You are a lucky man, lieutenant, to have such a man as your comrade, your commander, even your friend.'

'Yes, sir, indeed I am.'

'May I invite you, both of you, to dine with me this evening? It would be my great pleasure.'

Keane nodded. 'I should be delighted to dine with the most distinguished marshal of the empire.' He turned to Archer. 'Won't we, Charles?'

'Of course, sir, it would be an honour, a real honour.'

Keane was aware that Marmont had been born into the

minor French nobility. It was well known, and it had not occurred to him, when he had suggested Archer as his companion, that the two of them would be invited to dine with the man. He wondered how good Archer would be at passing himself off as an officer. He knew that he came from a good background and that his father was a doctor somewhere in Scotland; should he be suspected to be something other than an officer, it would jeopardize their entire mission.

For the next hour or so Keane and Archer stayed in one of the castle's many rooms. A dragoon kept watch, seated in the corner, his hand on a loaded carbine while two more stood at the door. It was clear, thought Keane, that the French had no intention of allowing their distinguished guest to escape.

He began to think about how he might make use of the coming encounter. How he might work into their conversation subtle questions, which when answered, could, if he found a way of doing so, pass back to Wellington gobbets of otherwise unobtainable information. He wondered how much the marshal might unwittingly reveal.

At eight o'clock the door to the room was unlocked and Keane and Archer were conducted by a different aide de camp – in the rather more glorious sky-blue and silver uniform of that to a marshal of the empire – along a corridor and down a wide flight of stairs. At the bottom stood four flunkies in dark blue livery, their hair powdered and tied in a queue. The aide continued on his way, leading the two men into a grand dining room where, beneath a grand chandelier, at a long, highly polished oak table sat Marmont and two other officers. To Keane's relief, de la Martinière was not among them. The marshal spoke to them in French, which suited them both, Archer having been chosen specifically for his command of the language and Keane too being fluent.

'Captain Keane, Lieutenant Archer, wasn't it? Do sit down, here and here.'

He placed them on either side of his own chair, and both flanked by one of the generals.

'May I present General Foy, General Maucune? They know much of your exploits and were anxious to meet you. Now, a glass of wine?'

He nodded to one of the servants, who filled their silver goblets with red wine. Keane took a sip and was delighted to find that, rather than the local red, it had the fine flavour and bouquet of a claret.

'Excellent wine, sir.'

'Thank you. You know your wine then, captain?'

'I like to think so. I can't recall claret this good since the peace of '02.'

'Yes, it is particularly fine. I have it brought to Spain from my estate in Bordeaux.'

While Marmont spoke to Keane, the latter listened in with one ear to Archer's conversation with General Maucune. The man was asking him about the British army – where it was and what was its strength. Keane was pleased to hear Archer duck the question and turn it against the general with his own counter-request for the whereabouts of Marshal Soult's army. The general laughed and said that he was uncertain. But it was clear that the game was up.

Marmont snapped his fingers and one of the flunkies brought more wine and at that moment four more servants entered with silver plates which they set before Marmont and

Keane and the other diners. Other waiters appeared until the table was covered with silver dishes. To Keane, used to the occasional excursion to the officers' mess while on campaign, with its 'pot-luck' array of food dependent on their supplies, the quantity on the table seemed huge and he compared it to their meal of the previous evening in Morillo's camp. Archer, as a private soldier, more used to the 'stir-about' ration of oatmeal into which the occasional piece of meat might find its way, was noticeably shocked. Keane hoped that it would not betray his real position.

The first dish to arrive on the table had contained salted fish, possibly cod, and the next boiled potatoes, covered in butter. Beside these were quickly set a roast saddle of mutton and alongside that a plate of stewed beef. In the centre of the table a whole chicken sat surrounded by roast potatoes, together with a huge boiled ham.

As soon as their guests were seated the two generals began to attack the food. They tore at the chicken with their hands and then ladled and shovelled whatever they could onto their plates. Marmont, Keane noticed, was the exception. He ate delicately, with almost feminine precision, picking carefully at his food before eating it and chewing it thoroughly as if, thought Keane, to extract every ounce of flavour.

'It was General Foy here who took the news of the composition of the army back to the emperor himself from the lines of Torres Vedras. But of course I forget myself. You know that already, Captain Keane, do you not?'

Keane smiled. 'Indeed, sir. I myself was shadowing the general on his route through Portugal. And for that service he was promoted to his present position.'

'I think that we have met before, Captain Keane.'

'General? I'm sorry I'm afraid that I can't recollect it.'

'Oh yes. You were at Oporto, were you not?'

'Yes, indeed.'

'You led the army across on the wine barges. A surprise attack. It was I who spotted you, and I who led the 17th regiment in the attack on your position in the monastery.'

Keane shook his head. 'That I did not know, general. It was a valiant attempt. Many were killed.'

'Yes, you put up an excellent defence and we were ordered to retreat.'

Keane was puzzled how General Foy might know the identity of the defender of the bridgehead at Oporto when the general spoke again, 'But we also met again – at Busaco.'

'And I have to applaud your saving of six hundred of your men in such testing circumstances. When badly wounded. Single-handedly.'

Foy applauded. 'Your information is really most remarkable, Captain Keane. I see that reports of your abilities have not been exaggerated.'

Keane looked across to Archer, who was laughing convivially with General Maucune. The young private had not made any mistakes with the etiquette of the table and was adept it seemed at the necessary skills of making amusing conversation as he ate. Compared with the manners of the two French generals, Archer looked every bit the English officer born and bred. Clearly Keane's choice of him had been right.

Keane too had held back, difficult as it was, not wishing to seem to appear hungry, although he was ravenous. He was aware that they were being observed by the French and every little detail informed the enemy. That would certainly confuse the French, who believed that Wellington's army was starving.

No sooner had the three Frenchmen finished off the chicken and most of the beef than the flunkies reappeared and removed the dishes. Archer looked briefly crestfallen and Keane smiled at him and gently shook his head.

Sure enough Archer's face brightened when the servants entered again bearing more salvers which they set on the table. This time there were roast partridges, a rice pudding and a plate containing five omelettes.

Helping himself, Marmont turned to Keane. 'Do you know if there is any truth in the rumour we have heard here about your men coming up from Badajoz? You must have taken terrible casualties, captain. I have heard that as many as twelve thousand of your men were killed and wounded.'

Keane said nothing. Then, 'I think that is something of an exaggeration, sir.'

'Oh really? How many were there then? What would you say?'

'I really couldn't say. There were many, certainly, but nothing like that number.'

'Nevertheless, it must be shattering for your army. To lose so many British soldiers.'

'There were many Portuguese casualties, sir. Don't forget that.'

'Of course, your brave allies. But surely the dead were mostly Englishmen?'

'Irishmen and Scotsmen too.'

Marmont laughed. 'Yes, my fault. I'm not very good with that. The Scots of course we know well. Your Amazons in their skirts. Men of the mountains.'

He paused and took a long draught of red wine, considering his next comment and its possible effect.

'Surely, captain, to have suffered such great losses would mean that Wellington cannot be intending to send men north against me. Wouldn't you say so, captain? Surely it seems unlikely.'

Keane was well aware that Marmont was trying, somewhat clumsily, to extract information from him and he was damned if he was going to give anything away. 'I really couldn't say, sir. I would not like to predict what my commander in chief has it in his mind to do.'

'But surely that is exactly what our profession entails, captain. To predict the movements of commanders based on information you have gathered and what you know of their characters?'

Keane said nothing and Marmont tried another tack. 'No more than two divisions, I would say. Wellington can have no more than two divisions which he will be able to send against me. Would you agree?'

He grabbed a partridge, ripped it apart and began to gnaw at it.

Again Keane circumvented the question. 'Perhaps. Who can say? He might be intending to send the army elsewhere. You are not alone. What of Marshal Soult?'

Marmont, still chewing, spoke quickly. 'Oh, Soult's closer to Wellington.'

'Is he? Are you quite sure of that?'

Marmont stopped eating and stared at Keane. 'You know otherwise?'

'Did I say that? I don't think so . . .' He paused, teasing Marmont. 'Two divisions would be about right, I think.'

The marshal, he could see, was becoming angry, riled by the lack of direct answers to his questions and clearly now somewhat muddled. But, pushing his luck and his host to the limit, Keane decided to have some sport and to see what else he might be able to learn.

'You must find it somewhat tiresome, sir, to have two armies here in Spain with no single commander. I mean, to have to be constantly in communication with Marshal Soult, who is effectively your equal in rank.'

Marmont raised an eyebrow. 'My equal? Yes, perhaps he is. But it's not that simple . . . Tiresome? No, not really. I know Soult. We have no great rivalry.'

Keane frowned. 'That wasn't my understanding of the situation. I had thought that you and the marshal were both striving for the emperor's attention.'

Marmont froze and for a moment Keane thought that he might have gone too far and too fast. Their other dining companion, whom, it had emerged, was General Maucune, had noticed it too, and although General Foy continued his conversation with Archer, which had now developed on to the topic of colic, the three other men sat silent for a few moments before Marmont at last spoke again. 'I have no need, captain, to strive for the affections of my emperor. You see, the emperor is also my friend, has been my friend for many years, long before he was my emperor, long before he was even a general.

'Soult is not a good general. I don't think he will do for Spain. He sent a secret dispatch to Berthier telling him that it was my fault that Badajoz was lost.'

This was interesting, thought Keane. So it seemed that the rumours he had heard were correct. The marshals were fighting with each other. Here at last was the real evidence he wanted that Napoleon's great administration was beginning to pull apart. Then it occurred to him that perhaps Marmont was trying to mislead him. Trying to suggest that they were disunited when they were in fact as strong as ever. He would test it.

'You were about to explain your personal connection with the emperor. I'd love to hear about that. You must know him better than any other French general or marshal.'

Marmont smiled and shrugged in a way that implied agreement. 'I'll tell you. There were three of us at the beginning. Three of us, together: myself, Bonaparte and Junot. We lived hard in Paris. Young men hungry for work, for power and glory. Toulon. That was where we had met. And the emperor saw at once my talent. Made me his aide de camp. In Malta I captured the flag of the Knights of St John and they made me a *général de brigade*. I was by his side at the coup d'état of the 18th Brumaire, and at Lodi I was with those who faced the grape and musket balls on the long bridge. And we took it in a great headlong rush. It was the stuff of genius, born from bravery and madness. A young man's war. Then the first real disagreement.'

'You fell out?'

'I don't know. You are a spy, Captain Keane, but I refused to become one. We planned to invade England, and the minister of war wanted a spy to go and supply information on the British preparations for such an attack. Bonaparte offered to send his own aide de camp, me. Well, naturally I refused. It went against everything, every code by which I had lived and been brought up. To go stealing secrets. To go in disguise. To become a thief and a liar and a cheat. It was not the conduct of an officer.'

Keane smiled. 'No, indeed. I share your sentiments, sir.'

'I am an honourable man. My father was noblesse. You understand. A man of title and property. I did not favour the Revolution. Yes, something was needed, but not that. Not all that blood.'

'And you refused to become a spy.'

'Yes. So instead they made me commander of the artillery. Then a *général de division*. And all the time, all the time, I kept my brain alert to all the new innovations of the world. I suggested to Bonaparte that we should start to use steamboats. Did he take up my suggestion? No. And if he had, perhaps we would have taken England and you and Wellington would not be here.'

'Then they gave me the army of Holland. But a marshal's baton? No. Instead it was Bessières who got it. The emperor had a simple explanation. "You have never once led an army as commander in chief. I cannot make you a marshal." But I know why it was. He loved me too much and the others knew it too. He didn't want to be seen to indulge his favourite. So I waited. I was content to wait.

'So in 1805 I received the command of a corps. We walked into Ulm. Took the surrender.'

Keane spoke. 'Wasn't there something about money going missing during the occupation?'

Marmont looked surprised. 'It's lies of course – all lies. Napoleon made me governor of Dalmatia. Five years I spent there. In 1808 he made me Duke of Ragusa. But still I had to wait another year before I held a marshal's baton.'

'The emperor likes to make you wait.'

'In 1809 I commanded the army of Dalmatia. Then at last it came. The baton I had craved. On 12th July. I had it. All I had ever really wanted.'

He took a long drink before continuing, 'But what now? I was a duke and a marshal. But what did the emperor give now to the others? He made them princes. Princes? It was obscene. My old comrades – Berthier, Davout, Massena. Princes!'

'I can see how you might be annoyed. Did he do it on purpose? Was there, do you think, a message?'

Marmont did not seem to care what he said now. In encouraging him to speak, Keane had broken down the barrier of discretion. 'Do you know what he said? "Between ourselves, you have not done enough to justify entirely my choice." Not enough? What else could I have done? There were two others at the same time. Two more new marshals, and do you know what the army rhyme said?'

'I'm not sure I do.'

'They said MacDonald is France's choice, Oudinot is the army's choice and Marmont is friendship's choice.' He sat back, laughed and took a long drink. 'Friendship's choice. That's me. What do you think of that, captain?'

'And is he still your friend? The emperor. After all of that. All that you've had to endure?'

'I was pleased to be called to Spain. Massena had done a poor job and it was a bad business. He deserved to go. He brought his mistress with him, you know.'

Keane smiled politely. He knew well enough. Henriette Lebreton. Knew her all too well. But did not imagine he would ever see her again.

'Yes, I knew that.'

This was just as Keane had expected. Massena was not much loved. Marmont had been the obvious choice as his successor. The firm hand of an old friend in place of that of the devil himself. And it said more still. He noted the fact that there was more infighting, more splits within the high command. More envy.

Marmont went on. 'It is a great joy to be in the field again. You must miss real soldiering yourself, captain, don't you?'

Keane sensed that the tables were being turned again. He was now back under scrutiny and he wondered if the marshal had guessed his irritation at working as a spy.

'I do miss the front line, sir. Yes. But I have good men and the chance to do something that makes a difference.'

'A difference? You are important, Captain Keane, but do you really consider yourself that important? Do you think you can change the course of the war? We will win. France will win. Obviously. Our armies are the greatest the world has ever seen. Look at the empire.' He smiled, patronizingly, at Keane. 'I think that you will have to make a very big difference.'

It was fighting talk and Keane wondered how much of it was bravado. Clearly the marshal had lost his slavish devotion to the emperor. Keane wondered now if he would ever turn against him. After all, Marmont had admitted that he had been born into the noblesse. Was proud of the fact. Was his loyalty to France or to the Corsican? He would not be a part of their current plan, but Keane wondered on whose side Marshal Marmont might eventually come out.

'I have not been in the field for two years. Do you think that's too long to be away from battle?'

Keane thought about it for a moment. He himself had been away from the front line for three years and he wondered if you went 'stale', if you lost your edge. But his reply didn't betray his worries.

'No, sir. I don't think so. Soldiers do not change, they merely adapt.'

Marmont looked at him and smiled. 'Yes, I think you are
right. I think you are a very wise man, Captain Keane, which
may explain why your Lord Wellington trusts you so much.
But at this present moment you are my guest and we will see
what tomorrow holds.'

5

The following morning Archer and Keane were summoned by Marmont to his office in the fortress. The mood, Keane gauged as they entered, was somewhat changed from that of the night before. This he thought would be the time for Marmont to ask questions. The marshal might have realized just how garrulous he had become the previous evening, what he had revealed of himself, and by way of recompense would want something from them. Keane fully expected to see de la Martinière sitting with Marmont and was surprised that he was not.

Marmont looked Keane in the eye. 'You slept well, I trust, captain?'

'As well as might be expected, in the circumstances.'

'It was a pleasant evening, was it not? I suspect though that I spoke too long. I hope that I did not bore you.'

'No, sir, not in the slightest. I found everything that you said most interesting.'

They were playing a cat-and-mouse game and Keane knew now that Marmont must regret all that he had said. How, he wondered, would he begin their interview? They were, in

effect, at his mercy, and de la Martinière had hinted at the fact
that it would not be hard to find an excuse to hang or shoot
all three of them. Keane hoped that Silver was safe. They had
not seen him since their arrival and he could only presume
that he was being held under guard, without recourse to the
level of hospitality he and Archer had been fortunate enough
to enjoy at the marshal's table.

Marmont began, 'You learnt much of me last night, captain.
But sadly I still know so little of you. I don't suppose that there
is any way we might be able to remedy the imbalance in the
situation?'

'Sir, I very much regret that I am quite unable to give you
any information. You spoke last night of honour, and I believe
that we share a code which allows us to conduct ourselves in
time of war in an honourable manner. You mentioned the idea
of the spy and how abhorrent it is to you, and I find myself
in agreement. This might seem curious, for, as you say, I am
such a person, although I have never acknowledged the fact. I
have never adopted disguise –' a lie here, he thought – 'and it
rankles with me to win a war by any such clandestine means.
But if I acknowledge the fact that I am somehow involved in
such a business, then at the same time I must apply to it my
own code of honour. Thus I hope that you see it is impossible
for me to impart any information.'

'Well put, captain. Very well put. Certain of my subordinates
would choose to use other means to extract such information
from you. You have encountered Colonel de la Martinière. This
is not my way. I tried my best last night, and now I see that
you are a man of your word. So that is how I will treat you. I
ask you, gentlemen, both of you, to give me your parole. Your
word of honour as officers and gentlemen that you will not

attempt to escape when in French custody. Will you give me that assurance?'

Keane was pleasantly surprised but not entirely shocked. Grant had led him to expect that he might be offered parole. Certainly such a request would not be made to men about to be hanged as spies. He was also well aware that should he and Archer refuse Marmont's offer, they would in effect be signing their own death warrants. The French were inclined to be especially harsh with British officers who refused to give their word not to escape. He was quick to take up the offer before it was withdrawn.

'Yes, sir, of course, we would both be happy to give you our word as officers in His Majesty's army.' He looked at Archer. 'Won't we, lieutenant?'

Archer smiled back. 'Yes, of course, sir. Only too happy.'

Keane felt an enormous sense of relief but with his natural sense of suspicion began to wonder whether this might not be some new plan of Marmont's to catch him out. Thinking quickly, he supposed that the two of them, hopefully along with Silver as their servant, would be taken to the French headquarters in Salamanca. Here, as officers on parole, they would be allowed to walk the streets. Keane knew that one of Grant's agents, Patrick Curtis, was in Salamanca, where he was a professor at the great university, and he needed somehow to pass him the information that Marmont had unwittingly imparted the previous evening, regarding the division that clearly existed between the marshals, along with Marmont's own tenuous relationship with Bonaparte and his potential royalist sympathies. It was too good an opportunity to miss, and also it was the best that Grant had hoped for in their journey to their eventual destination of Paris.

Marmont smiled, evidently similarly pleased now that he would not have to hand over this man to his less than savoury associates. He passed Keane a sheet of paper, which Keane read. It was a draft letter of parole, with spaces left for his full name, rank, regiment, the date and other details. Marmont handed him a pen across the table and Keane filled it out:

I, the undersigned, James Keane, captain in the 27th regiment of English foot, taken prisoner by the French army on the 1812, undertake on my word of honour not to seek to escape or to remove myself from my place of captivity without permission; nor to consent to be released by the guerrillistas in the course of any journey through Spain or France. I also undertake not to pass any intelligence to the English army and its allies. In fact, not to deviate in any way from the duties which an officer prisoner of war on parole is in honour bound to perform; and not to serve against the French army and its allies until I have been exchanged, rank for rank.

The words rang in his head '. . . not to pass any intelligence . . . in honour bound to perform' . . . 'in honour bound'.

He pressed the pen to the paper and signed the document, and as he was signing, the door opened and de la Martinière appeared. For a moment Keane panicked, thinking that they had in some way been tricked. But then Marmont spoke. 'The colonel here will act as your witness, captain. Yours too, lieutenant.'

De la Martinière said nothing, but leaning over Keane took the pen from him and appended his own signature below his.

Marmont handed a second piece of paper to Archer and the process was repeated. Keane prayed that Archer would remember his new rank and not sign as a private soldier. De la Martinière took the second document and as he had done with the first held it up to his face. But his purpose was not to scrutinize any given-away mistakes of Archer's, but merely to blow the ink dry. The colonel turned to Marmont and spoke in a low tone of acceptance which betrayed his obvious disapproval of the offer made by his commander to two men he considered should be shot as spies. 'All in order, sir.'

Marmont turned to Keane. 'Thank you, gentlemen. I had planned to remove you to Salamanca tomorrow, but we have a slight setback in that the Agueda is flooded and the waters have carried away our bridge at La Caridad.'

Keane smiled. 'You're stranded?'

'Yes, captain. That amuses you?'

'What if Lord Wellington is on his way?'

Marmont shrugged and grinned. 'Then of course we stand and fight. With losses of 12,000 at Badajoz, how many effectives can he have now? 30,000 men? He would need double that to attack my 20,000 in a fortified position.'

'How do you know we lost so many?'

'Because you told me, captain.'

'I most certainly did not.'

'But you did, Captain Keane. When you said . . . let me remember, how did you put it? "I really couldn't say. There were many, certainly, but nothing like that number." Do you really think that I would be fooled by such a reply. It's obvious that your army was horribly cut about. I will hold off Wellington here and then Marshal Soult will take him in the rear. His army will be crushed, like an insect between two rocks.'

So, thought Keane, Soult was coming up to join forces. It was what they had feared. The necessity of getting word to Wellington had now become crucial.

Marmont continued. 'As soon as the river is once again fordable you will be taken to Salamanca and thereafter to France. I shall remain with the army.'

Keane was relieved. If they could reach Salamanca and Don Patrick, then there was a chance of getting the news to Wellington. There was something else on his mind too. 'Might I enquire as to what is to become of my servant?'

'The soldier? Yes, at present he is a prisoner. Of course we cannot accept the parole of a man who is not an officer. He will have to remain here and share the fate of the other prisoners.'

'If I vouch for his good conduct, surely you might permit him to travel with us. He is one of my soldiers and my responsibility, as well as a servant. I should hate to lose him.'

Marmont thought for a moment. 'Very well. But I am surprised at you, captain. I would not have expected an English officer to speak up for his servant in such a way. You are truly quite unique.'

'I told you, sir, I am not an Englishman; I'm Irish. It makes a difference.'

The room was comfortable enough as a cell and the two men managed to share the wooden bed quite easily sleeping head to toe. On the third day there was a commotion at the door. The staff officer entered. 'You are to come at once. We're leaving.'

Keane turned as he threw on his red coat. 'Why, may I ask?'

'The English are coming. Come on.'

This had not been in the plan. The last thing that Keane wanted was for them to be rescued by Wellington's advance guard. He had known of course that the commander would not allow Marmont's army to escape. The British and Portuguese would be closing all the time, exhausted as they were.

Keane spoke to the officer. 'But I thought the river was too swollen to cross. And the bridge had broken.'

'The waters have gone down enough to allow us to get across.'

'Marshal Marmont said that he would stand and fight.'

'That was when we did not know the size of Wellington's army.'

'I could have told you. In fact, it seems that I did.'

The man said nothing but ushered them out into the courtyard. They found Marmont mounted on his Arab stallion and surrounded by his staff. The marshal called to them, 'So it seems that you were right, captain. Your army did not lose too many at Badajoz. Wellington is approaching and he will not take me, or you. I shall see you no doubt in Salamanca.' He turned and swept with a flourish from the courtyard, followed by his staff in a clatter of hooves on cobbles.

The staff officer pointed Keane and Archer towards an under-strength half-troop of dragoons who were standing mounted a little distance away. Keane, noticing several riderless horses with the dragoons, looked about the place and spoke to the staff officer. 'Where is my servant? Have you seen him?'

The man shook his head, and at that moment Silver emerged from a door in the great keep. He looked as white as a sheet, but his face brightened on seeing Keane.

'Blimey, sir. I'd given up on seeing you again.'

'I might say the same about you, Silver. You remember Lieutenant Archer?'

Keane pointed to Archer, and Silver smiled and nodded. 'Yes, sir. Of course.'

'How did they treat you?'

'Passable. Place was damp and right old. Didn't sleep that

well, sir. Food wasn't bad though. Do themselves well, the French, don't they, sir?'

Keane looked at Archer. 'Indeed they do, Silver. There's no denying that. Wouldn't you agree, lieutenant?'

He looked back to Silver. 'The good news, Silver, is that you're to come with us.'

'That is a relief, sir. I didn't know what they'd do with me and I feared the worst.'

'Well, you're quite safe, for the moment at least. We're bound for Salamanca, on our parole, and then up and into France.'

They mounted up and left a few minutes later, riding in close formation out of the great gate of the fortress. Each of the three men rode in the midst of four troopers, their horses tethered by a rope to that of one of the troopers riding in front. The escort consisted of some fifty troopers with their three officers riding in front, and slowly the party began to make its way from the hillside town back onto the road that led to Salamanca.

It took them five days to reach the city. They rode throughout the day, with pickets posted on their flanks to watch out for guerrillas, and at night made camp quickly and silently. Keane and the others sat on their own around a fire, close to that of the officers and guarded by eight of the troopers. There was no opportunity for Keane to speak with any of the officers, let alone attempt to strike up some sort of a rapport with any of them. They nodded to each other and exchanged pleasantries, and although the officers seemed amiable enough they were taciturn to say the least and hardly repaid his attempts at conversation.

At length Salamanca came into view and as they rolled in through the old gate of the ancient city Keane felt relieved that no attempt had been made to rescue them and supposed that word must have been sent out in advance by Grant to the guerrillas not to make any effort to do so.

They quickly found themselves billeted in a room in the Fort San Vicente in the south-west of the city. Here they were completely secluded from the rest of the city. But, to Keane's delight, the fort was no more than five hundred yards from the Irish College in which Don Patrick Curtis had his base. Their rooms themselves were if anything less salubrious than those in which they had been held in Almarez, although Silver found himself on his own in relative comfort.

As before, an officer was stationed permanently in Keane and Archer's room as well as a guard outside. On the first night Keane, determined to act fast, struck up a conversation with the man, a young infantry officer from Nantes named Dupont, who shared his knowledge of farming. It was interesting, Keane said to Archer, when Dupont went outside to relieve himself, where a common interest in the best soil required for growing beans could get you.

By the second night they were on good terms. Keane suggested that perhaps on the third day the two captives might be allowed to promenade in the area outside the fort.

'No, sir. I'm afraid that is expressly against Marshal Marmont's orders. You are not to have any intercourse with the outside world.'

'But that's inhuman.' Keane frowned. 'You know, Dupont, that I signed my parole. I have given the marshal my word as an officer that I will not attempt to escape.'

'Yes, sir. I am aware of that. But it is the marshal's order.'

'And what do you think of it? You're an intelligent young chap, as good an officer as any in the emperor's army. What is your opinion of the marshal's order?'

Dupont hesitated for a moment, then, 'For my part, it would not be the way I would handle the situation. I should respect your parole, sir.'

'I thought as much. You see, Archer, here is a fellow with true decency. It is just what you and I surmised. French officers are no different from our own. We are all decent sorts. It is the few, an unfortunate few, who while they might have admirable characters otherwise, give the bad impression we have of the French officer.'

Dupont became interested. 'You have a bad impression of us?'

'Yes, didn't you know? The word among the British officers is that French officers are cruel, without principle and without our sense of honour. I will ensure, as soon as I arrive back in England once I am exchanged, that this impression is reversed. Assuming you are typical of your kind.'

'Thank you, sir. That is most considerate. In truth I am very much against the order to confine you here. But I think there is little I can do about it. If you were to take the air even, outside the fort, I should be put on a charge.'

'No, no. I should not want to put you in danger, lieutenant. It is a pity too that we cannot receive any visitors. In particular for me as I am a religious man and I have not seen a priest these past two months.'

The officer shrugged. 'Let me see what I can do. Perhaps it might be simpler if I were just to have to take a break from my duties at certain times. I am not a monster, sir, and I would not want to be considered as such. To treat you as prisoners when you have both given your parole must be seen as a stain on my own honour as an officer. Leave it with me, gentlemen.'

And so it was on the fifth day of their incarceration in Salamanca, while Lieutenant Dupont was taking his lunch, the door to the cell was opened by the guard and a man entered, wearing the dress of a Spanish priest: a long dark brown cape and a huge, flat black tricorne hat.

He was tall, with a slightly swarthy complexion, and looked to be in his late sixties or early seventies yet in good condition for his age. He said nothing as he entered but looked hard at both Keane and Archer before closing the door behind himself. When he spoke it was in a soft Irish accent. 'I am told that there is an officer here who requires the services of a priest. Is that correct?'

Keane knew him in an instant, but said nothing except, 'Yes, father, I imagine that would be me. How did you find me?'

'Oh, I have my means, captain. There are many people in this city who are great admirers of everything you have done. Your fame does not travel only to the French authorities. I was told by one of my friends that your custodian was happy to allow visitors. Unlike his commanding officer.'

Don Patrick Curtis was by any accounts an extraordinary man. A polymath, a priest, a linguist, able to converse fluently in many languages, he was also professor of astronomy at the University of Salamanca, a philosopher and not least a spy. What was more, he had never aroused the suspicions of the French authorities.

Of course Keane had heard of him many times before, and the account given to him by the Irish Portuguese brigadier,

Nicholas Trant, in particular stuck in his mind. Trant had told
Keane that Curtis, or as the Spanish called him Patrizio Cortes,
held some valuable clues to the identity of his father. A question which had long troubled him and which this war gradually
seemed to be revealing. It was hard, however, looking at this
quiet, elderly man, to believe that he was one of Wellington's
most adept agents. And did he really know the truth about
Keane's father? But that of course would have to wait.

Curtis spoke again. 'Can you tell me, captain, who you are,
and then tell me why I should believe you?'

It was what Keane had expected, and Grant had equipped
him for it.

'I'm Captain James Keane of the 27th and the word that you
need is Zenobius.'

Curtis smiled and nodded. Zenobius, thought Keane, the
code word given to him by Grant. He had explained that it
referred to the Catholic Florentine saint of that name who
was venerated for several miracles of restoring the dead to
life. It seemed appropriate enough for a man who among
his accomplishments had managed to engineer the escape of
several of Wellington's spies from certain death at the hands
of the French.

'Zenobius, indeed. So, Captain Keane, I'm delighted to make
your acquaintance. Your fame precedes you. And your companion here, lieutenant . . . ?'

'Archer, sir.'

'This is Mister Archer, Don Curtis, one of our more recently
made-up officers.' He smiled as he said this and Curtis nodded.

'Very good. Now, what can I do to help? I believe that you
have the names you need for your ultimate destination?'

'Yes, I believe so. Although any other information would be

most welcome. I knew our destination as a boy but I'm sure that it has changed beyond my recognition and at Bonaparte's hands.'

'I will see what I can give you. I'm sure that I can help. Is there anything else?'

'Yes. I have certain things to pass on. Can this be done through you?'

Curtis nodded. 'Yes, but I will show you how to do it.'

He had just finished speaking when the door opened and Dupont entered.

'Ah, father. Good to see you here. You see, captain, I am good to my word.'

Keane smiled at the French officer. 'Indeed you are, lieutenant. Thank you. I now feel at one with God once again. You might say that I have been afforded a small glimpse of salvation.'

He turned to Curtis. 'Until tomorrow, father?'

'Until tomorrow, my son.'

The following day Curtis came again, at the same time, when Dupont was absent at his lunch. Keane and Curtis were less cautious now, but still careful not to use any particular proper names of places or people, lest the guard outside the door should hear them and report them to a higher authority.

Curtis began to speak of religious matters, and for a moment Keane wondered what he intended. But then he realized that as he was doing so his hands were showing Keane something very different. He took a pen from his pocket and a small scrap of paper, then, writing on the paper, finished and took the scrap and twisted it into a thin spill, the sort of taper one might use for lighting a candle. He took the paper and rolled

around it a piece of brown leaf, which looked to Keane like the
wrapping of a cigarillo. Curtis finished by tucking in the ends
and then licked the open edge to seal it. He then presented
it to Keane.

'You like these, I believe. The finest cigarillos. I find them
a great aid to thought. It is surprising what comes into the
mind. Perhaps you would like me to bring some to you. Make
sure that Lieutenant Dupont is aware of this.'

Curtis placed the roll into the pocket of his cloak and from
the other produced a handful of cigarillos. Then handing all
but one to Keane, he took the remaining one and gently slit
it up one side with his fingernail. Rolling it open, he removed
the tobacco inside and then reached into his pocket and
brought out another piece of paper. He performed the earlier
operation again, inserting the rolled paper into the leaf, but
this time placed some of the tobacco inside before licking
it shut.

'There you have it. I cannot vouch for its construction but
I'm sure in your hands its content will improve.'

Keane smiled. 'Ingenious, father. Truly enlightened.'

Over the next two days Keane took delivery of dozens of
'cigarillos' from Curtis and although he smoked a few, to
give the illusion to Dupont, most of them he opened and
filled with the information he had gained from Marmont.
Everything about the infighting among the high command,
about Soult's intentions, Napoleon's character and plans and
even the fact that they might at some point expect Marmont to
turn.

And all of these he passed back to Curtis to give it to his
network of agents, who between them would inform Grant.

*

It was two more days before Curtis appeared again and Keane duly passed on the latest cigarillos. He had just done so when it struck him that now might be the time to ask the priest the question which had been on his mind since their first meeting.

'Father, there was something that Colonel Trant told me in Coimbra. Something about yourself.'

Curtis looked interested. 'Indeed? Now what would that be?'

'To do with me, in fact. A matter of some personal importance.'

Curtis looked at Keane and smiled. 'The matter of your father? Yes, I do know something of that.'

'You are able to tell me his identity? Good heavens. How long has this day been in coming. You will tell me?'

'I don't know the half of it. But I'll tell you some things I do know. If you're sure that's what you want.'

'Why should I not? I want it more than anything in the world.'

'Firstly, I do not know his name. I do know that he was a British general of some fame in the American War and that he might be one of two people. One of my brothers in the Church had some dealings with him, I believe, on his return from the Americas, at the time of your birth. They were together in Ireland, and when your mother fell pregnant, my friend looked after her when your father was unable to do so.'

'Unable?'

'You understand, Keane, that it could not be admitted that he had begotten you. It would have brought shame on your two families.'

'Shame on my mother?'

'Yes, and on her family, themselves a noble line.'

Keane paused. 'My mother's family? But they're mere farmers. We have no great lands. We are not a noble line.'

Curtis shook his head. 'No, you are wrong there, my boy. Your mother comes from one of the noblest lines in the land. In fact it was she who had most to lose.'

'But what of our position now? We need for money. Always have done. I worked the farm myself.'

'Yes, I dare say so. But her family has no need for money. None at all. It was they who cut her off.'

This was a revelation to Keane. He had come to Curtis hoping for news of his father's identity and now had been given quite different news. His mother disinherited by a noble family. But why? he wondered. True, she had sinned, but to cut her off utterly, when other steps might have been taken. Why would his grandparents have done such a thing? Far from shedding light on his origins, Curtis's words had merely made his roots all the more mysterious.

'I'm afraid I can offer no more. My friend knew the whole story. Indeed he knew you. But I lost touch with him some years ago. I believe that he like me, and like so many of my fellow priests, became involved in this business. He may still be, if he has not already been caught and shot as a spy. I am sorry, captain. I hope that you were not building your hopes too high.'

'No, father. Not at all. Anything I can learn about my family is a bonus. Thank you.'

But both men knew that not only had what Keane had heard not been of any help to him, but that among so many lies and counter-lies it had only compounded the facts about his origins and that his own great mystery had now become even deeper.

He was pondering this and at the same time wondering how long they would stay in Salamanca and what plans Marmont had for him when, on the sixth day, Curtis produced a letter. He held it out to Keane under cover of his cloak.

'What's this?'

'A letter, to Clarke, the Duce de Feltre, Bonaparte's minister of war, in Paris. Look at the signatory – you might recognize his name.'

The letter was written on thin grey paper and bore the stamp of an Imperial crown. Keane scanned to the bottom of the page and saw that the author of the letter was one Colonel Charles de la Martinière. He nodded. 'Ah, yes. I do indeed.'

'Then I think you had better read the contents.'

Keane cast his eye more closely over the letter. It was headed:

'Armée de Portugal, Salamanca, 28th April 1812.'

It read:

His Excellency the Duke of Ragusa has ordered an officer of his army to accompany as far as Bayonne the English captain James Keane, of the 27th regiment of foot. This officer was found with two companions close to the headquarters of our army. On him were found papers which indicate his importance to the English army. He was captured in the uniform of an English officer and the marshal has treated him with great consideration and has received his parole of honour. I enclose a copy of this undertaking. But His Excellency thinks now that he should be watched closely and be brought to the attention of the police.

It seemed simple enough. A note from de la Martinière to the minister of war explaining Keane's presence on French soil.

Don Patrick spoke. 'Do you understand what it means, captain?'

'I think so.'

'Read it again. Read the final sentence.'

Keane read it again. 'Yes? Am I missing something?'

Curtis nodded. 'Do you detect the actual meaning of those words? What they actually imply concerning your fate? Try this.

'"Captain Keane is a spy and a dangerous one. We could not hang him because he was wearing uniform when caught. We will escort him just as far as Bayonne. Then let the police arrest him there and dispose of him and his two accomplices."'

Keane gasped. It was plain now. It was as good as his death warrant. De la Martinière and Marmont were washing their hands of him. Handing him and the other two over to Napoleon's notorious secret police, the organization by which Bonaparte kept internal control of his subjects.

Keane shook his head. 'But that's impossible. I gave my word.'

'Not impossible, captain, no. Because, you see, it has been done.'

'Where did you get this letter?'

'It was intercepted by one of my agents. A guerrilla leader, Don Ramon Sanchez – I believe you are acquainted with him.'

'Yes, of course, I know Sanchez well. So there is no doubting its authenticity?'

'None at all. They undoubtedly intend to kill you. All of you.'

The news to Keane of his own impending execution was alarming but in a way strangely welcome. It was useful, he thought, since, assuming that Don Patrick's interpretation was correct, its existence absolutely and instantly released him from his promise to keep his parole. The French had broken their part of the bargain and had arranged to have him and the others 'disappeared' at the hands of Napoleon's police thugs. On the other hand, it meant that when it was discovered that they had not been disposed of as intended, Keane and the two others would possibly be the most wanted men in France.

Keane put down the letter and, rising from the chair, began to pace the floor before turning to Curtis. 'What do you advise, father?'

'I would suggest that it is imperative you do not give any indication that you suspect anything. Go with the escorting officer on the road to Bayonne and then you must somehow contrive to escape. Major Grant had hoped that you might receive safe passage all the way to Paris, but he was clearly optimistic. This is the best you can now manage. You must go to Bayonne, playing along with their game, and then, before you are handed over, somehow make your escape. After that I can help. I have contacts at Bayonne, royalists who can assist you and get you to Paris.'

He reached into his cloak and produced what looked like two small pieces of paper. On one were written three names and addresses. Keane noticed references to Bayonne. The other, which on closer inspection was a piece of silk, opened out to a considerable size and proved to be a map, tiny but meticulously drawn, of the centre of Paris. 'This might help. I would advise you to cut a slit in the seam of your coat and hide them in there. You can never be too careful with the French.'

6

The main road to France from Salamanca ran by way of Valladolid and Burgos to Vitoria and San Sebastian.

Keane and Archer travelled inside a military coach, facing their guard of two armed infantrymen and an officer. Silver travelled up on the roof, alongside the driver, with his hands shackled to the bar at the side of his seat. Two further guards rode at the rear of the coach and they had been given an escort of forty dragoons.

Whether or not their guard knew what their intended fate might be was unclear. It seemed to him likely, however, that their commanding officer must know, as it would be he who would be handing them over to the police when they reached their destination. Perhaps, thought Keane, he might be able to work the same trick upon him as he had with Captain Dupont. He would, he reasoned, certainly have time to try.

Curtis had told him that it was some 320 miles from Salamanca to Bayonne by coach, and he had calculated by experience that in a coach this would take them some forty hours. It was customary to arrange changes of horses after every forty miles, and Keane reckoned that travelling at between eight and ten miles an hour, they would make six stops. One every four or five hours, the first for perhaps two hours, the second overnight at Valladolid, and then at Burgos, at Vitoria and at San Sebastian. He had just two and a half days in which to arrange their escape from certain death.

As dawn broke over Salamanca, the coach rattled out of the north gate of the old city and began to trundle up the road to Valladolid. No sooner were they clear of the environs than Keane began his attempt on the officer. He began with simple introductions. The man, a captain of infantry, was called Wenger and was originally Swiss, having joined the French army in 1809. He was clearly in awe of Keane, of whom he had heard much, and this provided the perfect opportunity. Over the next few hours, pausing occasionally to sleep or simply be silent, Keane entertained him with tales of his adventures, heartily embellished of course and in some cases entirely fabricated. He drew in Archer, who began to tell something of his own exploits, and soon the officer was staring at both of them, his attention and imagination held in their grasp.

As Keane had predicted, they halted after five hours, at a small inn at Alaijas, near Tordesillas, and having posted sentries went inside and ate, the two captive redcoats sitting apart from the others and Silver on his own, massaging his wrists which were chafing from the irons. Keane managed to persuade Captain Wenger to change the irons for a rope, and after an hour and a half they were on the road once more.

As they pulled away, Keane decided on his tactic. He would not be so forthcoming now as he had been before, but, having whet the Frenchman's appetite, would feed him just one more story and get him to ask for more. It worked. By the time they came within sight of Valladolid, two hours later, the captain was hanging on Keane's every word.

'And there I was, standing in Marshal Massena's own quarters in Almeida. I tell you, even I was terrified. But the only thing to do was bluff it out. So then I approached Marshal Massena and, still maintaining my dignity, refused point blank his invitation to take on my services as a spy. And of course he had to capitulate.'

'And his mistress? What of the lovely Henriette?'

'Well, of course we became lovers. And she left Massena. But this was not to be the last time that I would see her. Oh no.'

'No?'

'No, not by a long mile. But that of course is another story.'

The captain looked crestfallen. 'Oh, I say, come on. Carry on, Keane. You can't leave us there.'

The 'us' referred to one of the guards, who had been listening all the while and was now almost as captivated by the tales as his commander.

'I'm afraid that I shall have to. Look, we are arriving at our halt for the night.'

They rolled into the courtyard of a small coaching inn on the north side of the town and within minutes the French had posted sentries.

Keane and Archer found themselves sharing a room for the night with Captain Wenger, but despite his entreaties Keane was obstinate and would not tell any more tales that evening, claiming that he was far too tired. So far his plan was working perfectly.

The following morning an early start brought them to the third stage of their journey. Now, thought Keane, now was the time at which to deal his masterstroke.

As they drove along the road that flanked the Pisuerga river, rising from the plains around Valladolid to the foothills of the Cantabrian mountains, he began.

'I can tell you now, captain, that I have it on good authority that once you have turned us over to the police at Bayonne, we shall never be seen again.'

Captain Wenger stared at the floor. 'Yes, it was my fear. How do you come to know this?'

'I'm not an idiot, captain, as I would have thought would be evident from the tales with which I have been entertaining you. I have my means, as you will now be aware.'

Wenger looked troubled. It was exactly the reaction Keane had wanted.

'I have to say, I am a little surprised. I had reckoned Marshal Marmont above such things. De la Martinière? Well, I'm sure that you know his character as well as I do. It must be his doing. But to murder in cold blood officers who have given you their parole, their solemn word of honour, it's unthinkable. Wouldn't you say so, captain?'

'Yes, Captain Keane. If you must know, I am wholly in agreement with you and when I saw the order I was appalled. Worse than that, sickened. Surely such a plan is not necessary. But I'm afraid that I think there is nothing I can do to help you. Your fate has been decided.'

The remainder of that stage of the journey was passed in silence, and when they stopped for lunch at the same time as the previous day Wenger clearly felt too awkward to make conversation. As they sat in the little inn at Palencia, eating a meagre lunch of bread and broth, and Wenger turned to give the guards an order, Keane spoke quietly to Archer.

'You know, I think we might just have a chance here. He's

a very suggestible fellow and clearly his conscience is troubled about delivering us to the firing squad.'

'But, sir, he can't go against the order. He would simply exchange places with us. It would be him at the end of the guns.'

'True, but if we can persuade him to allow us to effect an escape without implicating him, then all might be well.'

The next stage of the afternoon brought new revelations. They had not gone more than ten miles when Wenger spoke. 'I apologize, captain. I feel that I have been less than gracious. You took me into your confidence and I have nothing to offer you. I am deeply embarrassed by the behaviour of my countrymen.'

Keane smiled at him. 'You are very kind, monsieur, but your apology is not necessary. As soldiers we accept our fate, do we not, Archer? We are quite resigned to what awaits us. I am only surprised as it was not what I would have expected from the sort of honourable Frenchman with whom I have had the pleasure to be engaged with in battle these past twenty years.'

Keane looked at Wenger's face and for a moment he thought the man was going to burst into tears. Clearly something he had said had struck a note. And he thought that he knew what it might be.

At length Wenger spoke. 'I have to tell you, captain – Lieutenant Archer, you too – I do not like Colonel de la Martinière.'

He paused before going on. 'He is not a popular man. Do you understand what I mean? In the army. He is a most unpopular man. In fact I would go so far as to say that he is hated. Yes, hated, captain.'

Keane said nothing and inside was jubilant. This could

not have been a better reaction. He prayed that it would develop.

Within a few minutes Wenger spoke again. 'I admire your courage, Captain Keane. You are an extraordinarily brave man and a great soldier. And you too, lieutenant. In Captain Keane here you have a great model to live up to.'

He looked puzzled and then looked away, as if suddenly realizing that as both men had a death sentence upon them Archer's aspirations would never be realized.

He spoke again, with some feeling in his voice. 'I feel that in the past two days, you and I, captain, we have become close. Almost friends?'

Keane looked back at him. 'Yes, captain, I would dearly like to think so. I would like to count myself your friend. It would matter to me a great deal before I go to meet my maker, as has been ordained by your superiors.'

Wenger looked at him and for a moment Keane saw in his eyes almost his own image. It was the look of a man who, faced with an insufferable truth, will try his best to overcome that impossibility. The look of a man who would take on the world to help his friend. The look of a man who would help him.

But it was not until the three of them were alone in their shared room that night in the inn at Burgos that at length Wenger spoke. 'Captain Keane, I know enough about you to know that you are a man of honour. That whatever you have done against the empire counts as little in the face of the fact that you are an officer and, if I may say so, a quite extraordinary man. It would be against my nature and against all the principles and codes by which I stand to allow you to be murdered by Fouché's thugs.'

'Fouché?'

'The emperor's ex-chief of secret police, who still effectively controls Paris, if not all France, with his own men. To that end, I have decided that when we reach Bayonne, you will escape.'

Keane smiled and clapped him on the back in a gesture of thanks.

'I thank you, captain, for delivering us from Monsieur Fouché. I am forever in your debt. To Bayonne!'

The plan appeared to have worked.

The following day, their last full day travelling together, was spent in more storytelling. Keane, anxious to preserve the companionable mood in which he had put Wenger, spoke warmly of their relations with some of the French they had encountered. He told him in particular detail of the fight at Coimbra in which he and his men had defended the French garrison from the onslaught of Portuguese militia. He also, gauging his moment, related the story of the French spy and his underhand and barbaric methods. It caused the predicted revulsion.

They stopped for just over an hour at Miranda, and crossing the Ebro they passed through Vitoria in the late afternoon and began to climb steadily into the mountains beyond. After twenty miles they came to a halt at the village of Bergara. Not wanting to revisit the same territory they had traversed so heavily the previous night, and sure in the certainty that Wegner would now do everything he could to allow them to escape, Keane decided that the best way for them to pass the last evening was with several bottles of wine. But at the same time he would ensure that the French captain drank more than he and Archer.

As they sat down in the otherwise quiet tavern, Keane pulled a bag from his pocket, took out four gold coins and pressed them on the landlord. The man, clearly astonished that a prisoner of the French should do such a thing, was only too pleased and produced two of his finest bottles with which to wash down their supper of roast rabbit and tortilla.

Wenger sat with the two English officers a distance away from the dragoons, whose officers sat together, close to the sergeants. Silver as usual messed on his own, and engaged the landlord's wife in conversation in Spanish.

Occasionally the dragoon officers shot Wenger a disapproving glance, but he was beyond caring. As far as he was concerned, Keane and Archer were in his care and he would choose how to deal with them. Wenger was only too happy to accept Keane's hospitality. It seemed almost as if he had been waiting for this excuse. He raised his glass to toast Keane's health.

'You are very kind, captain. I am sorry that we shall lose you tomorrow.'

Keane froze for a moment. 'Lose us?' His blood ran cold.

'Yes, when you leave us at Bayonne and I return to my duties at Salamanca.'

'Yes, of course, at Bayonne.'

He hoped that in his cups the Frenchman would not say too much, particularly with the dragoons looking on. 'Lose' was rather too obvious a word, although to anyone overhearing their conversation it might also have meant the worst interpretation of de la Martinière's orders.

Wenger had promised to give Keane an idea of how and when might be their best time to make a run for it, but had not done so to date. The wine was enough to loosen his tongue.

'There is a place as we enter the town. I know it well. We will arrive in the late afternoon. We will all be tired. The place will be sleepy. It is a very small square, not much used by the troops of the garrison. When I was there we hardly ever went there and certainly not at that time of day. I will halt the coach in a square and the men will be looking for somewhere to spend the night. I can guarantee that when we get there the thoughts of the dragoons will be upon quite different things. We will have no trouble from them. We will dismount from the coach and I will dismiss the escort and then, while the men are getting your sergeant down from the roof and putting themselves in order, you will take me prisoner.'

'I will?'

'You will. You will take my pistol and hold it to my head. You will then walk with me and your two friends as I direct you across the square and into an alleyway. There you will hit me.'

'I will hit you?'

'Yes, of course. You have my permission to hit me, captain.'

'I'm sorry? I'm to hit you?'

'Of course. How else are we to make it seem that I have not assisted you? You must assault me.'

Keane poured more wine. 'Very well. You're quite happy with this?'

'Of course. I consider it my duty as an officer. Captain Keane, we have discussed this enough. We both know what must be done to satisfy honour in this matter. This is the only way.'

Keane noticed from the corner of his eye that the two green-coated dragoon officers had risen from the table and were walking towards them. He nudged Archer beneath the table and nodded to Captain Wenger, who turned to them.

'Good evening, Captain Duvalle, lieutenant.'

'Good evening, Captain Wenger. You seem very happy to sit with our prisoners. Are they so very interesting that they persuade you to reject our company?'

Wenger stood up. 'Don't be silly, Duvalle, I'm not rejecting your company. I find Captain Keane's exploits highly entertaining, as you would too if you cared to listen.'

Duvalle bristled. 'I do not care to share the table with a man who colludes with the guerrilla. And nor should you, Wenger.'

'Oh, don't be such an ass, Duvalle. Captain Keane is no more a guerrilla than you or I.'

'But he does know them and has used them. And they in turn have profited from him and they have killed more of my men than I care to recall. He is no better than . . . a guerrilla in a red coat. He is a spy, Wenger. No more, no less.'

There was silence for a moment. Keane could not deny any of the facts. He had worked closely with the guerrillas, with Sanchez and Morillo and others. And the guerrillas had perpetrated ghastly atrocities against the French. In particular against the dragoons, who were often used as escorts for couriers, their prime target. Keane stood up and nodded a greeting at Duvalle. 'Captain, I cannot deny that what you say is true, although I take exception at the use of the word "spy". I am a British officer and courtesy demands certain etiquette. As regards the *guerrillista*, I, like you, abhor the methods of many of the guerrillas, as does my commander Lord Wellington. We have done everything possible to dissuade them from such practices.'

The dragoon officer shrugged. 'That may be, but it has had no effect. You might have seen some of my men. They're the ones you see hanging from the olive trees as you pass along the roads observing our armies and stealing information. The ones with no arms or legs, or genitals. Stripped, dismembered, disembowelled and blinded. That's the work of your Spanish friends. They're very talented butchers.'

'Yes, captain, and as I say, I am sorry for the atrocity. I have done all I could to prevent it. Although it is done, I might add, in response to the acts of your own countrymen.'

Wenger spoke. 'For heaven's sake, Duvalle, Captain Keane has told me how he personally intervened to stop a French officer being tortured to death.'

'And how did he manage that?'

Keane interjected. 'The only way I could. I shot him myself.'

Duvalle said nothing, but turned and walked away with his lieutenant.

Wenger and Keane sat down. Wenger spoke. 'I apologize.'

'There's no need for that. No need at all. I have seen what the guerrillas do. Of course. We all have. And I have tried. But this war is not like any other. It is a war of the people. A war in which your countrymen under their emperor are trying to conquer not just a great land but a great people. And that is why we are here. We are fighting for their freedom.'

Wenger smiled and took a drink. 'Perhaps also though you are fighting for your own country. Not for its freedom, but for its wealth. Isn't that true?'

Keane nodded. 'Yes, I can't deny that. But as a soldier I would rather think that I was risking my life and those of my men for something more noble than money.'

Archer grinned. 'That's true enough, sir. But you must admit that sometimes, for the men, gold can be the best motive.'

Keane looked at him and raised an eyebrow. What did he mean, 'for the men'? Clearly Archer had taken his role play as an officer to heart and now felt himself a class above the others. Keane played along. 'Yes, Archer, you're quite right. The "men" do appreciate the baser things in life. As Wellington says, the army is as loyal to its rum ration as it is to him.'

Wenger laughed, making the two dragoons look round at him. 'I should like to meet your Lord Wellington, whatever my commanders say of him.'

'Who knows – perhaps some day that might be arranged.'

Wenger lowered his voice. 'Now, just to make sure we have it right. Remember, Keane, I don't want you to play with me; I want to feel the full force. You must do it as if it is real.'

Keane smiled. 'Very well, captain. I'll do it as if it is real.' He turned to the landlord and called for another two bottles of the Rioja. 'And you had better pray, my friend, that you drink enough of this stuff to make you feel nothing.'

They reached the outskirts of Bayonne in the mid-afternoon of the following day, having made the twenty-six miles from Bergara to San Sebastian by midday and another thirty from there to Bayonne in three hours. They approached the coastal town from the Ustaritz road from the south, and the first thing that Keane noted was the strength of the walls of the citadel. Bayonne was a classic star fort, built by the great Vauban and well placed to defend the mouth of the river Adour on which it sat. Before a high castellated and turreted wall with seven bastions lay two defensive lines of triangular demi-lunes, split as was the town by a tributary of the river, while beyond these at half a mile lay more defensive earthworks, and to the right the natural defences of a large salt marsh with on the left a forest of pines. Rising up beyond the town, across the river, they could just make out the shape of the citadel, with more high bastions. It made Badajoz look like easy pickings and

Keane wondered if they would ever have the misfortune to lay siege to it. He stared hard, attempting to etch the look of the place in his head so that he might draw an image of it as soon as might be practical.

The coach rumbled on through the huge gate and past the towering cathedral on the left of the road. They had not gone more than a few narrow streets beyond the church, however, when Wenger rapped on the roof with his cane and shouted to the driver to stop. Looking through the windows, Keane saw that they were in a small square of tall, half-timbered houses rising above stone colonnades. The place was quiet, the inhabitants, presumably including the garrison, still taking their afternoon siesta.

The coach pulled up abruptly and Wenger looked at Keane and nodded before pushing open the door and stepping out. One of the guards motioned to Keane and Archer to get out and they did so in turn. One of the dragoons cut Silver free from his ropes and escorted him down to join his comrades. The rest of the dragoons had assembled in two ranks in the square and were being given orders by Captain Duvalle. Seeing Keane emerge, he rode across to Wenger.

'Captain Wenger, I think our job is done. The prisoners are yours.'

'Yes, Captain Duvalle. You are discharged from your escort duty. Thank you.'

Duvalle saluted and, with a last glaring glance at Keane, turned to face his men. After a few commands they were off, riding in column of twos across to the far side of the square, where they left down the widest of the side streets in the direction of the bridge across to the barracks at the citadel.

Looking across to Wenger, Keane saw that the French captain had tucked his pistol into his belt. Wenger glanced at him and he knew the moment had come. He looked back at the second guard, who was only just dismounting from the coach, and in a single swift action moved close to Wenger and took the pistol from his belt, cocking the hammer and placing the muzzle close against the captain's temple.

The four guards instinctively raised their muskets, but stopped quickly when Keane spoke to them in French.

'Do nothing. Put down your guns.'

Wenger, feigning fear, nodded and the guards obeyed. Keane motioned to Archer, who picked up one of the muskets and, using the bayonet, herded the guards together, making them stand in a huddle beside the coach. Silver was with them now. He took two of the guards and used the rope with which he had been tied to bind their hands together before forcing them to mount the step and climb into the carriage. Then, using the driver's whip, he bound the hands of the other two guards in the same way and made them do the same before shutting the carriage door. At the same time Archer moved his musket from the guards to the driver, who sat above the horses, terrified. Then, making sure that the driver continued to watch, Keane slowly walked away from the coach with Wenger, all the time keeping the pistol close up against the captain's temple. Wenger had told them to make for the street at the northern corner of the square and this they did. A shutter opened and a face appeared, only to disappear instantly at the disturbing sight which greeted it.

Entering the side street, Keane relaxed the pressure of the gun on Wenger's head and after a few yards dropped it entirely. Archer, who along with Silver had picked up two of the grounded muskets, made to hand one to Keane, who shook his head before turning to the French captain.

'Thank you, captain. I really can never thank you enough.'

'It is no more than I would do for any officer, of any army, in such circumstances. But for you, Captain Keane, it was a real pleasure.'

'Should the need ever arise, captain, don't hesitate to call on me. I am at your service. I truly hope that your actions will not have put your own life at risk.'

Wenger laughed. 'Don't worry, captain. All cats have nine lives. I must have at least three of mine left. Haven't you forgotten something?'

'You're quite sure about this?'

'Certainly. It's my alibi. May I turn away?'

'Please, and thank you again.'

Wenger turned from Keane, and as soon as he had done so, Keane, still holding the pistol in his hand, raised his fist and brought it down on the captain's head.

Wenger crumpled to the ground, unconscious, and Keane was pleased to see that his head did not strike too hard on the cobbles.

Silver looked at him. 'Blimey, sir. That was giving it to him all right.'

'Looked worse than it was. Old trick. I didn't use the butt of the weapon, just its weight. He'll have a nasty headache though, when he wakes up. Come on.'

Wasting no time, the three men turned and hurried away down the street. Keane tucked the French pistol inside his cloak and then, realizing that Archer and Silver were still carrying the muskets, told them to drop them.

*

Keane drew out from the slit in his uniform coat the piece of
paper given to him by Father Curtis and read the three names.
The most likely, Curtis had told him, was the first, a French
royalist by the name of Duplessis who lived at a house on the
east bank of southern Bayonne. That was where they would
now make for.

There was a sketch map on the reverse of the piece of paper,
and Keane used it to navigate them to the royalist's house. It
was part of a modest half-timbered building containing four
houses, all accessed through a common shady courtyard lined
with balconies and with a fountain in the centre. Fragrant
mimosa plants grew among the old stones and a single olive
tree stood near the fountain. The Duplessis house lay in the
far corner and Keane knocked on the door, conscious that
soon the town would be alive with troops searching for them.

With only six men able to identify them, and the captain
unlikely to do so, the likelihood of them being found in a town
of some 15,000 inhabitants was slim. But Keane didn't want to
take any chances.

After a while the door was answered by a woman. She was
small, in her sixties and neatly turned out in a plain white
dress of a style which had been in fashion some twenty years
before. She looked Keane directly in the eye and, seeing the
other two men, their cloaks worn over military uniforms,
spoke in a clipped accent with a hint of alarm in her voice.

'Yes? What do you want here?'

'Madame Duplessis?'

'Perhaps. Who wants her?'

Keane had taken pains to remember the password. 'Zenobius.'
The woman opened the door further and without a word

ushered them all inside before closing it behind them. In the dark it took Keane a few seconds before he realized that she was pointing a pistol at his heart.

'Who are you and what do you want? Speak fast and speak true. I won't hesitate to shoot if I doubt you.'

'We come from Father Curtis. My name is Keane. Captain James Keane. We are British soldiers. We escaped from the French less than an hour ago. We're on the run and need to get to Paris. Can you help us?'

The woman lowered her pistol. 'Yes, of course. I had word of your coming. Camille Duplessis. It seems strange to me though that three British soldiers on the run from the French should want to get to Paris.'

'It's rather hard to explain. Let's just say that we have a mission there. Is your husband at home?'

The woman smiled. 'Captain Keane, my husband passed away seven years ago.'

'Oh, I'm sorry. I thought—'

'You presumed that a royalist agent working in secret for a clandestine organization would naturally be a man.'

'I'm afraid that I did.'

'It's a common mistake. My husband was the contact before he died. I just took over. It's a better cover. Who would suspect a frail old woman of being at the centre of a group of royalist insurgents?'

'Very clever, madame. We are grateful for your help. I think it would be best if we moved on as quickly as possible.'

'I agree. You are two officers and a servant, isn't that right?'

'Yes, Lieutenant Archer and Private Silver.'

'That is what I was told. I have prepared papers for you. You are Irish, is that right?'

'Yes, madame.'

'And your lieutenant is a Scot?'

Archer spoke. 'Yes, madame. That's quite correct.'

'Good. On Father Curtis's instructions I have papers for you both in the names of officers of the Légion Irlandaise.'

She led them through the house to a small room at the rear where, opening a secret drawer hidden in a large oak bureau, she drew out several pieces of paper.

'Here you are, captain.' She handed a paper to Keane. 'And one for you, lieutenant, and another for your servant.'

The three men looked at their papers. Keane's was in the name of a Captain Williams. He was the same age as Keane and had been born in Newtownards, just a few miles away from Keane's own home town of Bangor. Curtis had done his job well. Archer's alias was that of a Lieutenant O'Connell, from Cork, while Silver was Corporal Lynch, a Derry man.

'Thank you, madame. These look splendid. You have done a fine job.'

'It comes naturally. I trained in the fine arts and had planned to become a painter of miniatures. Then the Revolution came and that world vanished for me. For everyone.'

'The arts seem to flourish under Bonaparte.'

The woman looked at him with hatred in her eyes. 'That man – that monster – he makes a sham of art. He uses art for his own purposes. Just as he uses everyone and everything. Come with me.'

She took them into the next room where, to Keane's surprise, they found hanging on the wall a small portrait of a man in French military uniform. On his chest he wore the Légion d'Honneur and his tall shako marked him out as an officer of the Imperial Guard.

'My son, Charles-Louis Duplessis, captain in the Tirailleurs of the Young Guard.'

Keane spoke softly. 'He fought for Bonaparte?'

'Yes, he fought for Bonaparte. When we all believed that Bonaparte might be the answer. When we believed that man would right the wrongs of the Revolution and give France back her soul. But what did he do? He sent France to her grave. A million soldiers. Half a million dead. That is what we hear. Half a million of our sons. And my son was one of them.'

'I am sorry for your loss, madame.'

'Thank you. Now you see why I hate that man and all that he has done for France. You will need to change your uniforms.'

Keane shook his head. 'I don't think so. Father Curtis didn't mention that. The moment we change our uniforms we assume disguise, and in disguise we can be taken for spies and shot.'

'Nevertheless, if you are to pass as Irish then you cannot wear the red coats of your own army. You will have to wear the green of Ireland.'

Keane thought for a few moments. 'Very well. But how are we to find green coats?'

'I have them here for you.'

'How could you know our sizes?'

'Father Curtis is most thorough.'

Madame Duplessis left them to change and they were quick to slip off their cloaks and exchange their red coats for those she had so unexpectedly provided. A white waistcoat and a green tailed coat, trimmed with yellow facings, gold lace and gold buttons, for Keane and Archer and a less ornate green coat for Silver, with a single NCO's stripe and a long-service badge.

Keane was not surprised that, while far from perfect,

they fitted well enough. Their grey overall trousers they would keep, these being similar to the French model. As to headdress, while Madame Duplessis offered Keane a shako that had belonged to her son, with an altered brass plate and green pompom, Keane and Archer were happy enough to keep their black military bicornes, merely exchanging the black Hanoverian cockade of the British army for the tricolour worn by Napoleon's troops. Silver, rather than a cumbersome shako, would make do with a simple green and yellow forage cap in the French style.

Of course Keane had adopted disguise before. First at the attack on Oporto and later to infiltrate Massena's headquarters at Almeida. But this was different. Now they would be behind enemy lines, on French home territory. Donning the green coat he felt instantly vulnerable, although of course he did not say anything to the others and tried to make light of it. He looked at Archer.

'It's extraordinary, Archer, if I didn't know you better I would say that you look an even better Irish officer than you do an English. And as for you, Silver, you fit the bill exactly.'

The men laughed. Archer felt the gold bullion epaulette at Keane's shoulder. 'You do look very smart, sir. Quite the Irish officer yourself. They don't stint on expense, do they? In Boney's army.'

'His army thrives on glory, Archer. Everything is for show. It does not matter to us in the British army. We don't care for show. It's the fighting man that counts.'

Silver shook his head. 'It's all very well being got up as Paddies, sir, if you'll excuse me, but I don't see how that's going to help us. To tell you the truth, I don't really understand it, sir. All this Irish stuff. I mean, you're Irish and so is

Wellington himself and that's good because Ireland is really a part of England, isn't it? But why would there be Irishmen in their own regiment in Boney's army?'

'We're supposed to be in the Irish Legion, Silver. Irishmen fighting in French service. It's like this. Back in '98 there was a rising in Ireland and our clever government in their wisdom, having put it down, sent all the ringleaders over to France in exile. And what happens? Bonaparte comes to power and says to himself, Let's invade England. And while I'm about it we'll go for Ireland too. Hold on, weren't there a lot of Irishmen hereabouts? I know, we can make them into a unit and send them over to raise their countrymen against the English. So that's what he does. He starts the Irish Legion, the Légion Irlandaise. The men of '98 become the officers, and there are soon enough Irishmen to make a regiment.'

Keane carried on. 'That's about it. Major Grant told me about it. It was back in '05. The Irish Legion was to be the core of a much larger invasion force of 20,000 that had been earmarked to take Ireland, known as the *Corps d'Irlande*.

'It came into being in 1803 under a rogue named MacSheehy who was an adjutant-general in Boney's army. The whole idea of it was to turn Irish patriot hearts to the French cause in the imminent invasion of Ireland.

'But we all know what happened next, don't we, Silver?'

Silver grinned. 'Trafalgar, sir. I was there.'

'As you never fail to remind us. On the *Victory* itself, wasn't it? Admiral Nelson's flagship.'

'That it was. Up in the rigging. Marine sharpshooter.'

'Yes, well, Trafalgar happened and so the French were stuck. The invasion was off. So Boney abandons his idea of taking England, and that includes Ireland into the bargain.'

Archer, straightening the lace on his new coat, spoke again. 'What happened to the legion then, sir?'

'He didn't disband it. It was too useful to him. Good as a snub to England too – to have that many Irishmen fighting against the Crown. He kept it together on the French coast on garrison duty and coastal defence. He sent some to Spain too. I never fought them, but I'm told they fought well. As you'd expect from my countrymen. They put down the Spanish rising on 2nd May and fought at Astorga. It was the legion that led the assault on the city that took it. They say that one of the drummer boys carried on beating the attack even after having both his legs blown off. And they fought against us at Fuentes last year under Massena.'

'So it's not a bad lot that we're supposed to be a part of then, sir?'

'No, Silver, not a bad lot at all. You can be proud of your adopted regiment.'

'Well, that's a relief. And I can tell you I'd rather be an Irishman, even a bad one, than a bloody Frenchie. I hated those uniforms you made us wear at Oporto, sir.'

'There are different sorts of Irishmen, Silver. Always have been. There are those who like King George and those, shall we say, who don't. There are Catholics and Protestants.'

'So really what you are, sir, is you're an Irishman pretending to be an Irishman?'

'I'm a sort of Irishman pretending to be another sort of Irishman. The sort of Irishman who wants Ireland not to be a part of England, as you put it, and is prepared to fight for Boney to make that happen.'

'That ain't right, sir, is it?'

'No, Silver, I don't think it is right. But it's damned useful as it means that now I can move freely around France. And so can the two of you.'

'You mean I've to pretend to be an Irishman? A bad sort of Irishman?'

'Yes, exactly. As has Archer.'

'I'm still Lieutenant Archer though, sir, aren't I?'

'Yes, Archer, don't worry, you are still an officer until further notice. You're doing a good job so far. Just don't get too used to it.'

7

Having adopted their disguises, Keane was well aware that all three of them had to familiarize themselves with their aliases. He had managed it well enough when masquerading as a Spanish wine merchant to infiltrate Massena's headquarters at Almeida two years ago, but this time he knew he would require something more. If they were all to carry off their new characters, they would have to have the facts about these men at their fingertips and be ready to answer some basic questions if and when they were asked.

Curtis had done his work well. Each of their aliases suited them perfectly.

Keane stood before his two men. 'We have to get this right. If we're suspected, there will be no way back. No second chances. Let's try the accents.' He switched to character. Captain Williams was an Ulsterman. It had been Keane's native tongue, although he had in recent years grown to speak more as the English officer he had become. Yet there was still in his own accent an underlying base of the native Northern Irishman.

He tried it now, managing several sentences before Archer

and Silver dissolved in laughter. 'Sir, that's very good.' Archer grinned. 'Very good indeed.'

'This is serious, Archer.'

'Of course, sir. I know. It's really very good.'

'Silver?'

'Very good, sir. Just right.'

'Yes, well, it's your turn now. Archer?'

Archer, as a Scot, was better suited to carry off the voice of the man from Cork with its softer, lilting tones. He spoke a few sentences and Keane couldn't help but smile. 'You're a natural, man. A real man of the south.'

'Thank you, sir. I'll do my best.'

As a private, Silver would not have to speak so often. So he was to be a Derry man, and Curtis had banked on the fact that his natural English accent, coloured by years on campaign, would serve well enough.

The only worry would be if they were to encounter any genuine Irish Bonapartists. Keane knew that there were a fair few about. Even Napoleon's minister of war, the Duc de Feltre himself, Clarke, was an Irishman on his father's side. So, apart from their accents, their stories would have to be perfect too. To this end Curtis had sent to Madame Duplessis, through his agents, a sheaf of written notes for each of them. Facts which they would have to learn, simple general facts about the Légion Irlandaise and other details regarding their own backgrounds.

He handed the relevant pages to the others and began to read his own.

The history of the Légion Irlandaise read roughly as he had explained it to Archer and Silver. In 1809 the first battalion had fought the British at Walcheren Island and had retreated to Flushing with heavy casualties but put up a gallant defence. The French surrendered and the entire garrison of Flushing were made prisoner and transported to England. However, a small number of men managed to escape. Among them Captain Lawless, who travelled by boat to Antwerp and Paris, where he was received by the emperor himself. He was given the Legion of Honour, promoted to *chef de bataillon* and given command of the first battalion of the Irish regiment. The second battalion joined Murat's army in Spain and were among the French troops used to suppress the revolt in Madrid of 2 May 1808.

In 1810, the battalion was assigned to Junot's army of Portugal. It saw action at the siege of Almeida, Bussaco and Fuentes de Oñoro. It was from this unit that Keane and his men purported to come. Their story was that the battalion had been broken up in December 1811. The officers and sergeants, corporals and drummers had been kept together, and the privates had joined another regiment as replacements. While the other officers and NCOs had arrived at the new regimental depot at Bois-le-Duc in southern Holland in April 1812, Keane and his two companions had been engaged in regimental business in France since then and were now on their way to Holland. It sounded plausible enough, thought Keane, and hoped that he and the others would be able to recall the regimental history.

It would not be long before they had a chance to find out. Keane had supposed that they should travel from Bayonne to Paris by coach, and Madame Duplessis confirmed this. There was a 'diligence', the regular express coach, due to run the following morning and it was imperative that they should not stay in the town for any longer than they had to. The papers provided by Doctor Curtis contained military travel passes which permitted them to move freely by public transport throughout the empire, at no expense.

After they had become better acquainted with their parts, they ate a simple supper and slept on beds provided by Madame Duplessis, with Silver and Archer taking turns at standing sentry just inside the front door, listening for the merest hint of any footfall which might signal a search party. But none came. Dawn arrived and with it the rare chance to arrange their appearance. Keane and Archer shaved and washed to present themselves as officers who might have spent the past few months on home service rather than the renegades they were. Even Silver managed to give an impression of orderliness in a fresh shirt and his new green coat. They retained their blue boat cloaks, but Madame Duplessis wrapped their scarlet uniform tunics in paper, ready to be collected by one of Father Curtis's agents. There was now no going back. They had broken their parole and were wanted men who might be shot dead by any of the enemy at any time.

They left the Duplessis house at intervals of a few minutes, heading through the narrow streets in the direction of the inn which was the terminus for the Paris diligence, and Keane prayed that there would be sufficient seats inside the coach for all of them. Heading out from the maze of alleyways into a wider street, Keane stopped for a minute, momentarily frozen by the presence of a group of blue-coated French infantry in conversation on the corner. One of them noticed him and indicated to the others. It was a moment of truth, but it seemed that the disguise had worked, for all three of them stood to attention in the presence of an officer of the famed Légion Irlandaise.

Buoyed up by the reaction, Keane decided to push his luck and, walking directly past them, returned the salute. He carried on, waiting again for the shout of 'halt' and the click of hammer on lock, but neither came and he reached the end of the street. He could see Archer now, coming towards him from the opposite end of a small alleyway, and greeted him with a smile.

'Any problems?'

'No, sir, it seems to work.'

'Yes, I just got a salute from three Frenchies. Have you seen Silver?'

The private was Keane's biggest worry, and they found him making his way towards the inn, looking a little unsettled.

'Still don't feel right, sir. Green coat? Feels queer to me.'

'Well, you look every inch the part, Silver. Just try and act like an Irishman.'

'Would that mean acting like you, sir?'

'You know what I mean. Think yourself into the part.'

'I'll do my best, sir. I just try to follow you, do I?'

'As you will, Silver. But remember, you're still a private.'

'Just like Mr Archer here, then, sir.'

Archer scowled at him.

Keane led the way to the inn where the coach was waiting and called to the driver, who was standing talking to the landlord. 'Any seats left? To Paris?'

The man turned, and on seeing Keane's uniform his scowl changed. 'There might be, sir. The general's commandeered the whole coach, but for you . . .'

Keane nodded to him. 'The general?'

'General Souham. He's inside, sir.'

Keane turned to Archer and spoke quietly. 'Here we go. Wish me luck.'

He would rather have delayed until the following day, but Keane knew that there could be no backing down now. He walked towards the door of the coach, which stood open, and peered inside.

There were four other passengers and two empty seats. One occupant wore civilian clothes; the others though were French officers. One of them, his shoulder encrusted with gold bullion and the cross of the Légion d'Honneur on his chest, was clearly General Souham, divisional commander in Marmont's army of Portugal.

Keane coughed. 'Excuse me, general. Captain James Williams, Légion Irlandaise. Would it be possible for myself and my lieutenant here to take the remaining two seats?'

The general looked at him. 'Yes, captain, that should be fine. You are going to Paris?'

'Yes, sir. Regimental business. That is extremely kind. My servant can travel up beside the driver.'

With their travelling bags stowed on top of the coach behind Silver, Keane climbed into the compartment, followed by Archer.

Once settled, Keane smiled at the general, who was sitting directly opposite him and who returned his smile and spoke. 'Good morning, captain. You're most welcome to share my coach. May I enquire as to the nature of your business in Paris? I had thought that all of your regiment had been moved to Holland two months ago.'

'We were left behind, general. Tying up regimental affairs in Spain. You know the sort of thing.'

The driver goaded the horses to start, and the coach rocked into motion.

The general nodded. 'Yes. We too have been away from the army. On the Esla, while Marshal Marmont raided into Beira.'

'Oh yes, things are getting quite hot here. It would have been better for the regiment to have remained in Spain, I think. I don't think we'll see much action where we're going. Still it will be good to see Colonel Lawless again after so long.'

'Yes, I wonder how he is. Do send him my compliments, won't you? And I wouldn't be too sure about the lack of action, captain. The emperor's big offensive can't be far away. I'm sure that you will have a part to play. Your regiment is well known for its bravery.'

There was a disturbance outside the coach, which came to a halt. Souham looked vexed. 'What now? We've hardly started.'

One of the staff officers spoke. 'It's the sentries. They're checking papers. I think it's to do with that business with the escaped prisoner.'

'Oh yes, the redcoat officer. Someone said something about a spy.'

As he said the word, a face appeared at the carriage window followed by a hand thrust inside. The sentry spoke: 'Papers.' Then, seeing General Souham, the guard withdrew his hand. 'General, my apologies. I didn't realize it was you. Please, carry on.'

The general smiled and waved the man away and the coach rolled on, through the town gates, northwards towards Paris. Keane realized that his unplanned choice of travelling companion could not have been better, providing of course that his cover was not broken.

*

They moved up the road at an average speed of around ten miles an hour through Bordeaux to Angoulême and then from Poitiers to Tours, where they crossed the Loire over the old bridge. And all the time the passengers exchanged pleasantries and polite conversation. And every time they reached a toll bridge or a police checkpoint on the larger of the highways, on seeing the general the guards did not ask for any of their papers.

From time to time each of them slept in turn, and Keane and Archer managed in this way to avoid long and involved conversations with the French officers and in particular with the general.

They travelled thus for twelve hours a day, stopping twice at inns at Bordeaux and Poitiers. It was curious to be driving, or indeed driven, through a country that had not seen the ravages of war. France looked, from the window of their carriage, as perfectly at peace with itself as he imagined England and his native Ireland must have looked these past three years that he had been away with the colours in Portugal and Spain. Late spring had touched the land with a riot of colour and the trees were all in blossom. Sheep with lambs and cows with their calves filled the fields, where in Spain such sights were now rare, such were the spoliations of the invading and occupying armies. It was strange too, even for Keane as an English officer, to have the sensation of feeling unthreatened on the road. Every road in Spain was watched, either by French scouts and cavalry patrols or by guerrillas, and at any moment a shout or a shot could signal an attack. And if he felt such a sense of relief, he could only imagine what it must be like for his fellow travellers to be back on their home soil.

At length, on the evening of the third day, the coach rolled into Orléans. They drove along the left bank of the Loire and turned into the Place du Marché, and it was with some relief that Keane bade farewell to General Souham outside the half-timbered inn which was to be the general's billet for the night. He and Archer retrieved their bags and with Silver behind them walked away from the coach towards the west of the town.

Archer spoke. 'By God, sir, I don't think I could have managed another day of that, do you?'

'No, not for one moment. For one awful instant I thought we had been discovered.'

'Yes, a little too close for comfort at times.'

Father Curtis had told them that one of his agents would be awaiting their arrival with three good horses, which would carry them to Paris. The map showed the rendezvous to be a short walk away and the trio moved fast and silently through the streets, focused on their destination.

'Another Irishman,' said Silver, and Keane had to admit that he was right.

Archer shook his head. 'How many of these Irishmen does Curtis run, do you suppose, sir?'

'Heaven only knows, but we should be damn thankful for them, don't you think?'

The agent offered them no name. He greeted them stiffly and with few words led them to the stables.

There were several horses in the stalls but their contact had tethered the three he had chosen for them together at one end. He offered Keane a tall bay, while Archer took a black stallion and Silver a slightly smaller roan with a vaguely Arabian look to her.

'We really can't thank you enough.'

At last the man smiled and spoke. 'Any friend of Patrick Curtis is a friend of mine, captain. Plus the fact you're an Irishman yourself. Now, the road you want to take is the one north to Artenay. Don't use the main roads as there will be police checkpoints. The smaller, country roads are safer, and any gendarmes posted on those will have slipped off home to their beds by the time you reach them. Take the road to Angerville and Étampes and from there the road towards Orsay and Sèvres. It will take you a good four hours, maybe more, and don't push the horses. Come into the city from the north-west. The guards are less watchful there.'

They set off immediately. It was good to be on horseback out in the open after so many days penned up inside a carriage, although Silver did not seem to agree and let them know about it as they trotted through the city.

'Have you ever travelled up on top of a coach, sir? Can't say it's something I'd like to do again. Freezing cold and bloody dangerous, if you ask me.'

'At least you didn't have the general's conversation to deal with. If I hear one more time about Marshal Massena's exquisite taste and Marshal Marmont's wine cellar my brain will burst. I've sampled his wine cellar myself, for God's sake. How I'd love to have told him that.'

Archer added, 'And what about his snoring, sir? Every time I began to get to sleep, there it was again. Like thunder, every time.'

Keane laughed. 'Or his aide de camp's curious lack of hygiene. You'd have thought a bit of soap, or a pomander at least.'

Silver laughed. 'You should have been sitting next to the driver, sir.'

Three horsemen riding through the night make better time by moonlight, and the weather favoured Keane and his men. With their cloaks blowing out behind them they pushed on to Angerville. The little town was silent and, just as the agent had told them, the sentry box at the side of the road was empty of its guard. Étampes and Orsay followed quickly, and after three hours' hard riding Keane pulled up beside a brook which ran along the side of the road.

'A rest, I think. She's a bit heated.'

He jumped down and led his horse to the stream. Archer and Silver followed.

'We should be there soon. An hour and a half perhaps. Don't want to arrive too early. We should rest here too. Take a couple of hours. That would get us in nicely. Just after dawn.'

They tethered the horses away from the road, just as they would have in Spain, and with Archer taking first watch Keane and Silver lay down on the bank, wrapped in their cloaks, their heads resting on their packs. After an hour Silver took the watch and then they were away on the road to Sèvres.

They entered the environs of Paris just as the dawn was coming up. As usual in a public street, Keane and Archer rode ahead, with Silver tucked in behind them. Moving up through the village of Saint-Cloud they at last saw a few people, farmhands and a vagrant in a faded French uniform. But most of the shutters remained closed.

The suburb was unimpressive. He had thought that the entrance gates to Bonaparte's great Imperial city would be astonishing. But all he saw now were squalid streets of the like he was more used to walking in the Peninsula.

They could have belonged to any of the towns he had passed through in the past ten years, with narrow streets hung with washing and filthy central gutters where the sewage ran raw.

At length they entered a great wood. Keane turned to Archer. 'It's the old hunting forest of the kings of France. The Bois de Boulogne.' A hundred yards ahead two roe deer crossed their path and he turned to Archer again. 'It's a pity that Martin's not here. He'd have brought them both down.'

He wished he hadn't made the comment. All the way through Spain and France, under escort and later with the general, he had deliberately stopped himself from thinking about the rest of the troop, back in Spain. It was curious, he thought, how one thing, the sight of two deer in a forest, could trigger something in the mind. He did not want to admit the fact, but there was no denying that he missed the men. He wondered how they were getting on without him and the others. Sergeant Ross was a fine NCO and would have them working at something, he was sure, and Grant would probably have set them some task by now. He'd have them out observing, reconnoitring, making themselves useful. His main concern was that during his absence the unit might be broken up and the men attached to others battalions.

He chided himself for such a thought. Grant would never allow that to happen, nor Wellington. But if they were otherwise occupied, he worried, perhaps those elements at HQ and St James's who wanted to discredit the commander in chief might take the opportunity to issue an order . . .

Keane brought himself to his senses.

*

They were emerging from the wood now and he pointed ahead in genuine astonishment. 'Look, over there.' For quite suddenly they had found themselves in a very different world from that they had seen before the trees had closed them in and one utterly changed from the Paris that Keane remembered.

Ahead of them stretched a wide, tree-lined road leading to a huge open square, also encircled with short fruit trees, in the centre of which dozens of workmen appeared to be toiling to raise some sort of structure. Whatever it was, it looked as if it might be built from marble. It was topped with a statue of a goddess in a chariot pulled by three horses.

Archer exclaimed, 'Good God, sir. It's just like ancient Rome. Like those engravings we used to have at the university. It's extraordinary.'

Silver gasped. 'Well, I'll be blowed. That's something I ain't never seen. That is something, I'll say.'

Keane said nothing.

And as they approached it became clear that this was not just any building but an arch. A triumphal archway, thought Keane, such as the Caesars had in ancient Rome. Archer had caught the parallel perfectly.

'It's fantastic, sir. It'll be colossal when it's finished.'

'That it will. And that is exactly what the emperor intends. He is building monuments to his own greatness. Creating his own myth. And will you try occasionally not to call me sir? Look out – there's the gate.'

On two opposite sides of the round *place* that contained the rising arch, a huge white marble neo-classical building commanded the road. These were the toll houses which after the Revolution had been constructed along the new city wall, the farmers' wall that encircled Paris. Between each of the buildings and the arch stood two sentries clad in the uniform of the City Guard, watching the traffic as it passed in and out.

It was now coming up to 5 a.m. but already the wagons were moving into the city. They would be farmers mostly, Keane supposed, taking produce to the markets.

The three of them rode towards the entrance gate on the right side of the arch, with Silver once again dutifully behind, taking his part as their servant. As they approached one of the guards stepped out, his musket brought to a challenge, and indicated that they should show their papers. They reined up and Keane reached into his pocket and handed the man the passes that they had been given by Madame Duplessis, praying that they would do the job. The guard looked at them all carefully, then up at Keane, taking in the uniform and peering beneath the cloak at the green tunic. He looked back down and then up at Archer, giving him the same treatment before moving round to Silver. He returned to Keane and muttered at him in a guttural patois, 'You're a long way from your regiment, captain.'

'Yes, sergeant, that's why we're here. We're on our way to Holland.'

'Where have you come from?'

'Orléans, but before that we were in Spain. On campaign with Marshal Marmont.'

'It's a long route to take, isn't it? Through Paris.'

'Yes, but I have business here on the way.'

'Very well. I hope you find your regiment.'

He waved them on through the gate and once they were out of earshot Archer spoke to Keane. 'He seemed suspicious, sir. Do we need to worry?'

'No, I don't think so. Just doing his job. He'll have been told to keep an eye open for deserters. I think he wanted to make sure we were officers.'

'Lucky he spoke to you, sir.'

'Don't underestimate yourself. You would have carried it off.'

He was not concerned. The man had been doing his duty and there was nothing out of the ordinary in the three Irish soldiers making their way into the city from Orléans. Curtis and Grant had both told Keane that Paris was teeming with unusual, even bizarre characters and that the three of them would attract little attention in such a varied population.

As they passed the arch, Keane noticed that while one side was indeed made from marble with carved relief sculptures, the other was merely constructed from painted canvas hung on a wooden frame. There to impress but with no reality. He wondered how much more of the great empire's façade might be similar.

It had struck him that the sergeant of the guard had taken a curiously familiar tone with him. A British sentry would have peppered his conversation with 'sir's. It made him think.

He turned to Archer. 'Archer, I've been thinking. It may go against your nature, but perhaps it might be a good idea to just occasionally address me as "James".'

Archer looked puzzled. 'Really, sir?'

'The French, since the Revolution, are more informal than we are. I may be your superior officer as a captain, but as Irishmen we might look more convincing if we were a little more familiar with each other.'

Silver grinned. 'That go for me too, sir?'

Keane shook his head. 'No, Silver. Your part is that of our

servant and as such you may still address me as "sir". In point
of fact, you had better do the same to Archer.'

Archer smiled. Silver shook his head. 'What, call him "sir",
sir?'

'Yes, that's precisely right.' He changed the subject. 'Were
you aware that I had been here before, Archer?'

'You have, sir? Sorry, James. You have?'

'As a boy. My aunt lived here and I was sent to live with
her. I had left school and my mother needed me away from
the farm for a while.

'It always seemed a little curious to me that my mother's
sister should have come here. She had grown up in Ireland but
had married a Frenchman. A Parisian nobleman. She and her
husband became almost like parents to me. He in particular,
fatherless as I was. They had a wonderful house. It seemed like
a palace to me, coming from a farm in Ireland. Such paintings
on the walls and a library filled with books. Most in French of
course. But I had a little Latin. I would spend hours in there.
They seemed to live a charmed life. And I, for a while, became
a part of it.'

'How long did you stay here, sir?'

'Two years, but it seemed like a great deal longer. You know
how it is when you're that age. I came in the summer of '90.
I was twelve.'

'What did you do for friends? Could you speak French?'

'Not at first, but you learn quickly at that age. Besides, I had
a cousin, Sophie, who was almost the same age. She helped.'
He smiled.

'A girl? What was she like? Where is she now?'

'I have no idea. My whole world here collapsed when the
Revolution came. I was still here in '92 when they arrested old

King Louis and his family. My uncle too. He followed the king and queen to the Conciergerie. It was a huge prison back then, filled with aristocrats and nobles and any political prisoner that citizen Robespierre and his cronies chose to name and condemn. And then the king and queen and all their children went to the guillotine. And my poor uncle lost his head too. Unfortunate man. I was lucky to escape with my life.'

'I had no idea, sir – James. What happened to your aunt?'

'She got me away. How she managed it I still don't know. After the night when they took my uncle she knew it wouldn't be long until they came back for us. One night she woke me and Sophie and got us dressed and then I remember a carriage outside the house with the blinds drawn. We left everything behind. Everything. All of the paintings and furniture, all the books I had studied. Even our clothes. We drove for the coast, I suppose, but I couldn't tell you where. She handed me over to a soldier, an officer in a redcoat, and I remember waving goodbye to her and Sophie and the next thing I knew I was back in Ireland on the farm with my mother and somehow we had money again.'

Silver too had been listening as they rode deeper into the city. 'Where was the house, sir?'

'In the old quarter, the east. The Place Royale. Although of course it won't be called that now. If it's still standing.'

Keane wondered if he had said too much. Given too much away about himself. But these were the men alongside whom he had fought for three years. And if he couldn't tell them these things, then who could he possibly tell? The two women he had loved, one English, one French, had gone. Grant was in Spain, and Don Curtis, the man who he knew had information on his father, was there too. Being in Paris, he thought, might be a chance to revisit his past. The past about which he yearned to know more. And to visit the old house would be a starting point. Of course everything he had known of it would be long gone now. But curiosity and the fate which had directed him here had got the better of him.

On this first impression, he was now beginning to wonder how different he would find the great Imperial capital from the Paris he had known. The pre-revolutionary city had been a warren of tiny lanes and high apartment blocks where people slept in houses stacked on top of each other. His family's house had been set in a beautiful square of four identical terraces, each resembling a country house. Beneath two sides, colonnades held restaurants and street cafés, and in the centre a lawn was framed by fruit trees. Could all that really have gone?

They were riding now down another tree-lined avenue, away from the arch and taking them, he presumed, straight into the heart of the city. He was conscious that this too was a new creation. It was wider than any such road he could recall seeing or riding along, allowing two carriages to pass in each direction and any number of horsemen. It was not hard to perceive why Bonaparte had had it built. This was a triumphal avenue, intended for great victory processions and large enough to accommodate column after column of marching men, twenty or thirty abreast.

Silver was in awe. 'Is it true that it is the centre of all the evils of the world, sir? That smart ladies go almost naked to the theatre and that whores can be bought and had in the public gardens?'

Keane smiled, and nodded. 'Yes, I've heard the stories too.

How would I know the truth of it? They do say that in the Place Louis XV, where the guillotine was for so many years, the stench of blood is still so great that the cattle and horses refuse to cross it. This place has certainly seen its fair share of blood in the last twenty years.'

As they approached the end of the avenue they came to a wide square, with neo-classical buildings on one side, the other being bounded by the river. As they entered it Keane's horse began to grow nervous and refused to go on. The others too seemed to be having problems with their mounts.

Keane spoke. 'I'll be damned. This is it. This is the Place Louis XV, as was. God knows what they call it now. But this was the Place de la Guillotine.'

Pulling on the reins, he managed to push his horse right, along the side of the square closest to the river.

As they moved further away from the centre and the horses became more relaxed, the cityscape began to open out before them, unfolding a skyline of tall buildings and in the distance to their right the towers of a huge cathedral which seemed almost to be floating on the great river.

The water was spanned by endless bridges, and across these the sun gleamed on the domed roof of another huge building which stood in its own landscaped gardens. They continued to ride along the river in the direction of the cathedral, and as they did so the townscape changed again about them. Apart from the one great street, as they began to peer to their left up the numerous side streets there seemed to be another world behind the pomp. More like the old Paris he knew, or Lisbon, or Salamanca or Burgos. Here again were the squalid slums where children played on the broken flagstones, and as the three men rode through the streets, women whistled at them from the upper floors from where they displayed their wares and called out the usual invitations.

Keane turned to Archer. 'Just like being in Portugal, Archer, eh? And another thing I don't think has changed since I lived here all those years ago – I can tell you, the Parisians think of us as idiots. All Englishmen are red-faced drunken boors. I suppose the Irish might be seen in the same light. Well, I'm not going to disabuse them. We don't fit the caricature image. We should blend in nicely.'

8

The agent Grant had told him about, Andrew Macpherson, lived in one of the better streets of the old quarter of the Faubourg Saint-Honoré. To Keane's eyes it was a very public street, filled with merchants and their customers coming to and from the new market of Les Halles, built by the emperor for his people.

'Bit conspicuous, sir, isn't it, for a spy?'

'Quiet, Archer. For heaven's sake don't breathe that word. Actually, I think that's the beauty of it. It's too obvious. It's a double bluff. I think our Mr Macpherson might turn out to be a very interesting person indeed.'

Arriving at the door of 320 rue du Faubourg Saint-Honoré, they dismounted and Keane knocked. For some time no one answered. They heard nothing. No hurrying steps, no creaking of doors, no calls. Nothing. And then, quite suddenly, the door opened and there stood a woman. She was in her fifties, of rosy complexion, and stared at Keane with shining green eyes. She spoke in a subtly Scottish accent, with the intonation of the Western Isles.

'Yes, what would you be wanting?'

'We are here to see Mr Macpherson.'

'And who might you be?'

'If I said the word Zenobius, would it mean anything to you?'

'Nothing whatsoever. Wait, I'll call my father.'

She turned back into the corridor, all the time keeping a hand on the door. 'Father, it's some gentlemen to see yourself. Someone called Zenobius.'

There was a noise from within, and from the darkness of the hall a man appeared.

Andrew Macpherson was just as Grant had described him. He looked as if he was in his sixties, but Grant had said that as a boy in his teens he had enlisted to fight for Prince Charlie in the '45 rebellion. That, thought Keane, would make him at least eighty-two, in which case he was in remarkable condition. Macpherson was small in build, with a long, angular nose and the same bright green eyes as his daughter, almost like emeralds in their intensity.

'Good day, gentlemen. What was the name you used?'

'Zenobius.'

Macpherson looked at them, focusing principally on Keane. 'Yes, that would be right. That's the very word. Do come in, won't you? Kirsty, will you make these gentlemen at home?' He closed the door to the street as he spoke. 'They have come a very long way to see me so I think some coffee would be in order, or tea perhaps. Or something stronger, gentlemen?'

Keane shook his head. 'No, thank you, sir. We have ridden throughout the night. Tea would be perfect.'

Kirsty Macpherson left the room and the old man smiled.

'It's good to see you safe here, gentlemen. I had been expecting you. Major Grant sent word. I trust that all went according to plan?'

'It went beautifully, thank you. It's a pleasure to be back in Paris again.'

'You know the city?'

'I was here as a boy.'

Macpherson shook his head and smiled again. 'I did not know that. I'm afraid that you will find it much changed. I myself can hardly recognize whole areas. You will presume to know your way around?'

'I did, but as you say, even from what we have seen it is much changed.'

'It's Bonaparte's doing. This is his showpiece. All show.'

'We noticed the arch as we entered the city. Half built.'

'Yes, it will be carved with the names of all his victories and all his generals. Who can say when it will be finished?'

'You believe that the empire will last?'

'No, I believe that the empire is doomed. When you reach my age you have seen many such enterprises come and go. It is the folly of vanity and as such it will fail. Although of course we might help it on its way. It is up to you gentlemen to determine how quickly that comes about. The people of France are becoming tired of war. Paris is an indicator. Look at what Paris thinks and you will see the spirit of France. There was a poor harvest last year. Look more carefully and you'll see the first signs that the empire is not all it seems. It's starting to crumble, captain. And you're here to help speed up that process.'

It was a curious thing to say, thought Keane, delivered almost as an order.

'Yes, I'm aware of that. Part of my brief was that we are to encourage and assist an attack on the empire at its heart and destroy it from the inside. And that is just what I intend to do. With your help. Can I ask, Mr Macpherson, if you hold military rank?'

'You can ask, certainly, but how shall I answer you? Shall I tell you that many years ago, as a very young man, I held an officer's commission, bestowed in the field by the prince himself, in the Jacobite army that fought to bring down the very government that I now support? Shall I tell you that later I held rank in the war in the Americas and fought against the revolutionaries? Does that surprise you? Of course I wished to uphold the old order. But shall I then tell you that I also held the rank of a captain in the Revolutionary Army of France? Well, I did. And why? To undermine the Revolution from within. But I doubt whether any of those would be the sort of military ranks for which you are hoping. Let's just say that I do now hold a rank, but I am afraid that you will not be privy to it. Let us also say that that rank is above your own, captain.'

It was enough to satisfy Keane. 'I quite understand, sir. Can you brief us on the current situation?'

Macpherson's daughter entered with the tea and after she had left, closing the door behind her, he began.

'Paris is alive with rumour and speculation. Marshal Marmont is beaten in Spain. The Prussians are re-arming and will attack France. The emperor plans to attack Britain again and there's an army of 500,000 men at Calais waiting to board the invasion barges. All the usual stuff. And there are the crazy ones too. The empress has had an affair with a Bourbon. Nelson has been seen alive in Cherbourg.

'I've been trying to feed the madness. That's how you bring down a regime. You destabilize it from within. Make the people and those who govern them believe their own lies.'

'Fascinating. How do you manage it?'

'I have agents. A number of them, throughout the city. Royalists, émigrés, republicans. I'm not fussy. I'll use anyone who wants to bring down the tyrant.'

'That must be a delicate game to play.'

Macpherson laughed. 'I'll say it is. You have to keep on your toes.'

Perhaps, thought Keane, that explains why the man seemed to have kept his youthful spark.

Macpherson continued. 'Fouché's men are everywhere. He may now be the ex-minister of Napoleon's secret police and that fool Savary in his place, but Monsieur Fouché still rules Paris. In truth he shouldn't really be here. He was banished from the city by Bonaparte two years ago after they fell out. Bonaparte was trying to make peace with Britain, but Fouché wanted the war to continue. Bonaparte sent him to Tuscany. But now he's back and he still has power. The man is a monster – born of the Revolution and nurtured by the policies of Bonaparte.'

'So we need to avoid him.'

'On the contrary. I think it is imperative that you make contact with him. With Fouché himself.'

'You're serious? I should really meet Fouché?'

'Yes. You are a card player, are you not, Captain Keane?' It was the first time he had addressed Keane by name. 'You must be aware that in this game the best defence is attack.'

'Yes, I understand. I was explaining to my men that is the reason you live on so public a street.'

'Precisely. You must hit the enemy where he expects it the least and when his guard is down.'

'And where do I find Fouché? This monster with the need for war.'

'I will think of that. I will arrange a meeting.'

Keane thought that he might rise to Macpherson's terms and suggest the ridiculous. 'And what of Bonaparte himself? When should I meet him?'

Macpherson seemed to take the suggestion as an obvious possibility. 'Oh, he's gone. He left the city for Dresden on 9th May.'

'So the rumours that we heard in Spain were right. He's going to invade Russia.'

Macpherson nodded. 'Yes, quite right. He is not poised to invade England. And he's certainly not heading for Spain. He's had his fill of that debacle, if you ask me. He is actually assembling what will be the greatest army ever seen in the modern world. Half a million men, they say, drawn from all parts of the empire. He intends to crush the Russians completely.'

'Have you sent word of all this to Wellington?'

'I need it to be absolutely confirmed. You must do that, captain. Then we shall send word.'

'And what of our disguise? Is it sufficient, do you think?'

'I have no reason to think otherwise. You know your stories, I presume, all of you?' He shot a glance at the others.

'Excuse me, sir, this is Lieutenant Archer, actually Private Archer, but he makes a very passable officer. And Private Silver. Two of my very finest men. I think they'll do as two of Boney's Irishmen.'

Macpherson looked at them carefully. 'The main thing is to know your stories inside out.' He looked at Archer. 'What's your name?'

'Patrick O'Connell.'

'Where are you from, Lieutenant O'Connell?'

'County Cork, sir.'

'And your father's name? Your mother's too?'

Archer hesitated and looked at Keane. 'I . . . I'm not sure, sir.'

'Well then, you had better make sure. Your accent is convincing, but you must know everything. Everything from your mother's maiden name to your tailor.'

He looked at Silver. 'Your name, man? What is it?'

'Joseph Lynch, sir, at your service.'

'Well, Lynch, tell me about yourself and how you come to be in Paris?'

Silver looked at him and spoke in what he hoped would pass for an Irish brogue. 'Well, sir, you see, your honour, I'm just a private soldier, sir. I've no idea who my father was and my mother was a whore from Derry. I was raised in the gutter and taken from there by the British army to fight in Spain and it was there that I deserted, sir, and joined the French, who put me in the Irish Legion. I'm now the soldier servant to Captain Williams here. It's good work and I love it, because I hate the bloody English, I do. But in my heart of hearts, sir, I can't wait to get back and see old Ireland again.'

'Who's your commanding officer?'

'Colonel Lawless, sir. Never was a braver man. Wounded that many times leading us, sir. And did you ever hear about his heroic escape from the English in Holland? If you've the time, I'll tell you, sir.'

'No, that will have to wait. Where did you fight with the legion?'

'Bussaco and Fuentes, sir. And many other places besides. To tell you the truth, I didn't want to leave Spain. I'd have stayed on and finished the job.'

Macpherson laughed. 'There, captain, he's got it. Brilliant, Lynch. *Vive l'empereur*.'

Silver grinned and used his broadest Irish accent. 'Oh yes. *Vive l'empereur*, sir. Right enough.'

Macpherson spoke seriously again. 'I can tell you, captain, that the French intelligence service has had no word of your escape as yet. Either that or perhaps your erstwhile captors are keen not to let the news get back to Marmont and his associates, lest they find themselves on the end of a rope. Either way, you're safe for now. I have a trusted contact on the inside. He's with the police. A royalist. He serves me well, captain. He will warn us of any suspicions long before Fouché's men think to come looking for you. And before that happens we need to ensure that you make the acquaintance of their leader.'

They rested for the first day in their new lodgings in Macpherson's house, Silver and Archer in the attic, and woke the following morning feeling refreshed. It was a sleep such as Keane had not enjoyed for years. He had grown used to lacking the luxury of a proper bed, clean sheets and pillows. There was something else too. The noise outside his shutters was quite different to that he was used to in Spain. There were no shouted orders, no guns being cleared and cleaned, no drums or bugles. Instead he heard the noise of the Paris street. The cries of the street vendors, the shouts of children at play and the rattle of carts on cobbles. It made a welcome change but also made him feel uneasy. As if suddenly it would all vanish and he would be transported back to the vision of hell that had been Badajoz, or any other Peninsular battlefield. But it didn't vanish. He threw open the shutters and let in the sunshine and watched the people down below. Real people in civilian clothes going about their everyday business. It reminded him of when he had been part of that society, and suddenly the urge came upon him to seek out his aunt's house.

Dressing quickly, he found the other two at breakfast, which had been provided by Macpherson's daughter.

Keane sat down and dunked a hunk of bread into sweet coffee, eating before turning to Archer. 'Have you seen Mr Macpherson this morning?'

'Yes, sir. He said something about becoming acquainted with the city and that he would give us a tour of the places we needed to know.'

'It's a good idea to have some sense of the streets. Keep a watch for dead ends and potential short cuts. Think of the city as a battlefield. How to use its terrain. I'm sure that we'll need to do so before long.'

Macpherson entered. 'Good morning, captain. Your men will have told you my plan for the day. I intend to make you all natives of the centre of this city. By the time I've done with you you'll know every alleyway and every building. You'll know the cafés and what sort of person visits each one and you'll know where to find Fouché's hired thugs and where best to lose them. Some are still in the police. Some he keeps himself. They're no different to each other. Just as lethal.'

They finished breakfast and were about to leave. Archer and Keane strapped on their swords. Silver reached for the musket which he had brought from Bayonne. Macpherson took it from him gently. 'I don't think that will be needed.'

Silver turned to Keane. 'But, sir, surely, I need a weapon?'

'Not a musket, Silver. Not in the city.'

Macpherson reached up and unhooked from the wall a short sword, fitted with a white belt. 'Here, take this. It will do the job as well as anything else.'

Thus equipped they left the house and walked into the street, which was teeming with people of all classes and conditions. Macpherson led them to the left, towards the east, and at once began to talk. 'Captain, forgive me if I tell you what you already know. There have been many changes and it's easier to talk in general.'

Keane nodded and the old man continued.

'It's simple really. The city's built on two banks of the river Seine, left and right. At present we're on the right bank. There are seven bridges and more being built.' They passed a church on the left, up a flight of stone steps, pockmarked with what looked like bullet holes. 'That's Saint-Roch. Where you might say it all started. That's where a young artillery officer called Bonaparte fired grapeshot into a crowd of civilians and stopped the Revolution.' Ahead of them lay the Place de la Carousel. Macpherson continued. 'You won't have seen any of this, captain. This is all Bonaparte's doing. Monuments to French military glory. You should see this place after he wins a battle. Parades? You never saw the like. Thousands of soldiers. Infantry, cavalry, cannon. And this isn't the only place. You've seen the new arch up at the Porte de Maillot? Well, there's a new square behind us, Place Vendôme. He's put up a huge column there. Copied from one in Rome. Finished two summers ago. It took four years to build and they say it's made from the iron of cannon captured from the Russians and Austrians in 1805, at Austerlitz.'

Keane shook his head as they entered the rue de Rivoli. 'I certainly don't remember this street.'

'Nor would you. Rue de Rivoli. Named after another victory.'

The street was wide and cobbled and without the stinking central gutter common to the other Parisian streets. It was also absolutely straight, and standing on it Keane looking east was able to see all the way to the Bastille, the old prison that had been the focus of the early revolutionaries.

'Good heavens, that's the Bastille, isn't it?'

'Yes, only ruins now, of course. The road runs all the way from the Place de la Concorde, where the guillotine used to be, to the Place de la Bastille, which he renamed after the battle of the Pyramids.'

Looking to his left Keane recognized another huge building. 'The Palais-Royal.'

'Correct again.'

It was almost impossible to walk in the narrow streets of Paris, due to the mud and traffic, and the Champs-Élysées did not yet exist.

As they walked, in the centre of the street, avoiding the gutter, they had to dodge the traffic. It was heavy going as the cobbles bore a thick covering of mud and horse manure.

Keane cursed. 'I don't recall the streets being as bad as this.'

'This? This is passable. You wait until the rains. Actually Bonaparte has improved the streets.'

'Really?'

'Really. You have to admire much of what he's done here. And his vision. It might be fuelled by pride and megalomania, but look at it. And he's made huge improvements to the city's sewers and water supply. A canal from the Ourcq river, and a dozen new fountains. The palace of the Louvre is now the Napoleon Museum; it takes up a whole wing and is crammed with works of art he's brought back from his campaigns in Italy, Austria, Holland and Spain.'

Keane interjected. 'Yes, we know all about that. All the works that he's "liberated" from churches and museums across Europe.'

Macpherson smiled. 'And then there are the schools. He's put them on a military basis and re-organized them to train engineers and administrators. It's all been done to furnish all the people he needs to fight his wars and maintain his empire.'

Keane was puzzled by the sudden wave of enthusiasm. 'You sound as if you approve, Mister Macpherson.'

Macpherson nodded. 'Perhaps I do. But that does not mean that I condone the whole system. Nor the man. You know my views on Bonaparte. You have seen at first hand the misery that he has brought upon this country to create this new wealth. You met Madame Duplessis?'

'Yes. Her son—'

'Yes, her son and the sons of thousands, hundreds of thousands, perhaps millions of others, eventually, if he is allowed to continue.'

Keane was aware that, being in a strange city, an enemy city, he should know the places to avoid. At the same time he wondered where this new aristocracy created by Napoleon chose to make their home.

'Sir, can you point out the areas where Bonaparte's men are in greatest numbers. Is there any particular area of the city where they congregate?'

'Well, obviously the Palais-Royal. But you can see them on the boulevards. There are uniforms everywhere, and those out of uniform too. Four thousand cafés for them to choose from.

It's not hard, captain, to find Bonaparte's chosen few. It might interest you that many of them live on this very street.'

He produced a piece of paper. 'Here you are. A list of the houses of Napoleon's great and good. The wealthiest Parisians in the western neighbourhoods of the city, along the Champs-Élysées, and around Place Vendôme, where the column is, you remember? The poorest are concentrated in the east, in two neighbourhoods; around Mont Sainte-Geneviève, in the Faubourg Saint-Marcel and the Faubourg Saint-Antoine.

'The wealthiest and most distinguished have bought houses between the Palais-Royal and the Étoile, especially on the rue du Faubourg Saint-Honoré and the Chausée d'Antin.'

'But that's here, isn't it?'

Again, thought Keane, the ability to hide oneself by placing oneself among the very people who spell the greatest danger.

Macpherson handed the paper to Keane, who took it and studied the names and addresses. It made fascinating reading.

Joseph Bonaparte, the older brother of the emperor, was at 31 rue du Faubourg Saint-Honoré, fifty houses from Macpherson. His sister Pauline was in the same street at number 39, Marshal Berthier, Napoleon's chief of staff was at number 35, Marshal Jeannot in number 63 and Marshal Murat in number 55. In the Chausée d'Antin, General Moreau was at number 20, and Cardinal Fesch, Bonaparte's uncle, at number 68. Other members of the emperor's inner circle seemed to prefer the left bank and the Faubourg Saint-Germain. Eugène de Beauharnais, son of the Empress Josephine, lived at 78 rue de Lille, and Napoleon's younger brother Lucien at 14 rue Saint-Dominique. Marshal Davout was just some twenty houses along the same street. Keane looked at Macpherson. 'But this is superb. What a document. Are there more?'

'I have every address of every one of Bonaparte's inner circle. Of course you must realize, Keane, we have a new social order here now. The core of the new aristocracy was provided by those who'd escaped execution during the terror and fled abroad to England, Germany, Spain, Russia, all over. Even the United States. Most have now returned, we believe, and many have found themselves positions in the new Imperial court and government. But it's not just all the generals and marshals. The names you have there, they have been joined by a new aristocracy created by Napoleon. This is a new class of wealthy Parisians. They've made their money selling supplies to the army, as well as by buying then reselling property taken by the Revolution. Then there are the owners of chemical factories, textile mills and machine works. I have all the papers here. Look.'

He handed a sheaf of handwritten manuscripts to Keane. 'Count them for yourself. Generals, ministers and courtiers, bankers, industrialists and arms dealers. There are about three thousand people in all. This is your new enemy, Captain Keane. You will find it everywhere and impossible to commit to battle.'

Keane looked again at the pieces of paper. Scanned through the names. Three thousand people. Some of them in uniform, many civilians, some in disguise. This was an army, but a very different sort of army, and here in Paris, he realized, he would be fighting a quite different sort of war.

9

Keane and his men had one day to acquaint themselves with Paris. They reeled beneath the bombardment of facts and figures provided by Macpherson. Keane had thought that it might be easier for him, having a good knowledge as he did of the old city. But he, as much as any of them, had been befuddled by Macpherson's unrelenting guided tour.

He had planned this well, thought Keane. With true military precision. He wondered about Macpherson. What rank he held. He presumed he must be of senior rank. A brigadier at least or a major general. But this had been done, was being achieved, so well and so thoroughly that he began to think that he might even be superior to that. And it occurred to him very strange indeed that someone who had fought for Prince Charlie, as they called him, and then in the Americas and had gone undercover, should now choose to be a spy.

A good one certainly. But why should such a man choose a profession which Keane himself found to be distasteful. A profession which over the last three years he had had such trouble reconciling with his ideals of what it really meant to be a soldier. Suddenly he had a tremendous respect for the old man. He could have been enjoying the fruits of his labours in retirement in England or Scotland. Or even, if he chose to, sitting behind a desk in St James's, deciding the fate of Keane's fellow officers. Instead he was here, in his eighties, risking his life to bring down the Bonapartist regime.

Now, as they sat together in Macpherson's dining room after dinner, the old Jacobite began to explain more about the details of the mission on which they had been sent.

Macpherson turned the glass of brandy in his hand and spoke again. 'Monsieur Fouché is extremely dangerous. Make no mistake, gentlemen. Should he suspect any of you for one moment, he will contrive to have you all arrested and that will be the end of it. You will join the legions of the "disappeared" and we shall hear no more of the intrepid Captain Keane and his men.'

Keane took a long drink and as the Armagnac trickled down spoke in reply. 'Yes, of course, I understand. So what else should we know of him?'

'Firstly, you will know him by his appearance. Joseph Fouché is, shall I say, "sinister" in his look. He is foul-mouthed, slovenly, badly dressed. Repulsive.'

'You make him sound endearingly attractive.'

'There's more. He has the misfortune to have the most hideous wife you could possibly imagine.' Keane was not sure how to take the last comment. But Macpherson continued: 'He has collected all manner of information on all kinds of people. It is said that he has a dossier on Napoleon himself, as well as all of the expected files on spies, dissidents, writers, ministers and generals.

'He has been known to use information to "turn" enemy

agents into double agents, working for him. That is what we must now exploit.

'Although he undoubtedly possesses a talent for accumulating and organizing large quantities of information through his unparalleled network of scurrilous informers, I believe that his real genius may lie in his sceptical approach to the information he manages to obtain. He doesn't trust much of what he hears. But we need him to trust you, Captain Keane.

'He is something of a contradiction. He was banished for years by Napoleon to Tuscany. But he has somehow managed to creep back to Paris. He used to live quietly with his wife and four children, but now they are estranged and he lives by himself in the rue du Bac area of the city, in the Faubourg Saint-Germain. He still keeps up a façade of being a normal, happy family man even as he sifts through intelligence reports in search of royalist plotters. It might interest you to know too that Monsieur Fouché was once a priest.'

'No? But that's extraordinary. How would a man who had taken vows of priesthood become someone so feared and so reviled?'

'It's simple really. He renounced the Church. He turned his back on God and with it on any idea of salvation. So you see, anything that Fouché does, anything, is not answerable to a higher power. As far as he is concerned, he is that higher power.'

'So he believes that he has the right to do anything to anyone?'

'Yes, precisely. He is a very dangerous man, captain. But he is the key to the downfall of Bonaparte's empire.'

'Really, are you sure of that?'

'I am quite certain. You must meet Fouché and you must get him to take you into his confidence.'

'There is an opportunity. My man in the Sûreté tells me that Fouché will be hosting a ball in the Palais-Royal tomorrow evening. Is that time enough for you?'

Keane nodded. 'It seems that it will have to be.'

'Good. You will attend the ball. I have a ticket for you. My agent will also be there. He will make contact and at a given moment he will ensure that you meet Fouché, among others whom I think you might find of use.' He smiled. 'I'm sure that you will find it fascinating and quite diverting.'

Keane wondered what he meant to imply, but was sure that he would discover soon enough.

The ball was not due to take place until five o'clock in the afternoon, but Keane thought that he should familiarize himself with the location and so shortly after lunch left the house and ventured into the street. It was a short walk to the Palais-Royal. Passing the Place Vendôme, with its towering column and the pockmarked church where Napoleon had begun his career, Keane found himself in the place and turned left into the gardens of the palace.

Although it had originally been a royal palace, the huge neo-classical building was now a collection of galleries and colonnades where upper- and middle-class Parisians took their promenades. It was filled with people. Smartly dressed men and women along with soldiers, mainly officers and NCOs, he thought, in their characteristic dark blue uniforms. He was acutely conscious for the first time of his livid and distinctive green and knew that it must attract attention. He presumed though that this was all part of Macpherson's plan – Grant's plan. The notion that by making oneself conspicuous you were in fact double-bluffing your enemies. Attempting to act as if he knew every inch of the ground, Keane made his way along the left-hand colonnade of the *palais* and pretended to look in the windows.

The shops of the Palais-Royal contained boutiques with glass show windows displaying jewellery, fabrics, hats, perfumes, boots, dresses, paintings, porcelain, watches, toys, lingerie and every type of luxury. Between these were grand offices. Keane read the nameplates of lawyers, doctors, dentists and opticians, offices for changing money. Then every so often there would be a salon for dancing, or a bar for playing billiards and cards. Men wandered in and out of these less highlighted doors and more than once he was tempted to enter.

There were countless cafés too, as well as street vendors' stalls in the gardens themselves, selling waffles fresh from the oven, sweets, cider and beer. The smell was as overpowering as the noise.

Keane walked around the arcades for a good two hours, taking a coffee at one of the cafés and observing the passing Parisians. It was a million miles, he thought, from where he had been so recently – the Peninsula with its stretches of arid plain and mountain, its olive groves and its vineyards. He thought of the rolling fields of crops which Wellington had ordered to be destroyed to prevent them falling into the hands of the advancing French armies. And of the bloody battlefields, the charnel houses of mangled bodies and dead flesh.

One thing was clear. Napoleon might be hard pressed in the front line in Spain. But here in his rejuvenated capital there seemed to Keane to be no shortage of anything. You could obviously get whatever you wanted, from Indian silks and spices to fine cuisine and even finer women. The wealth of Bonaparte's Paris was conspicuously vulgar. And for more than a moment, although it went horribly against everything he believed that he stood for, Keane began to wonder whether the emperor might not actually have got it right. And the thought worried him more than he had expected it might.

At shortly after five in the afternoon, he left the café and walked slowly through the arcades back to the main salon of the *palais*, where the reception was due to take place. As he approached the sixteen-paned glass garden doors, it was abundantly clear from the noise of music and chatter that the soirée was already in full swing. Keane entered the room and was instantly aware that he had walked into something quite special. As the flunky at the door asked his name and took the engraved invitation card which had been delivered earlier that day, Keane paused in the doorway and took it all in.

Even though it was still daylight outside, on an early summer's afternoon, the room was lit from above by three huge crystal chandeliers, each set with over a hundred candles. Mirrors on two facing walls amplified the numbers present, but there seemed to Keane to be some three hundred people in the place. While a dance was taking place in one corner, scattered groups of men and women stood in conversation while in another corner a group of men stood watching some spectacle. Keane walked across to them and discovered it to be a woman, a pretty girl in her early twenties with long blonde hair and emerald eyes. She was clad in a spangled leotard that barely covered her torso and allowed her breasts to protrude, and the crowd around her were marvelling at her feats of acrobatics, some of which bordered on the lewd. It was hardly the sort of thing Keane had thought that he might find at a ball in Napoleon's capital. But he stayed and watched for a while until she caught his eye. Then he turned and left. Clearly this was going to be far from any ordinary ball.

He had not gone more than forty paces when a man walked up to him. He had short hair and wore a fashionable olive-green coat, purple-striped waistcoat and dark brown trousers. His shirt was trimmed with ornate lace, which protruded from his cuffs, and was finished at the neck with a silk cravat kept in place with a diamond stick pin. His hair was a long jet-black mane of cascading curls and his face was curiously pale with heavy black eyebrows and bright red lips and it was only as he approached that Keane realized that it was make-up.

The man spoke. 'Hello, I don't believe I've had the pleasure.'

'Captain James Williams, Légion Irlandaise.'

The man smiled. 'One of our brave Irish volunteers. My name is Choiseul. Baron Francis de Choiseul. How wonderful to meet you. What brings you here? I had thought that your regiment was in Holland.'

Keane wondered how on earth such a man – clearly a fop, and what his contemporaries in the army would, if being polite, call a 'beau' or a 'dandy' – knew such a thing.

'I have just returned from Spain. I was left behind at Marshal Marmont's headquarters – on special business.'

'Special business? That does sound dangerous. I suppose you can't tell me any more?'

'No, I'm afraid that I can't.'

'So, captain, tell me, what do you think of our little soirée?'

'It's wonderful. I haven't been in the capital for some time.'

'Really? And do you find it changed? How does it look to you, fresh from the battlefields of Spain?'

'It looks very well. The emperor has accomplished a great deal in a very short time.'

'Yes, hasn't he? And not just in Paris. Think, captain, about what we have. What the emperor has done. He is truly enlightened. He works in the great tradition of Frederick the Great, Maria Theresa. Before we had petty officials in local districts. Now we have unity. We have the Code Napoléon.

'The Grande Armée is the greatest agent of political change the world has ever seen. We have religious toleration, equality in the face of the law, a system of uniform weights and measures and even currency. Not far from here, just across the Channel, our enemies in England still have peasants with a duty to their landlords who pay taxes and swear feudal allegiance. The same in your own home country of Ireland.

'That is gone from France. Gone forever. We are not a medieval society. Everything is done by merit. Not birth. It's as if all the dreams of the thinkers came true. All the ideals of the Enlightenment have been channelled into this one man.' The man beamed a smile.

Grand ideas, thought Keane, but had this man ever seen the other side of the Grande Armée's enlightened spread of Napoleon's doctrine? Had he seen the burnt-out Spanish villages, the women and girls raped and then butchered beside their tortured and mutilated husbands and children? Where, Keane wondered, did that fit into this golden vision of Napoleonic Europe?

'Of course it is a wonder. But it does not come without a cost.'

'No indeed, captain. As you and I well know. I'm sure that you have seen your fair share of war, of horror. And as for me, do you think I choose to paint my face this way and look like a freak? I lost my face, most of it, at Wagram. And so I cover up the scars with this.'

He put his finger to his cheek and some of the white make-up came away. Beneath it Keane could see raw red flesh. Scar tissue. It obviously covered most of the man's face. And it was then that he noticed two more things. One of his eyes, the left one, did not move, and his hairline stopped with curious abruptness. The man spoke again. 'Yes, I have one glass eye and no hair. This is a wig. Without any of these things, I would look like a monster. With them I can pass for a clown. It is the price we pay for all of this and for my title. A gift from the emperor. He is most gracious with his gifts.'

Keane nodded. 'Sir, it is an honour to have met you and I admire everything you have given for your country.'

'A pleasure to have met you too, captain . . . ?'

'Williams,' Keane managed just in time. 'And now, baron, if you will excuse me.'

The man nodded and smiled and Keane turned away, attempting to make it look as if he had seen someone on the other side of the room. As he strode away there was a tap on his shoulder and he turned, fully expecting to see again the white-painted face of the baron, with another, more pene-trating question, perhaps to catch him out. Instead though he was met with the face of a different man. A stranger.

'Captain Williams?'

'Yes, I'm Williams, and you are?'

'Chef-Inspecteur Jadot.'

'Do we know each other?'

'No, but I believe you are acquainted with a friend of mine. He goes by the name of Zenobius.'

'Yes, how extraordinary. I do know of him, chef-inspecteur.'

'Can we talk? In private?'

Keane nodded and Jadot led the way across the room and into the entrance hall. Leaving the palace, they walked into the gardens and across to the less busy of the two colonnades that flanked it. There was a darkened shop in the arcade and Jadot turned the handle and the two men walked inside and straight through to the rear, where another door led into a small courtyard, enclosed on all sides. Jadot shut the door behind them and began to speak. 'I see that you have met the baron. It's his soirée this evening. He is most generous with his hospitality.'

'And also most inquisitive. How does he know that my regiment, that is the Légion Irlandaise, is in Holland?'

'He makes it his business. He knows much. After all, as Fouché's sidekick, wouldn't you expect it?'

'That man is Fouché's second in command?'

Jadot nodded. 'Yes. What better man to have as your deputy than someone who has lost everything in the service of France?'

'Yes, you're right. Good God. He was fast off the mark. He saw me as soon as I entered the room.'

'No less than I would have expected. He has an eye for spotting any newcomer. That man knows everyone in that room. And he knows much of the detail about them. Before the evening is finished he will know much more about you, captain. You are ready for that?'

'Yes, your friend has done a good job on me and my friends.'

Jadot nodded. 'He is most thorough. It is good that you should have been spotted by Choiseul. It will make my task of getting you to Fouché himself much easier. We must seize the moment. You should contrive to find Choiseul again. Bump into him at the buffet perhaps. Answer his questions and give him some hint as to why you remained in Spain. Intrigue him, make him curious. That way he's bound to introduce you to Fouché. He likes to show his master that he's on top of things. How much he knows.'

They left the room and the building separately with an interval of fifteen minutes and Keane walked as directed by a different route to that which they had used before. He crossed the gardens and entering one of the shops in the arcade pretended to browse through some pieces of silk until the shopkeeper began to pester him. Then leaving abruptly, he moved across to the palace and entered the ballroom. The place was as it had been before, although the guests seemed to Keane to have become less inhibited and some of them were clearly drunk. The men gathered around the acrobat girl, who had been joined in the audience by several women, were more animated now, and were shouting suggestions as to what positions she might adopt. Obligingly, quite naked now, she went into further contortions, indulging their requests. Again Keane watched, but this time when she caught his eye he did not look away but kept her fixed in his gaze as she moved her hands over her body and drew the crowd to new raptures. At length she looked away and Keane turned back to the room. He was sweating and needed another drink.

The dancing in the centre of the room was more frenetic and the buffet had become a sea of revellers, pushing and shoving to get at the food. Keane saw Choiseul among them. He moved quietly through the guests and insinuated himself into the crowd at the buffet until he was standing shoulder to shoulder with the baron.

Sensing Keane's presence, the man turned. 'Captain, hello again. Are you having fun? What a splendid evening, isn't it?'

'Absolutely captivating. And such a wonderful range of guests. It's a wonder they are all friends of your ex-superior.'

Choiseul froze, but only for an instant. 'Oh really? So you are aware that Monsieur Fouché is sponsoring this ball?'

'Isn't that what you told me?'

'Did I say that? Well, yes, of course, that's right. But I did have a little to do with it. You know, the boss would never have a clue about where to get her.' He gesticulated towards the acrobat, who was now lying on the floor, naked, in a somewhat more than revealing 'splits' position.

Keane grinned. 'No, quite, I did wonder. I had heard that Monsieur Fouché was a family man.'

Choiseul grinned. 'Of course he is. But do you think that his wife would ever come to an evening like this?'

'Quite frankly I have no idea.'

'I can tell you, captain, she most certainly would not. We live in a fascinating society, do we not? A society of two worlds, in effect. You might say that as the emperor's men we have built a new world. Think about it. It is far from uncommon for our new aristocracy to form alliances by marriage with old families, who undoubtedly after the Revolution need money. Only last year I overheard that stalwart of the old noblesse the Duke of Montmorency in conversation with Marshal Soult, of all people. Soult, who had been made a duke by Napoleon.

'Montmorency says with a grin, "Well, marshal, how's this to be? You are a duke, but you have no ancestors!" To which Soult replies, "It's true. But today we are the ancestors."'

Keane laughed and felt that he might have been accepted. But Choiseul's next question was worryingly to the point.

'Captain, you seem extraordinarily interested in what is going on in Paris. May I ask why that might be?'

'Oh, I suppose it comes from having just returned after so many years. I find it fascinating.'

'And tell me about Spain. How was it? What about the emperor's decision to replace Marshal Massena with Marshal Marmont?'

Keane realized that this was it. He was being put on the spot and everything depended upon his answers. 'Well, you know Marshal Massena was a great commander. We all had respect for him and he led us well, I believe. I truly do. But it was the right decision. It was the emperor's decision. It was most certainly right. Marshal Marmont is at present carrying out a fine job. And I believe he might manage it. He might even throw Wellington out of Spain and Portugal and destroy him and his armies completely.'

'You think so? I had always thought that he was not the one for the job. You know, I think that Marshal Ney is the man who can meet Wellington on his own terms and defeat him utterly.'

Keane nodded sagely. 'Oh, of course, Ney is unquestionably the man. But what about the politics? If we can get him then the army would profit by his appointment. But do you really think that the emperor will ever give him a position of serious power?'

'Well, I had hoped so. I really do. Michel is such a wonderful man. But you know, he is so very temperamental. I told him so only recently. Have you met him?'

Keane paused but only for a moment. 'No, I'm afraid I haven't.'

'It's rather a shame that he's in Dresden at the moment with the emperor. Well, you knew that of course. But what a pity. You know, I'm sure that you two would get along famously. After all you both have Irish blood.'

Keane laughed. 'Yes, that would have been wonderful. I have always wanted to meet the marshal. I am full of admiration for him.'

'You know we almost grew up together? He was from Alsace as I was. We were both hussars. There are an extraordinary number of cross-overs.'

For the first time Keane detected an air of jealousy in Choiseul's voice and slightly trembling tone. It wasn't difficult to work out the cause. Ney was the emperor's favourite. His blue-eyed boy. A marshal of France and destined in effect to inherit the world. And Choiseul. Well, thought Keane, perhaps he had grown up alongside Ney, but the man had lost out in the lottery of life. He had lost his face in the horror of battle and with it his command. Certainly he had gained a position and the emperor's trust. But what did that amount to when you were effectively cast out from the system of advancement of the army? The man was no more than a glorified policeman. For the first time Keane felt real pity for him.

Choiseul paused. 'Captain, may I say you seem remarkably quick on the uptake? It is scarcely an hour since we met and yet you appear to have the measure of me.' He fixed him with his stare and laughed. 'Indulge me for a moment. I wonder, are you perhaps a spy?'

Keane's blood ran cold. 'A spy? Sir, what do you take me for? I am an officer in the Légion Irlandaise. Nothing more.'

'I apologize of course. It's merely that you seem to me to

range widely and know a great deal more perhaps than you should, certainly more than you at first evince.'

'My apologies, my fault. It is my manner. But one thing I will say to you Monsieur Choiseul: I would count it a great privilege were I ever to be able to meet with your superior officer.'

Choiseul laughed. 'Oh, you take me back. Superior officer? Of course I can introduce you to Monsieur Fouché. Leave it to me. You will amuse him.'

Choiseul led Keane away from the buffet and towards the doors into the garden and for a moment he thought they might be about to leave the room. But just then the baron glimpsed something in one of the huge mirrors and, grabbing Keane by the arm, dragged him back across the room.

At the same time from across the room a man advanced towards them. He was tall and imposing with a square set jaw and a steely-eyed stare. Instinctively Keane knew that he was going to bring trouble.

Choiseul moved to greet him. 'Colonel Harrison, what a great honour. I had no idea that you were here tonight. Of course I knew that we had invited you, but to have your presence here. How good it is to see you.'

It was, thought Keane, obsequious in the extreme. Harrison – he could only presume that the man was American or, at the worst extreme, Irish. When the man spoke he was at least relieved.

'Monsieur Choiseul, it is all my pleasure. My great pleasure.'

Choiseul spoke. 'Captain Williams, allow me to introduce Colonel Harrison, late of the 4th Maryland Light Horse, one of our esteemed American allies in the war against oppression.'

Keane clenched his teeth at the expression and contrived

to appear as revolutionary as he could. 'Colonel Harrison. It is my pleasure to meet you. James Williams, Légion Irlandaise.'

'Why, sir, it's a great honour to meet anyone who fights for the Irish Legion. My God, how is your dear commander? I saw him last a year ago. Is he still as well as he was then?'

It was Keane's worst nightmare brought to life.

'Colonel Lawless is as good as he ever was, sir.'

'You know, it is quite natural that we should be allies with France against our common enemy, your ancient enemy the English. By God, we may have won our freedom, but they are still our oppressors.'

Keane summoned up in his memory everything he could about the native Irish, with whom he had very little in common. He thought back to his teens and to the 1798 rebellion that had driven the country apart; to the bitterness he had seen and experienced in those times – men, women and children put to the sword and, more hideously, to the pike. Now, he thought, now is the time to pour it out. My God, he prayed, let me for once appear to be a patriotic Irishman! And then he began.

'I have so much admiration for you, colonel. What you managed in 1776, our French friends managed in '89 and surely we ourselves might manage soon enough. You have forged an entire new nation out of your revolution. These noble Frenchmen have to thank the emperor for what he has done for them. And we Irishmen are just biding our time. Our colours are tied firmly to those of the emperor and we fight in the green of our homeland for the better good of France, knowing that in time it will be for our own good.'

Keane was rather pleased with his impromptu oration, and to judge by the Frenchman's nodding, smiling face, it seemed to have paid off with Choiseul.

Harrison replied, 'So you are aware that my country is now at war with England?'

'Of course, colonel, how could I not be? It has been my greatest hope. Perhaps we might manage to recruit a new battalion of the Irish Legion to fight with yourselves. There are after all so many Irishmen in your country.'

Harrison nodded. 'That is not a false hope, captain. In fact it is something about which I have already hinted to our president.'

Choiseul looked enraptured. 'You have?'

'Why certainly. It makes perfect sense. Perhaps you would lead the contingent yourself, captain?'

'Perhaps, colonel. That would be a great honour. Of course I would have to be appointed by my colonel.'

'Naturally I would clear it with Colonel Lawless. In fact I'm intending to travel to Holland to see him when I have finished in Paris. Who knows – you and I might visit him together.'

'That sounds an excellent idea, colonel. And I could then plead the case for an American battalion.'

Harrison clapped him on the back. 'Capital. It's a superb notion, captain. Shall we talk again soon? Perhaps we might meet tomorrow?'

'With pleasure, colonel.'

Keane smiled at Harrison. He would go along with the American and get from him whatever information he might have. But he would come up with an excuse at the last minute not to travel to Holland with him and prayed that his own business in Paris would be concluded long before Harrison had the chance to see Lawless and in doing so learn the truth of his identity.

Choiseul clapped Keane on the shoulders. 'This is excellent

news. I think that I need to introduce Captain Williams here to the ex-commissioner, our host. Now where did I see him? Excuse us, colonel.'

He gently manoeuvred Keane away from Harrison and as soon as they were out of earshot began to speak.

'I think it is a splendid plan, an Irish Legion for the Americas. But I also think that you might be more useful to the empire here in Paris, and I suspect that Monsieur Fouché might agree.'

They found Fouché at the buffet table, eating a plate of small chocolate patisseries. He was not at all as Keane had imagined him from Macpherson's description. His face was pale in the extreme with a long nose which seemed out of proportion with the rest of his features and a thin mouth whose pallid pink lips seemed to have been painted on in a strip. He had thick eyebrows and brown eyes and his high forehead was framed by thinning dark brown hair cut in a fashionable fringe and finished with a pair of wide sideburns. He wore a black coat with a black velvet collar, a white waistcoat and high white stock which reached up to his chin. Seeing Choiseul he smiled and his gaze moved to Keane. He stopped and, as his eyes became fixed on Keane's, put down the plate and the small pastry fork with great care. He moved closer to Keane, so close that Keane could smell him. Cologne mixed with sweat.

Keane was aware that Harrison had not left them and was looking on from close to where they stood. Not moving his eyes from Keane's, Fouché spoke. 'Good evening. It must be Captain Williams, is it not?'

He spoke slowly, in a cultivated Parisian accent. Keane was alarmed by his directness, but hardly surprised.

'Yes, sir, and may I thank you for your hospitality this evening.'

'It's nothing, nothing at all, and I was delighted to welcome a member of such an illustrious regiment as your own.'

The words were said without a hint of irony, yet instantly Keane was put on his guard. 'You are too kind, sir.'

Fouché smiled at Keane, his upper lip curling in a fashion that gave no hint of his true feelings.

'To tell you the truth, I am only too pleased that we were able to meet this evening. I suspect that you and I might have something in common, Captain Williams.'

Keane blanched. Could he know? This man was surely the most enigmatic fellow he had ever met. Macpherson's warning had been right. He simply could not read him. How had Fouché, if he had done so, guessed at his business? How could he know he was not just simple Captain Williams of the legion but Captain Williams the spy or, worse still, Captain Keane, the escaped British spy?

'We trust no one.'

Keane's heart started again. So perhaps he did not know. Had not guessed. What then?

Fouché continued, still staring at Keane. 'My lieutenant, the Baron de Choiseul, tells me that you are remarkably astute, Captain Williams.' Again the last two words were said with effect, as if challenging Keane to contradict his own name.

'I couldn't comment on that, monsieur.'

'He is an excellent judge of character.'

'Then I am honoured by his remark.'

'You are not a frequent visitor to the capital, captain?'

'I have been engaged in Spain, sir.'

'Although your regiment is in Holland?'

'Yes, sir. I was on special business for Marshal Marmont.'

'Special business? How very exciting for you. The marshal must think very highly of you. Are you at liberty to tell me what business exactly?'

'I am not, sir.'

'As you will. And what now? What now is your business?'

'I am bound for Holland, sir. To rejoin the regiment.'

'Ah, the good Colonel Lawless. What a man, captain. What a man. I do not think your regiment is part of the emperor's invasion force?'

It was a question, but said with a raised eyebrow that was again loaded with meaning.

'No, sir. We are not to have that honour.'

'You may be more fortunate than you know, captain. What do you know of the great enterprise?'

Keane took a chance. 'Only that the emperor's mind is set on Russia.'

Fouché looked at him and again the eyebrow rose. 'Very astute, captain. It is a presumption in the streets of the city. But few have the detail.'

It was a tease and Keane knew it. A challenge to somehow obtain the detail. And then what? he wondered.

Fouché smiled, wiped the chocolate from his lips and walked off with a nod of goodbye.

Keane, left momentarily alone once more, was considering what he should do next when the American colonel wandered up to him. 'Well, what did you make of Monsieur Fouché? He's quite a character, isn't he?'

'Yes, quite a character.' Keane smiled. 'You seem to know him very well.'

'Oh, I do, captain, I do. I like to think that I know everyone in this city. It is, you might say, my reason for being here. Fouché's information system is extensive. Better than anything the world has ever seen before. He has all kinds of information on all kinds of people. A file on Napoleon himself, they say, as well as the expected files on spies, dissidents, writers, ministers and generals. It was extremely foolish of the emperor to dismiss him.'

Keane realized in a moment to whom he had been talking. This man, Harrison, was no mere American colonel, nor any mere spy for Fouché. He was the eyes and ears of the American nation. The key spy in France working for the US president.

'Monsieur Fouché was telling me all about the invasion.'

Harrison looked at him. 'Really? Telling you?'

'Yes, the sheer scale of the thing is extraordinary. Don't you agree?'

'Well, of course it's a pity that he's not using it to attack England. That would have been opportune for us. But at the same time an invasion of Russia on such a scale can only divert allied resources and that will put a great strain on England.'

'Tell me more about your war. I fully intend to follow up our idea.'

Harrison warmed to him. 'Well, you know it's all about the Canadian territories. The British still think they have a claim, and we simply have to show them that things have changed. They can't just walk into us. We are a supreme nation.'

'Of course, it's very refreshing. And even more so when we know that the emperor is launching his great offensive against the tsar.'

Harrison was in full flow now. 'Oh yes. I have enough intelligence on that to show my bosses in Washington. 700,000 men. Just as Fouché must have told you. What an army! Frenchmen,

Poles, Austrians, Italians, Saxons, Prussians, Bavarians, Swiss and God knows what else. Hundreds of thousands of horses and thousands of cannon. Are my chiefs going to be impressed! Napoleon intends to subjugate Russia. And when he does, what will we have?'

He was jubilant now. 'My God, man, we shall have the greatest alliance the world has ever seen. The empire of Napoleon Bonaparte and the United States of America. What an alliance. What power. Together we will crush Russia and Britain. Between us we will rule the world.'

'What a thought, colonel. What a vision.'

Harrison stared at him and in his eyes Keane saw the light of madness.

'Is it not, my friend? I would kill every one of those English dogs. All of them. If I had one now before me, I would tear him with my bare hands.'

Keane nodded. 'They deserve nothing more, colonel. I would do the same myself. Now if you'll excuse me, I have seen an acquaintance on the other side of the room. I trust that our paths shall cross again, colonel.'

'Oh, I'm certain of it, captain. Most certain. Good day.'

Keane went back across to the buffet. A servant walked up to him and handed him a full glass of champagne. Keane took it. He had lost count of how many he had drunk, but he still felt quite in command of his senses. He was proud of his 'hard head'. His capacity to take alcohol had saved his life a number of times in the trickiest of circumstances and he was certain that it would do so again.

He knew though when he was tired and now he was aware that he was mentally quite exhausted. Yet something in him remained dissatisfied. The adrenalin of the evening had given him an appetite and it was not one that was to be slaked with cheap champagne and chocolate gateaux.

Keane wandered across to where the acrobat had been performing and noticed that she was no longer there. Turning to one of the servants, he asked where she had gone and was directed towards the ante-rooms behind the salon. He walked down the row of mirrors and turned into the adjoining corridor, not quite sure what he might find. The place was full of the paraphernalia that it took to make such an evening work. Trays and trolleys, plates and dishes were stacked together as servants and chefs and footmen bustled around the corridor, attempting to make sense of it all. Keane peered through the chaos and at the end of the hall saw a glimpse of spangled clothing. He hurried on towards it and within a few moments was in another area of the *palais*.

It did not take long to find the little acrobat. She was prettier than he remembered. Her blonde hair cascaded around her shoulders and those sparkling green eyes that had held him in their gaze now fixed him again and he saw in them a glint of recognition and a complete understanding. Keane had been driven to her by a need for company, a need for companionship and a need for something else. A need in both cases fuelled by fear and brought to a head by danger. A sensation which he had not known for some months. He had known when he had first seen her that this was where he would find it and it was clear that she too had noticed him and had somehow sensed that need and knew that she shared it.

It was a short walk from the *palais* to her home, a tiny room above a café in the market area of Les Halles. Hardly any words were spoken. He did not even ask her name. But everything was understood.

Keane left the little room in the morning an hour after dawn, kissing the girl on the forehead as she slept, and took his time in walking back through the waking streets. Les Halles market was stirring into life and the meat porters who had been up half the night smiled over their glasses of wine at the Irish officer as he walked past.

The road towards Macpherson's house was an easy stroll and Keane knocked hurriedly and repeatedly at the door which was eventually answered by Macpherson's daughter. 'Let me in. Where's your father?'

'In the study, I think, captain. He's hardly awake.'

Keane pushed past her and found the old Scotsman.

'Extraordinary news. Extraordinary. Where are the others?'

Archer, awakened by the noise, joined them. They found Silver in his room, a half-empty bottle of brandy beside his bed.

Keane stood over him. 'Silver, sober up, for Christ's sake. You're riding out today.'

Silver looked up at him.

Keane looked to Archer. 'You know him. Get some water over him. Feed him coffee and make bloody sure he's in a fit state to travel today. He has to take a message back to Spain, to Wellington.'

Keane left the room with Macpherson and the two of them sat down in the old man's study.

'May I ask, captain, what all this is about at so early an hour?'

'You may, sir, and with some justification. I had the most

extraordinary conversation last night with an American in the pay of Fouché. A Colonel Harrison.'

Macpherson nodded. 'Yes, I know him. A cavalryman.'

'He confirmed that Bonaparte has gone to invade Russia.'

'That we know, captain.'

'But do you know the size of his army? And its extent? 700,000 men, sir. Of all the nationalities in his empire. In particular he confirms that Napoleon's army will invade Russia and not England. And that's just the start. According to Harrison, the Americans are making, perhaps have already made, a treaty with the French to bring down British Imperial interests. It's fantastic stuff.

'I have to get the news to Wellington. It's all he needs to go on the offensive and invade Spain in the knowledge that no reinforcements will be coming from France. Can you have a fast horse saddled? Silver will ride out with the message. And he'll need an escort.'

Macpherson nodded. 'Yes, I can find four good men. Royalists. Completely trustworthy.'

'Four men? Is that enough?'

'This is not Spain, captain. Four men will be quite sufficient in France.'

Keane smiled but inside he was tired. Last night had been a most extraordinary evening, quite apart from his liaison with the dancer. He had confirmed Napoleon's intentions and learned of his international strategy. He had made the acquaintance not only of the notorious Fouché and his right-hand man but of the key American spy in Paris. For any espionage agent it would have ranked as a major gain. But something rankled within Keane. Silver was about to set out for Spain carrying the vital news which Wellington had been so desperate to get. But Keane wished that it might have been himself who would be making that journey. He knew though, more than ever now, that he could not do any such thing. His place was here, in Paris, masterminding the whole affair and taking the royalist rebellion through to its conclusion. It was the staff officer's lot, writ large. The life of the spy. The man behind the lines. How he longed to be rid of it and to rejoin the army and once again to lead a company into action. But for now such things were to be only the stuff of his dreams.

10

Later that morning, having slept for three hours and feeling
as rested as might be hoped, Keane found Macpherson sitting
again at the kitchen table.

The old man smiled at Keane as he entered. 'You are feeling
better now? You seemed exhausted, captain.'

'It was a very busy evening.'

'Yes, of course. And you did well to learn so much. I trust
that the rest of Monsieur Fouché's soirée was to your liking?'

Keane smiled. 'It was fascinating. Highly entertaining. Your
agent is extremely adroit.'

'Yes, Jadot is an asset.'

'He managed to get me to Choiseul and then to Fouché
himself. He is as you described him. All of that, and more so.'
Keane paused for a moment and drummed his fingers on the
table before speaking again.

'I'm not convinced that he quite believes in me yet. I had
to lie to Harrison to get the information on the invasion. If
they compare notes on me they might put it together. At all
costs I can't afford to look scared now. I have to brazen it out.
I need to go in from the front and convince him that I really

am something more than just a captain of foot. That I'm the real thing. A spy. Perhaps even a double agent that he can turn. That would make him very happy.'

Macpherson nodded. 'Perhaps. If that's how best to tackle him.'

'I need to impress him. He's bound to test me, but I can play him at his game.'

Macpherson nodded. 'There is perhaps a way in which I can help to convince him of your commitment to his cause. And of course to your own pocket. I have an idea, but it will mean losing two of my agents.'

Keane shook his head. 'No, let me do something of my own first. I want to see how far he's prepared to go.'

It was clear to Keane that the best way to convince Fouché of his ability would be to impress him on his own territory, deep in the demi-monde of the brothels and gambling dens of the Palais-Royal. He contemplated how best to do it. Of course, to stage a show in a brothel would not be beyond his powers, he thought, but, enjoyable as it might be, it would be unlikely to have the desired effect. Far better and more obvious to put on a demonstration at the gaming table.

He looked at Macpherson. 'Fouché's a gambler, you said?'

'Yes, inveterate. He can't stop. High stakes too. And he operates his own gaming house. At least that's what they say. It might just be a story. But he certainly plays every night at the Palais-Royal.'

'Then that's where I'll meet him. On his own territory. Let's see if I can't take some money from him, the more the better. I suspect he'll want it back. Then we'll see where that leads us.'

Macpherson shook his head. 'This is a daring scheme, Keane,

and it might just work. But I wonder, is it not perhaps merely rash? Why not let me try my idea?'

Keane shook his head. 'And risk losing two good men? No. We'll do it my way. Trust me, sir. I know what I'm doing.'

He rose abruptly from the table. 'Silver should be on his way. We have an escort?'

Macpherson nodded. 'As I said, captain, four men. All trusted. They await my word.'

'Then you had best summon them, sir. We have no time to lose.'

They found Silver with Archer in the house's small dining room, nursing a cup of coffee.

'Are you ready?'

Archer replied, 'He's as ready as he'll ever be, sir.'

'What got into you, man? Brandy of all things.'

'I don't know, sir. I suppose I'm just unhappy. I miss my Gabby and I ain't cut out for this sort of life. I miss Spain and the boys, sir.'

'Yes, Silver, so do I. Well, you're in luck. You're going back.'

Silver looked up. 'Are we, sir?'

'Just you. Mr Macpherson here is providing an escort and you're taking this note to Wellington.'

Producing a paper from his pocket he handed it to Silver. It was folded heavily, bound with a red ribbon and sealed with red wax.

'Wellington himself, mind. Don't go giving it to anyone else. No matter how important they say they are. This is for Major Grant's eyes only.'

'Yes, sir. I understand.'

'Right, get your kit together. You leave as soon as the escort arrives.'

Half an hour later, Keane and Archer watched as Silver and the four horsemen rode along the rue du Faubourg, westwards, towards the boundary of the city.

Archer spoke. 'I know what you're thinking, sir. You're wishing it was you in his place, aren't you?'

'Yes, Archer, of course I am. Is it that obvious? And aren't you? Come on, we're late for our appointment with Lady Luck.'

It was approaching five in the afternoon as Keane and Archer walked together towards the Palais-Royal.

They entered from the rue du Faubourg and made their way quickly across the gardens to the arcade on the right, which housed most of the gaming houses. The most opulent lay in the centre of the galleries and it was here that they headed, in search of Fouché.

The entrance through the pillared colonnade was guarded by two huge liveried doormen and the two men had to pass through a smaller door to gain access to the entrance hall. Here a wide staircase swept before them to the upper rooms and they climbed, guessing that this was where the gaming tables would be found. Turning right on the landing they found themselves in a huge salon with a gilded ceiling and crystal chandeliers. A dozen large gaming tables draped in green cloths lay around the room, which was filled with people, men and women, all of them displaying conspicuous wealth. Keane knew instinctively that this was the place. But he also knew that this room would not be where Fouché would be found. He would have his own inner sanctum. That was Keane's goal.

He had not penetrated far into the room when he noticed Jadot seated at one of the gaming tables. The policeman saw

Keane and acknowledged him. Keane smiled but continued purposefully on to the *caisse*.

He had always been a gambler. When first in his old regiment, he had played cards on campaign with his fellow officers. Had learnt from them how to play and, importantly, how to cheat and how to trust to luck. It was one of the things he missed most since his new role had taken him away from the mess and he had had little chance to use his skills and his instinct.

He suspected that he would be a little rusty now but knew it would soon come back. After all, so much of it was luck. The trick was not to underestimate the imponderable. So far Keane's good fortune had held out although, as the old saying went, having been lucky at cards all his life, he had had little lasting luck with the fair sex. And he was quite aware that one day, either in the gambling house or on the battlefield, fortune would take a turn and his luck would run out. But he would deal with that day and its deadly consequences whenever it found him.

He had unearthed the five thousand francs that Grant had cleverly had sewn into the lining of the Irish uniform, and with this in his pocket he approached the banker.

He handed the man two thousand francs and was presented with a handful of tiny gold ingots as tokens. He returned to Archer, who was standing by one of the gaming tables in the large hall, staring at the game in progress.

Keane was taken aback at one aspect of the gaming room. He had been expecting the favoured game here to be *vingt et un*, but instead it was baccarat. The new fashion. It was similar to faro, his particular favourite, and he was well acquainted with the rules although he had played only a few times.

Archer stared at the cards as they flashed across the tables. 'It is fascinating, sir, isn't it? You can't help but admire their belief in themselves.'

'Well, perhaps you had better get yourself a little of that self-belief, James,' Keane said, and handed Archer a small handful of the gold ingots. 'There you are, lieutenant. There's five hundred to reinforce the illusion of your elevated social position. Shall I explain the rules?

'While each table is controlled by a croupier, each of the players takes a turn at being banker. They're all dealt two cards. You have to have two or three cards adding up to nine points, or as close to nine as possible. Court cards and tens count for nothing and aces are a point each. When you reach double figures it's the second number that counts. So a nine and a ten is nine, not nineteen. When two cards add up to nine it's called a "natural". If I have six or seven I can stand. Everything turns on the number five. With five in your hand you can ask for a card or you can choose not to. Are you following me?'

Archer looked bemused. 'Yes, sir, completely.'

'It's really quite simple. It's said to be a favourite card game of Bonaparte himself. All you have to do is make sure that you have more than your fair share of "natural" eights and nines.'

He looked at Archer. 'Wait here for me. I might be some time. That man over there –' he pointed to Jadot, who was looking away from them – 'you've met Jadot. He's Macpherson's mole in the Sûreté. If anything goes wrong here, go with him. Do whatever he says.'

'Sir, I —'

'Got it?'

'Yes, sir. I understand.'

Leaving Archer at the table to try his own luck, Keane walked across the room to Jadot, to whom he had sent a note with Archer, earlier in the afternoon. He pointed towards the inner sanctum.

'Get me in there, can you?'

'Of course. It's all arranged.'

Jadot gave Keane a small billet and then, getting up from his own game, parted company with him and walked over to where Archer had taken a seat at one of the outer tables.

Keane walked up to the entrance to the *salle privée* and after flashing the paper at the doorman was shown inside through the small doorway that separated the two rooms.

The inner room was hung with heavy crimson drapes, trimmed with gold bullion to give an air of opulence. Once inside, Keane walked across to the gaming tables. There were four in the room, all of them occupied and each one draped in a dark green cloth, in the centre of which was a rectangle made up of alternating red and white squares. The place smelt of stale sweat and alcohol and it all positively reeked of the new aristocracy of Bonaparte's Paris.

At one of the tables a young man had evidently just had a win, for the wine was flowing in greater quantity than else-where and those around the table were smiling and clustering close to the winner with the insincerity of those desperate to acquire a modicum of borrowed luck. The other three tables had the more usual tang of mixed nervousness and ennui. Keane chose the one with the fewest players and sat down, placing a silver snuffbox and his pile of ingots on the table beside him.

The table was busy, with six of the ten places taken. There

was a French general and next to him a man in outrageously expensive clothes. On his left sat a hugely fat man with spectacles and a bald head. The fourth player was a woman. Keane thought that he recognized her from the previous evening. She was attractive and of noble bearing, although age had left her face with heavy lines, and the figure that in her youth must have been so supple now sagged within her white dress which was nevertheless stunning, with a very low décolletage. As he approached she smiled at him and widened her eyes in an obviously flirtatious gesture. Keane nodded and smiled politely in response. Beside her sat a small man with a face like a weasel and orange hair to match and beside him was a splendidly dressed officer of the Chasseurs à Cheval. It was without doubt a wealthy table and Keane knew that he would have his work cut out to explain the presence there of a humble Irish lieutenant.

He found a chair at the sixth position, next to the ageing society beauty, who turned to him the moment he sat down, as he had known she would.

'How delightful. Another military man. We haven't met, I think. Madame d'Ecrambier.'

Keane nodded and kissed the hand she offered him. 'Of course, madame. Your fame outdoes you, but does not do justice to your beauty.'

She smiled. 'What gallantry, captain. One doesn't expect it from the military these days.' She shot a glance to the general, who pretended not to have heard. 'It is captain, is it not? I find military matters so confusing.'

'Yes, madame, captain it is indeed. Captain James Williams at your service.'

'You're Irish, I'll guess. Am I right?'

'Yes, madame, indeed you are. Fighting for the empire and the emperor, long may he reign.'

'Indeed, captain, long may he reign, and may the heavens protect him in Russia. Oh dear, perhaps I shouldn't have said that. But you're bound to know where he is, aren't you?'

She looked at him. 'Tell me, what can have brought you to our little table? You've certainly brought it some colour, and I hope some of your native luck.'

'Well, madame, I don't usually play cards in this way. But I have just inherited a little money. From my uncle. He had a farm, in the old country. And I thought I might indulge myself and try my luck.'

'You haven't played baccarat before?'

Keane shook his head. 'Sadly not, madame. But why not give it a try, says I? Anything once. Besides, it's not as if I can lose the whole of my fortune in one little game or one night, now, is it?'

The general sniggered.

Madame d'Ecrambier gave a warning. 'Captain, if there's one thing this is not, it is a "little" game. Just take care.'

At that moment a concealed door in the far wall opened and two men walked across to the table. Keane recognized one of them immediately as Fouché. The other, a thin man of around six feet in height and with long white hair which fell about his collar, he did not know, although from the deference which was shown him by servants and players alike, Keane guessed that he must be someone of national importance. They moved towards the table and without a word sat down, the tall, thin man at position three and Fouché in the banker's place, opposite Keane. Fouché placed a large glass of red wine beside his place and his guest did the same.

Fouché recognized Keane immediately and raising an eyebrow smiled and, turning his head, whispered something to his partner before speaking across the table.

'Captain Williams. We meet again and so soon. What a pleasure. Do you know Monsieur Talleyrand?'

So, thought Keane, Talleyrand. The arch spymaster and the most infamous turncoat of the empire. Keane had not known that he was in Paris and suspected that it was because Bonaparte was not in the city that he could show his face here. And perhaps there was another reason.

'An honour, sir. And may I thank you again for the ball last night.'

'The pleasure was entirely mine, captain. And I am pleased that you found it so diverting and were perhaps able to indulge yourself a little.' He looked at Keane with a grin which implied that he knew all about his interlude with the acrobat. Keane wondered how, but presumed that such information was bread and meat to Fouché.

Without further ado, Fouché cut the slab of six packs of playing cards which the croupier had placed on the table and laid the cards down on the green cloth, close to the squares.

The croupier announced the bank at one thousand francs. Fouché took one of the cards and moved it to the general before taking one for himself and repeating the moves.

The general lifted his cards very slightly, looked at them and turned to Fouché. He shook his head. 'Non.'

Fouché turned over his own two cards. Five of clubs and four of hearts. A natural.

The croupier said, 'Nine to the bank,' and removed the two losing cards.

The general asked for two more cards and Keane settled

down to watch the action. It was a long game, and by the time
the general had lost all of his money to the bank, Keane was
more than ready to begin.

'*Banco.*'

Fouché looked at him and smiled. 'Captain, welcome.'

He took the four cards one by one and dealt them, two to
Keane, two to himself. Keane flipped up the corner of each of
his cards and without hesitation turned them over to reveal
the five of spades and the four of hearts.

Madame d'Ecrambier gasped and smiled. The general shook
his head.

Fouché raised an eyebrow and turned over his own cards.
The ten of spades and the jack of diamonds.

The croupier spoke with almost religious zeal – '*Le baccarat*'
– before pushing the pile of ingot tokens across to Keane.

The game began again and Keane continued to win.

Before long he was conscious that a crowd of onlookers
was gathering. There were the usual pretty girls among them,
waiting to see who would be their benefactor for the night, a
few dandies, intrigued by the winner, and a couple of Fouché's
thugs. They stood out in the crowd. One was thin and sallow
with a face like a skull and the other heavy-set, with a bull
neck and a red face. With them stood Colonel Harrison.

Within the hour Keane had increased his two-thousand-
franc holding to no less than six thousand and he could see
that Fouché had lost heavily.

Curiously, Talleyrand had not taken any part in the game
but had merely sat and observed. It was almost as if the two
men had been expecting Keane to be there, to play. And the
only way they would have known that would have been if
Jadot had told them. Which, Keane reasoned, he must have

done. And he began to see how he, even he, was being manipulated like a puppet by other forces.

What he had thought was a scheme of his own making, a plan to impress Fouché with his sangfroid, had become something bigger. He was uncertain as yet as to what. But he knew that this was more than a mere attempt to infiltrate the staff of the ex-head of the secret police. Why else would Talleyrand himself be watching his every move?

Fouché smiled at him and nodded to the croupier, who spoke again in his best liturgical voice: '*Un banco de huit mille.*'

Keane calculated the state of his funds. The two thousand plus his winnings of four plus the original three thousand less Archer's five hundred. Eight thousand five hundred francs. He could either bet it all or walk away. If he lost, then he would be almost cleaned out. If he won, then Fouché himself would have lost tens of thousands. He looked across the table. Saw the raised eyebrow. It decided him.

'*Banco.*'

There was an audible gasp from around the table.

Fouché leant towards him. 'You're a very brave man, Captain Williams. I like that.'

Fouché dealt four cards. Keane looked at his own and turned them as one. The nine of diamonds and the three of spades. It was not a natural, but it might just be enough.

Fouché looked at his own cards. '*Carte.*' He drew another card and turned all three over. Two aces and a ten. Game to Keane.

Keane smiled as the croupier pushed the pile of ingots across the table towards him and looked at Fouché. 'Just one of those nights, I suppose.'

'You're a very lucky man, captain. Perhaps too lucky. You should take care.'

Fouché rose from the table, followed by Talleyrand and escorted by Harrison. Together with the two thugs, 'skull-face' and 'bull-neck', they left through the same door by which they had entered.

Madame d'Ecrambier shook her head and stroked Keane's shoulder. 'I thought you said that you had never played.'

'You should never believe everything that you hear, especially from an Irishman at a gambling table. Now, madame, if you'll excuse me, I have some business with the *caisse*.'

As he was exchanging his ingots for francs, Archer came up.

'You'll never guess, sir. I won.'

'Oh, really. How much?'

'Three thousand, sir.'

Keane turned to him. 'Three thousand? How on earth?'

'I just took your advice, and every time I won I just said "*suivi*" and put everything back on.'

Keane laughed. 'You're clearly a great deal madder than you look, Archer. Well done.'

With some difficulty Keane managed to decline the entreaties of Madame d'Ecrambier to join her for breakfast and, laden with their winnings, he and Archer finally left the Palais-Royal at close to two in the morning. They had gone no more than two blocks along the street, however, when he became conscious that they were being followed.

It appeared that his hunch about Fouché's reaction to his win at the tables had been correct. For there was soon no doubt in his mind that the heavy footfall which was following them belonged to Fouché's two thugs, who had now been

joined by a third. Undoubtedly their orders were to catch up
with the Irishmen and attempt to take his money back. Simple
enough of course, and he doubted if the heavies would realize
how little a value their employer placed on their lives.

If Keane and Archer were killed by the assassins, then
Fouché would know they were not worthy of a place in his
household and the money would again be his. If, on the other
hand Keane and Archer should win and dispose of the three
men, he could be confident that on that count they were
worthy of taking on as his own. Either way, he would win.
Either way, men were about to die.

Keane spoke to Archer without turning his head. 'Don't look.
Three men, across the street. Rear. Two hundred yards.'

They carried on in the direction of Macpherson's house and
Keane saw that up ahead of them a small close led off to the
right. He shot a glance at Archer and mouthed, 'Down here.' As
soon as they were level with the opening Keane turned down it
sharply, followed hard by Archer. The passageway was narrow
and led through to a square beyond. Houses lay on either
side, four and five storeys high with lines of washing strung
out across the void. The two men whom Keane recognized as
skull-face and bull-neck ran along the close and halfway down
took another right turn. Keane turned and drew his sword and
at the same time pulled a pistol from inside his coat. It was
pre-loaded. He saw that Archer had done the same. 'That's it.
One each with one shot, then the third.' They could hear the
men in the alleyway now and saw a shadow pass across the
end of the turning. The man walked past and then doubled
back and walked towards them. They could see him now and
beyond him the shadows cast by the others. He shouted to

them, and Archer, who had been holding his pistol out with his arm extended, pulled the trigger. The matchlock exploded and the ball found its target. The man doubled up, but neither Keane nor Archer could say where he had been hit. Archer cursed. 'Damn. Sorry, sir. Too quick.'

He was right, for the shot had warned the other two men and now the alleyway ahead of them stood empty. All was silent save for the groaning of the wounded man, who lay squirming on his side in the dirt of the lane.

Keane spoke. 'Reload. Take the chance while they work out what to do.'

Archer obeyed and Keane wondered what was going through the remaining two killers' minds.

'They won't charge us now. But they need to get the job done. They know we're stuck here. They might send for reinforcements.'

'What should we do, sir?'

'Only two things we can do, Archer. We can sit it out here and see what happens. Or we can take the fight to them. Personally I've never been one for waiting. Shall we?'

Gripping his sword and pistol he smiled at Archer and then together they ran the length of the alleyway, vaulting over the dying man. They turned into the main lane, one in each direction, and as they did so a shot rang out. The pistol ball smacked into the wall about an inch above Archer's head. He turned in the direction of the shot and, seeing the flash of a figure, fired. There was a shout as the bullet tore into the man's upper arm. Archer stood his ground and waited. Keane meanwhile could not see hide nor hair of his man and the assassin chose not to reveal his position. Keane sensed this man must be the leader, skull-face from the gambling house.

He advanced along the lane, and finding a barrel in his path ducked down behind it and listened.

He could hear heavy breathing, coming from, he estimated, perhaps thirty yards away to his left. On his side of the lane. Probably behind an outhouse he had noted on their way down the lane. He wondered how to lure the man out. Something thrown against the side of the building might do it. Or some other diversion. A sudden shot would be enough. He thought of Archer. Yes, a cry from Archer's side of the lane might goad the man into action, and then as he moved a stone thrown against the building would confuse him and Keane would have his moment. He was about to turn to Archer when from behind him came precisely the cry he had been about to encourage. It seemed that Archer had anticipated him. As he had thought, there was movement up ahead. Keane looked down and, seeing a loose cobble, picked it up and hurled it towards the wall of the outbuilding where it smashed into the bricks with a terrific crash. There was another cry from his rear.

Keane spun round and saw Archer pinned against the wall of the lane by bull-neck, the blade of a stiletto dagger held close against his throat.

The shout had been a cry not of diversion but for help. There was a noise from behind Keane and turning he saw the third killer, skull-face, standing in the lane, his pistol pointed directly at Keane's head. The man spoke. 'We've got your friend. Give us the cash.'

'You must be friends of Monsieur Fouché. I'm sure he's most anxious to be reacquainted with his money.'

'No clever stuff, or he gets it. In the neck. Hold him, Jacques. Give us the money or you both get it.'

'I'm sure that we'll both "get it" anyway. Besides, I no longer have the money. It's in a safe place.'

'I don't believe you.'

'Really? Come and search me then.'

The man hesitated. 'Not likely. Where is it? Tell me, or he gets it.'

'All right. I'll take you to it. But you must take the knife away from his throat.'

The leader nodded to bull-neck. 'Do it.'

Jacques pulled away the knife, but kept Archer's arm in a tight lock. Keane smiled. 'Thank you. And if you wouldn't mind lowering your pistol, it's not good for my memory. I'm likely to forget where I put the money.'

Skull-face lowered the pistol, but kept it pointed at Keane. 'Hurry up. We haven't got all night.'

'I presume your master told you to hurry back like good little thugs.'

'Don't be funny. We just want the money.'

'I know, or he "gets it". Got it, Archer?'

'Yes, sir. I think so.'

'Good. Follow me, gentlemen.'

With Keane leading the way, they moved carefully down the alley and back to the main street, where they turned left and began to walk back towards the *palais*. All the way Keane was forming a plan in his mind. At any moment the leader of the thugs would realize that he had missed a trick and that if his companion held a knife again to Archer's throat, Keane would have to allow him to search his clothes and then he would find the money. His best option, he thought, would be to take them back to the gambling house and hope that it was still busy. That being the case the men would have to hide their pistol and it would not be hard to overcome them. That at least was what he hoped. But what if the *palais* was not as busy and there was not a chance to tackle the two men? Archer's captor would snap his arm and the leader would shoot Keane before dispatching Archer. He weighed up the other options. There were none.

They were getting closer to the *palais* with every step. The streets were empty, save for a few drunks trying to find their way home, and no one gave a second glance to four men walking together. Indeed Archer and his companion might have been just two more drunks, supporting each other as they stumbled along, and skull-face had covered his pistol with a fold of his cloak and held it, as Keane was only too aware, pointed at his prisoner's back. The *palais* buildings were within sight now. The leader growled in Keane's ear, 'How much further?'

'Not long now. Be patient.'

In reply he felt the muzzle of the gun poke into his backbone.

They were entering the *palais* now and, to his horror, Keane saw that the place was almost deserted. Walking towards the gambling house he thought fast.

'The money's in a box just inside the door. I have hidden the key, and I'll need to bend down to get it. All right?'

Skull-face, standing behind him, grunted. 'Very well.'

Reaching the door to the gambling house, Keane began to bend down as if looking for something on the ground. Behind him, the pistol still covered with his cloak, his captor looked on with interest, absorbed in the hunt. Keane judged his moment and, just as skull-face was craning his neck to see over Keane's back, he turned and aimed a punch towards his groin. The man groaned and doubled up as Keane followed up with a left-handed chop to the back of his neck which sent him to the ground. Meanwhile, Archer had moved against bull-neck, whose attention had been taken by the attack on his partner. Breaking free from his grip, he tripped him with his right foot. The man fell backwards and landed sprawling on the cobbles. Archer wasted no time. Drawing his sword, he slashed at the man's throat, opening a broad lane of bright red. Keane drew his own sword and plunged it into skull-face's back, level with his heart. The man dropped flat to the cobbles and Keane withdrew the blade.

'That was close. Too close, I think. Come on. We should get home before they're missed.'

They had reached the junction with rue du Bac, almost at Macpherson's door, when Keane heard footsteps again, behind them. He turned to Archer. 'That's it. They've found them.'

'Should we stand, sir?'

'I don't see what else we can do.'

Together the two men turned and drew their swords. But it was not a group of assassins that greeted them, but Colonel Harrison, and he was alone.

Keane laughed. 'Colonel Harrison, don't tell me. Let me guess. This is another of Monsieur Fouché's little surprises and in a moment we shall be surrounded by his friends.'

The American smiled and shook his head. 'I'm sure that I don't know what you mean, Captain Williams. I am merely a messenger. Monsieur Fouché sent me. With a note for you, captain. I'm quite alone.'

There was certainly no sign of anyone else on the street, save a prostitute supporting one of her clients as he stumbled home and an old man urinating in the gutter.

Harrison handed a folded paper to Keane, who took it and opened it up to read.

It was in a slim, spidery hand and bore Fouché's signature. Keane scanned it:

My dear Captain Williams,
After tonight's fascinating sequence of events, it has occurred to me that perhaps you might be of some real use to the empire. Perhaps I might find a use for you that would prove to be to our mutual benefit. Do me the kindness to be at my office in the rue du Bac, Noon tomorrow.'

Keane folded the paper and tucked it inside his coat.

'Fascinating, colonel. Quite intriguing.'

'Monsieur Fouché is nothing if not intriguing, captain. I trust that he has offered you a position. Didn't I tell you he'd find a use for you? You've landed on your feet there.'

'You're forgetting, colonel. I already hold a commission in the army of France. I am fully employed.'

'Ah, yes, but with Fouché's kind of work you can do this at the same time as other jobs. In fact the two often go hand in hand.'

'You work for Fouché?'

Harrison nodded. 'Why not? It often seems to me that half of *le tout Paris* work for Fouché. You never know who's bogus and who's not. Take the gambling house for instance. How many of those people do you suppose were employed or paid by Fouché? I'll tell you. Almost all of them.'

'And the three thugs who tried to kill us this evening?'

'I'm sure I have no idea to what you're referring.'

'I saw you with them in the gambling house. The skull-face and the bull neck.'

'I'm sure that you're mistaken. I know no one like that.'

'Nor will you, colonel.'

'They don't sound like Fouché's people. He is discerning. He likes to choose those who are invited into his network with the utmost care.'

Keane nodded. 'Generals, society figures, the aristocracy? That's quite a network.'

'And I'm sure you have added to it, captain.' He paused. 'You seem to know a good deal about spies. How is that so, for a captain of infantry?'

'I might ask the same of a colonel of light horse.'

Harrison laughed. 'We had our fair share of spies in the revolutionary war. British ones in particular. Are you familiar with the name John André?'

'Yes, of course. Who isn't?'

'We hanged him. A double agent. What else can you do with a double agent. You can never know whose side they're on. Better off dead.'

Keane said nothing for a moment. How could this man know the truth of his own duplicity?

'There are many Americans in Paris at present, are there not? No one asks any questions and we move around freely. Do you wonder that the chief of the secret police chooses to employ me?'

'How can he trust you?'

'I might ask the same of you, captain? For my part I can prove that my father was a patriot in our great war and died at the hands of the British. I still don't know the full details, but I know I'm getting closer to them.' He smiled a cruel smile. 'I believe that there might be someone in this city. A girl, no, a woman, who might provide the information I crave. And as of today I have an idea where she might be found.'

He recovered his composure. 'That is what I get from using Monsieur Fouché's network. What do you get, captain, and for that matter, what can you tell me about your reasons for hating the British?'

Keane, puzzling about Harrison's references to his father's killer, smiled and almost said that he didn't even know who his own father was, but stopped himself in time.

'My father too was killed by the British, in 1798. He was impaled on a pike for speaking his mind and rioting in his own country. That is why I hate the British so much. My mother died then too. What else do you want to know?'

The American nodded. 'Then we seem to have something in common, captain. Let's not forget it.'

11

It was nine o'clock the following morning before Keane managed to tell Macpherson about their exploits of the previous evening. He produced the letter.

'It's precisely what I had hoped would happen. Of course he's bound to want his money back. But that's a small price to pay, I think.'

'A small price perhaps. Your presence in Fouché's network will be a great deal more important than that of Jadot. You've done well, Keane. I think now it is time to move on to stage two of the plan.'

He called to his daughter. 'Kirsty, run and fetch Elliott from his house and ask him to alert his brother that I have a guest they will wish to meet.'

Keane said nothing, although he was tempted to do so. He had not been aware that he had been part of a stage one, let alone that there was a stage two. For a moment he had the distinct sensation that he was being used by Macpherson and it offended his sensibilities. This was not what Grant had led him to believe. Macpherson's role was to have been that of an intermediary. A man on the ground rather than a spy. Yet here he was, using Keane as if he were a spymaster. Clearly something was wrong.

Kirsty arrived back almost an hour later and with her she brought a man. He was tall and lean with a long, aquiline nose and a scar on his chin. As he entered, Macpherson rose from his chair. 'Ah, Elliott, this is the man I was telling you about: Captain Williams.'

Keane noted Macpherson's use of his alias. The newcomer looked at him and nodded a greeting. 'I'm pleased to make your acquaintance, captain. Mr Macpherson speaks most highly of you.'

He turned to Macpherson. 'I have summoned my brother, general.'

'Rochambeau is coming here?'

'He is on his way.'

'Good, then we will wait for him. I'm sorry, Captain Williams, allow me to introduce François Elliott. Mister Elliott had a Scottish Jacobite father and his mother was of the French noblesse. Both perished in the Terror. If I tell you that he and his parents were part of King Louis's own personal household, then you will not need to ask me of his allegiances.'

'You are a royalist, sir?'

'I am indeed. A true royalist, loyal to the Bourbons and of a mind to depose the current ruler.'

'Then I'm pleased to meet you, monsieur.'

Macpherson interrupted. 'In fact, captain, it's monsignor. Sorry, I should have said.'

'Sorry, monsignor.'

The use of the title was interesting. In particular now as Keane had not been blind to the way in which the two men acted with each other, nor to the newcomer's use of the word 'general' to address Macpherson. So he was 'General Macpherson'. That explained a good deal.

They did not have to wait long for the other man to arrive. Elliott's 'brother' Rochambeau was physically the opposite of Elliott. As short as the other was tall and with a full physique which spoke of good living as much as it did of hard fighting. He was the sort of man who, if encountered on a dark night, might persuade you to cross quickly over to the other side of the road. He looked at Keane and squinted. 'Who's this?' He took a closer look at Keane's uniform. 'He's Irish? French Irish?'

Elliott nodded. 'Yes, Irish. But not for the French. Not for Bonaparte. This is Captain Williams, fresh from Spain. He's come to help us.'

Rochambeau continued to squint at Keane. 'Is he dependable?'

Elliott replied, as if the two of them were weighing up a piece of livestock. 'Completely. The general can vouch for him. He is one of Wellington's top men. A spy.'

Keane winced at the word and smiled engagingly at Rochambeau, who continued to stare at him while he spoke to Elliott. 'If you say so. I wouldn't trust any spy.' He fixed Keane in his gaze. 'What do you know of us?'

'Merely what I have been told by Mr Macpherson, the general here. Not much.'

'We aim to kill Bonaparte. A bomb. Before he begins on his new campaign, his latest madness. He is still in Dresden with the Grande Armée. The timing couldn't be better. He will be surrounded by generals, and no one will suspect that one of them will be bearing more than papers in his portmanteau.'

'You intend to kill Bonaparte with a bomb at his headquarters?'

'His field headquarters. Yes. Precisely. This coming Saturday. The general here tells us that you can help us. Can you?'

Keane looked quizzically at Macpherson. This had not been what he had been told his mission involved and he wondered what on earth his response should be. Macpherson merely nodded.

Keane looked back at Rochambeau. 'I'll do everything I possibly can to help. I have no great experience with bombs, and although I have a man with me who has special talents, I can't say I see either being of use to you. He's adept at both robbery and code-breaking. We'll do what we can.'

Rochambeau seemed satisfied. 'Good, we need anyone we can get who has experience of operating behind enemy lines. Your disguise is good too. The Légion Irlandaise is destined to be part of his force, we hear. When can you leave?'

Again Keane looked at Macpherson, who nodded. 'Captain Williams and Lieutenant O'Connell will be ready to depart with you just as soon as you are prepared to go.'

'Very good. We shall call for you tomorrow afternoon, captain. We ride to Dresden. Until then, goodbye, captain. Good day, general.'

The two men left the room and Macpherson's daughter showed them from the house.

Keane turned to Macpherson. 'Sir, could you possibly tell me what on earth that conversation was about? Dresden? I'm not supposed to go to Dresden. Am I?'

Macpherson shook his head and looked deadly serious. 'No, not at all, Keane. I'm afraid that you have just been used in a game. And I must say that you played your part very well.'

Keane's blood was boiling, his worst fears confirmed. 'What? Used how? What do you mean?'

'The bomb plot will fail. It must in fact fail before it begins. This morning you will travel to see Fouché at the appointed time. As your opening move as a new paid man on his team, you will tell him about the bomb plot. You will give him the addresses of Elliott and Rochambeau.'

'And they will be arrested.'

'Precisely.'

'But surely that will be to condemn them to death.'

Macpherson nodded. 'Yes, it will. But there is no alternative. You have done an excellent job of showing Fouché that you deserve a place in his confidence. Now we have to persuade him that, apart from being intrepid and resourceful, you are also loyal to your new master and ruthlessly disloyal to others. If it takes the death of two of my agents to do so, then that, I'm afraid, is what it takes. This time their luck has run out. We can't afford to give it another thought.'

Keane began to protest. 'But I thought that I was supposed to raise a royalist rebellion here in Paris. To help to bring down Bonaparte's regime from the inside. You yourself said so. How on earth can such a plan work if I show myself to be a traitor to the royalist cause. Which royalist will ever trust me again?'

Macpherson looked at him and smiled. 'Who said anything about any rising being an exclusively royalist insurrection? When we rid ourselves of Bonaparte, it will be by means of an alliance between all of his enemies, royalists, republicans, all sorts. They will work together. By sacrificing two royalists, we work for the greater good. Trust me, the royalists are used to such sacrifices and the republicans will see it as you proving yourself for them. It is the only way, Keane. Believe me.'

Keane did not know quite what or who to trust. He was genu-inely shocked by the man's candour and apparent brutality.

He wondered in passing if he might be destined for the same fate. If Macpherson's intriguing was so complex that he might himself be being used in some counter-counter plot. But at present there was nothing to do apart from go along with Macpherson's plan.

The bells of Notre Dame were striking twelve noon when Keane found himself in Fouché's office at the house in the rue du Bac. The ex-chief of police greeted him with a friendly smile.

'Captain, I am pleased to see you here as agreed.' He looked back down at the table. 'Now, to business. Monsieur Choiseul tells me that you already have information for me.'

Choiseul had ushered Keane into the room but had left on Fouché's bidding, leaving the two of them apparently alone.

'Yes, sir. I have information of an extremely sensitive nature regarding the well-being of the emperor himself.'

Fouché raised an eyebrow. 'Really? What kind of information?'

'Information regarding an attempt upon his life.'

Fouché's face became immediately animated and alert. 'An attempt on the emperor's life? Where and by whom? Tell me.'

'There is a royalist plot, sir. They plan to kill the emperor with a bomb. In Dresden, in three days' time. It is to be hidden inside the portmanteau of one of the generals.'

Fouché rang the little bell that sat on his desk and instantly the door opened and Choiseul entered, accompanied by two armed guards.

'Quickly, Choiseul, get a pen and paper. Now, captain, we need details. Every detail. When will this happen and who are the conspirators?'

'As I said, at Dresden. On Saturday. I do not know the identity of the general who will be carrying the bomb. But I can give you the names of his conspirators here in Paris.'

'That will be enough. We have means of getting any information we need.'

'Their names are Elliott and Rochambeau and I have their addresses here.' Feeling the very worst sort of traitor, Keane handed Fouché a piece of paper on which he had written, as directed by Macpherson, the names and addresses of the two men.

Fouché read it and handed it to Choiseul. 'Go and take both men and anyone else who you happen to find in their houses. If they resist, you have my express permission to kill them. But do your best to bring them in alive. Put them in the cellars. Then we shall see what they can tell us.'

For a moment Keane panicked. 'Sir, may I be allowed to leave before they are brought here? Should they see me here, it would all be up for me.'

Fouché smiled. 'Why of course, captain. That would not do at all. But first, would you be so kind as to tell me how you managed to get this information for us? Who was it entrusted you with it?'

'I did it myself, sir. I have my sources and the word was that something of the sort was afoot. I'm naturally inquisitive, sir. I just like to know other people's business. So in the last few days I began to make enquiries. A question here, a question there. You know how it is. It's not difficult when you wear the green and speak in an Irish accent as I do. There are many people on both sides who would take you as their friend. I simply made it known in certain circles, in certain cafés, that I was a royalist sympathizer and the next thing you know these two men were on me, asking me to help them.'

'And you agreed, of course.'

'Of course, sir, knowing that I might be able to impart to you some information which would save the life of the emperor.'

Fouché said nothing for a moment, and then, 'Yes, I see, captain. But put yourself in my position. You will see that from my point of view you might be lying. If as you say is true, and I know it to be so, there are Irish on both sides, then why should you not be on the other?'

'Then why would I have given you the names of two men whom I have now condemned to certain death? These men are royalists. They deserve to die. Why would I condemn my own type if I were one of them?'

Fouché considered the matter. 'I would like to believe you, Captain Williams, and so I shall. You may go before they arrive. Indeed you must go. You have done well, captain. Now, get out of here before the two unfortunates arrive.'

Within two hours, two companies of the city's National Guard, miraculously raised by Fouché using all the influence he still exerted in official channels, had surrounded the houses of Elliott and Rochambeau and the two men and their households were taken off without incident in covered wagons to the cellars of the rue du Bac.

The first that Keane heard of it was from Macpherson. He had returned home and was sitting in the library trying to puzzle out Macpherson's own motives when the old man entered. He looked sombre as he spoke.

'It is done. They've been taken.'

'That's it then. I can't say I'm pleased.'

'This is a long game, Keane. There's no room for sentiment. We're in it to win.'

And with that the matter was closed. Keane tried not to imagine the fate of the families and servants of the two men, but was nevertheless overwhelmed by a sense of guilt and complicity in an affair in which he took no pride.

And before long further arrests were made and publicised to Fouché's credit. And the remaining conspirators went to ground. Macpherson himself though remained untouched. It was said that another, nameless royalist agent, a double agent in the pay of Fouché, had come into Paris with an old grudge against one of the two men and betrayed him. That at least was the story being circulated by Macpherson.

Keane varied the times at which he visited Fouché and the days of the week. He did not take Archer with him, leaving him instead to use his own considerable initiative and explore the streets of Paris, listening, carefully and methodically and analysing what he heard.

In the evening he would report back with all the intelligence he had gathered from the heart of Napoleon's capital. Most of it was commonplace stuff. There were the usual lists of what regiments were stationed in what towns and how much bread was left in which storehouses. But over the next few days the gossip took a different turn.

A group of men and women had been arrested in the Place du Carrousel protesting about grain prices. It had not been reported in the press. Another similar group of angry, hungry Parisians had been taken in Les Halles, where they had overturned merchants' carts in protest at rising food prices. Either this was genuine popular expression or, as seemed more likely to Keane, someone was orchestrating these gatherings. And he had a fairly shrewd idea of who it might be.

He quizzed Archer on it. 'You're sure that no names were mentioned? Merely the fact that arrests had been made?'

'Yes, sir, but the curious thing is that some of the arrested people were seen the following morning going about their business as if nothing had happened.'

'What do you read into that?'

'That the arrests were bogus. Why would you arrest an insurrectionist only to release them by the next morning?'

'Yes, I agree. It's clearly a sham. I've a hunch this is Fouché's doing. But why on earth should he be behind it?'

It was as he entered the second week working as an agent for Fouché that Keane began to be aware, in the course of an apparently trivial and everyday conversation, that his master might not be quite what he seemed.

Keane had gone to Fouché's house at 83 rue du Bac late in the afternoon and entered by the secret way through a next-door café which led into a disused church. The previous evening Keane had attended another of Fouché's soirées at the Palais-Royal. It had been an enjoyable evening, although Keane's attempts to find the little acrobat had proved fruitless and he hoped that their liaison had not put her in any danger.

As he entered Fouché's office, the chief of police looked up from his desk. 'Good morning, Captain Williams. I trust that you enjoyed last night's soirée.'

'Very much, sir. It is good to be back in Paris after so long and to see how much the emperor has done for his capital and his people.'

Fouché gazed at him for a moment and once again Keane wondered if their game was up.

But Fouché went on. 'Yes, it is remarkable. But do you

realize how much of the success of his regime once depended upon me? You can see very clearly that was the reason why just this very year we created the Sûreté. But obviously I was wrong. When I was the emperor's man I had to deal with everyday matters. I had no time to devote my thoughts to higher things.'

It was a strange comment and to Keane's mind perhaps another hint that Fouché's thoughts were still on sacred matters. Although it was also perhaps a deliberate hint that he wished to be considered as a thinker rather than as the former head of the world's most notorious secret police organization.

'Do you know what I received one morning, captain, from the emperor himself? You're an intelligent man, captain. Look at this – look at it and tell me your immediate thoughts.'

Keane took the piece of paper and seeing the signature at the bottom almost dropped it. It was a letter from Bonaparte to Fouché, dated 1807. The top bore a simple address:

'*Palais Imperial de la Grande Armée, Wien*'

Keane read the letter. It began civilly enough with a cordial greeting and some comments about how well Fouché had done in controlling an outbreak of insurgency in the Vendée. But very soon it became a string of criticisms. Not enough was being done about the problem of British spies in Cherbourg. Where were the promised police reinforcements in Toulouse? There was lack of intelligence along the Westphalian border. And then there were a number of localized matters in Paris. In particular Napoleon commented on street lighting. Keane read carefully: 'I've learnt that the streets of Paris are no longer being lit. Fouché, this non-lighting of Paris is becoming a crime; it's necessary to put an end to this abuse, because the public is beginning to complain. And it is absolutely vital to me to maintain public approval at all times.'

Keane looked at Fouché. 'It seems very wide-ranging. Very concerned.'

'Yes, you might say that. Let me acquaint you with the facts, tedious though they are. In my time the main streets were illuminated by 4,335 oil lanterns hung from posts. These could be lowered on a cord to be lit without a ladder. But I had a problem, captain, with the quantity and quality of the oil being supplied by private contractors. The lamps were incapable of burning all night, and often they did not burn at all. Also, if the lamps were placed far apart, so much of the street remained in darkness. So the emperor was right. The emperor had a point. And the emperor was always right.'

Keane went on, pushing his luck and, he knew, Fouché's patience. 'Actually, I did notice the lack of lighting when I was walking home the other night. I had to engage the services of a *porte-falot* to illuminate the way.'

Fouché grimaced. 'Yes, it is still unresolved. Despite the existence of the Sûreté.' He spat the word out. 'Now, captain, you know that I am one of the emperor's most loyal and faithful servants. But look at how he treated me. How he treats me still. How has he rewarded me for everything I have done? For all my devotion?'

Keane handed the paper back to Fouché and nodded. This was no passing conversation. This was a test. Keane was acutely aware that he needed to stay two steps ahead of Fouché. This was not to discover if he was good enough to work in Bonaparte's war machine. This was a test of Keane's own loyalty to the emperor. Fouché seemed to Keane to be sounding him out as a possible sympathizer against Napoleon.

It was just as Macpherson had predicted. Keane was being turned into a double agent. My God, he thought, this man moved fast. Keane presumed that was how he had managed to engineer his own dynamic rise.

'Sir, I would not take against the emperor. After all he has done for his country.'

'*His* country? He's a Corsican, Williams. He's no more of a Frenchman than you.'

'But, sir, surely you don't mean this. You're merely out of sorts. Angry with the emperor for this slight. An old letter, a few ill-chosen words. I'm sure you'll feel different, after a while.'

'I know how I feel, captain, and I know that it has gone too far now for me to change my opinion. Do you understand what I mean?'

'Yes, I think so. Am I to infer from this that even after all that you and Choiseul have said to me, in reality you do not believe in the emperor's great project?'

'Great project? Huge folly is a better description. I lost faith in the emperor's "great projects" years ago. But trust me, captain, if I am at work here, it is because of my loyalty to France. And I think I see something of the same strain in you.'

'Monsieur Fouché, you realize this is treason?'

Fouché nodded and shrugged. 'And what of it? We are all men of the world are we not, Captain Williams? We take what it has to throw at us and if we need to adjust our allegiances from time to time, then so be it. This may be one of those times.'

This, thought Keane, was turning into a most bizarre interview. 'Then you're telling me that you're involved in an insurrection?'

'I can't really comment on that assumption, and of course I could never condone the sort of clumsy plan which our two friends managed to mastermind.'

'You intend to kill the emperor?'

'No, no. You're quite wrong there. I simply wish to question the way in which the empire operates.'

'By which you mean?'

'So many questions, captain. By which I mean I am not alone in wondering how far we have come in the last twenty years. And also, where we might be taken now?'

Keane nodded. 'Yes, I understand.' For a moment he thought that he might have allowed his guard to slip and his Irish accent to drop. But Fouché didn't appear to be any the wiser.

'May I ask how you suggest I should become involved in this?'

'All in good time, captain. All in good time.'

Walking back from Fouché's office, Keane decided that he would not mention the content of the meeting to Macpherson. He was unsure yet again about whom he should trust. Certainly not Fouché. But he was also concerned about Macpherson's ruthlessness. The man had effectively destroyed the reason for his presence in Paris. At least the purpose given to him by Grant. There would be no royalist underground movement to train and lead. He wondered if Grant was aware of what was happening and decided that he should somehow try to get word back to him. If only to receive further orders.

That afternoon, when Keane entered the house, Macpherson was waiting for him. 'We must talk. Now, come into my office.'

Macpherson led the way and locked the door behind them

and Keane wondered if he had heard about his meeting with Fouché.

However, he smiled at Keane. 'Things have changed. You are aware that Fouché is now playing for both sides?'

It was less a question than a statement, for Macpherson knew Keane's answer. 'Yes, he told me as much, only this morning.'

'For the Bonapartists and the opposition. As is Talleyrand.'

'Talleyrand?'

This truly was news. It was the first time that Keane had heard Talleyrand's name mentioned in the context of his mission, but now it made sense. Not least, his presence with Fouché at the gambling house. Of course, it was common knowledge that Talleyrand had masterminded many of the covert operations undertaken by the French secret service since the beginning of the war, but to date there had been no direct line back to him. This though was something quite different. It seemed that Talleyrand, the revolutionary firebrand and supporter of the emperor, had now turned.

Macpherson continued: 'I have good information that Talleyrand has by now switched sides and is intriguing against his former master, Napoleon.'

'Talleyrand is working with the royalists? It's hardly credible.'

Macpherson shook his head. 'No, no, captain. Not the royalists. That would be absurd. He's with the republicans, it seems. Now we have a three-way struggle.'

'So what now? How does this affect my mission?'

'It means that we have to be more cautious and we have to be pragmatic. It also means that the plans have changed entirely.'

'How? Why?'

'My fellow royalists and I have decided to abandon the notion of raising our people as an organized force and creating an underground network. There is a more immediate possibility.'

'What sort of possibility?'

Macpherson looked slightly smug. 'Well, I've had word of a republican plot to overthrow Bonaparte.'

Keane shook his head. 'But this is madness, surely, sir? We allied ourselves to the royalists, did we not? Not the republicans. I know we had to dispose of Elliott and Rochambeau. But you yourself said they were expendable. Fouché is the enemy, isn't he? Yet now you tell me that he and Talleyrand might end up being our allies. Whom can we trust? Are Fouché and Talleyrand to be trusted? What if they are simply attempting to get us to lead them to your fellow royalists?'

'I think that they have greater concerns of their own to worry about, Keane, don't you?'

'But seriously, sir, what if the whole thing is a huge bluff? We might have been persuaded into thinking that they are contra-Bonaparte when in fact they are as loyal as ever.'

'Are you suggesting, Keane, that I have been duped?'

The old man's eyes shone with fury and Keane decided that it was wise to back down. 'Not at all, sir, but just consider the possibility. We would all be killed.'

Macpherson shook his head. 'Captain Keane, believe me, we have a plan. At last. I have to know your intentions before I go any further. You are with us, captain?'

'Of course, sir. Tell me all.'

Macpherson sat down and motioned to Keane to do the same. 'There is one of Bonaparte's generals – General Malet. He has long been discontented with the regime. Well, now he is determined to bring it down.

'For the past two years Malet has been incarcerated in the prison of La Force, and during that time he has come up with what he considers to be the perfect plan to accomplish an aim which he has long harboured, the complete and final overthrow of Bonaparte. It will be accomplished in a daring coup d'état. The plan is simple. As you know, Bonaparte is currently attacking Russia, conducting a campaign which Malet, among others, believes to be utterly doomed.

'In two weeks' time, as Bonaparte engages the Russians, Malet intends to escape from prison. He will then announce the death of the emperor. Bonaparte will have been killed in an action on the Russian front. Other generals here in Paris will attest to it. Malet will then establish a provisional government and proclaim Bonaparte's death again using forged documents. We have every reason to believe that his word will be taken as the truth.

'It is important that my group is seen to be working alongside the republicans in this matter. So that after the fall of Bonaparte we can make sure that we have a part in the new France. You and your comrade have a vital part to play in this. I think you told me that your man Archer here is a good forger?'

'The best.'

'Good. I have promised General Malet's co-conspirators that we have a means of creating the documents that we need. You yourself, captain, will accompany General Malet in his escape and in the coup d'état.'

Keane nodded. 'Yes, I understand, and of course we will do everything we can to make it succeed, sir. And we have two weeks to prepare, you say?'

'Two weeks, Captain Keane. It must happen then or not at all.'

'How can we be sure that the republicans are not simply trying to infiltrate our organization?'

Macpherson smiled and it was that same cruel, cold smile that Keane had seen on his face before, just after the arrests. 'Take my word for it, Keane. After they saw us sacrifice Elliott and Rochambeau, they will not doubt us.'

He saw the look on Keane's face and Keane sensed that he must feel that at last the time was right.

He took a decanter from the sideboard and poured them both a glass of wine. 'You know, Captain Keane, I'm sure your father would be proud of you. You have done better than I ever expected.' He paused. 'And now it is time for me to do something for you. There is something you should know before we start on all this.'

Keane was mystified, but nothing, he thought, would surprise him. 'Yes? Tell me.'

'It's about your father. I knew him.'

Keane stopped and stared at the man, his eyebrows narrowing. 'You knew my father?'

'Yes.'

'Who was he? What was his name? Is he still alive?'

'We fought side by side in the American war. Not in the same regiment, but side by side.'

'Tell me his name.'

'I'm afraid that I cannot do. I swore him an oath of secrecy that I would never reveal his identity and I am bound to keep it.'

'Oh, come on, tell me. What harm can it do now? That was all in the past – it was thirty years ago. You must tell me.'

'I'm sorry, Keane, I cannot do that.' He paused again. 'I will, however, tell you certain things. Your father was the most honourable man I have ever known. He was a true gentleman in every sense of the word. A fine shot and a man of his word. A man of the utmost integrity.'

'With respect, sir, this does not much help me. These are things which I have suspected, indeed known in my heart, for some time.'

'Of course, I am merely trying to impart something to you of the essence of the man.'

'Do you know anything of me? Did you know anything about me?'

'Yes, in truth I did. Your father explained things to me and swore me to secrecy. I am so, so sorry Keane that I can give you no more.'

'But what of his military service? Please you must be able to tell me something about his time as an officer.'

'Very well, I can do that. We were both at the battle of Freeman's Farm and both at Guilford Court House. Very bloody affairs.'

'So I believe.'

'Your father saved my life.'

Keane paused. 'Really?'

'Yes. Would I pretend? We were standing in line and were charged by American light horse. It seemed to both of us that the line must fail. I recall your father shouting to his men to hold the line and then I was attacked by two cavalrymen. I attempted to parry their cuts but one hit me here.' He showed Keane a line in his face where the tissue had scarred. 'That was when your father came across. I have never seen such bravery. He took one of them from the saddle with a single cut. Almost cut the man clean in two. The other one he cut down with a thrust. The man fell from his horse. He saved my life.'

Keane's mind was whirring. So his father was a hero. It was astonishing. Although of course he had always hoped that it might be the case. And then he had a sudden thought.

'You said "light horse". You don't suppose that Colonel Harrison's father . . . ?'

Macpherson smiled. 'You know, captain, I could see that you were remarkably astute the moment I set eyes on you, but you have quite surpassed yourself.'

'Don't tell me that you engineered my meeting with Colonel Harrison?'

'Let's just say that it was a most happy coincidence.'

'You and I know, Macpherson, that there is no such thing as coincidence. There are merely people pulling the correct strings to ensure that we all operate in the way in which we are supposed to. We are all of us in this filthy game no more than simple marionettes, engineered to our own destruction.'

'Oh, Captain Keane, please don't be so overdramatic. It's not like that at all and well you know it.'

'Do I? At this present moment it would take some convincing to prove to myself that I do.'

But, thought Keane, he would go along with it.

The old man went off to his office and Keane, who had lately been so desperate to climb into his bed for a couple of hours, sat up a little longer, dwelling on what had been said. He was happy to go along with all that was unfolding and he realized that he had never been more resigned to his fate. Since arriving in Paris he had felt that somehow coming events might resolve some of his own inner questions, and with almost every hour now something else came to reinforce that feeling. Here he was, disguised as an Irishman in

French service and living cheek by jowl with an ex-Jacobite. These were strange things for a man of his northern Protestant roots. He wondered how the men of his old regiment, the Inniskillings, would have taken them.

All this and what Macpherson had told him and what he had observed had set him thinking about England. The England and the Ireland that he knew and that he loved. And he began to wonder what the new world might be like after Napoleon had fallen. Most fundamentally though, he had begun to ask himself the bigger question which he now realized in that new world all men would be bound to ask. Was he at heart either a royalist or a republican?

Keane left the room and found Archer at the rear of the house, where there was a small library. He sat down and shook his head. 'I don't believe it. It seems, Archer, that we're caught up in an intrigue far greater than any of us thought. Although I'm beginning to wonder if Macpherson hasn't been playing us all along.'

'Do you think this has anything to do with the food riots, sir?'

'That's a very good question, Archer, and, yes, it has everything to do with them. Now it makes sense. Fouché is trying to stir up the people of Paris against Bonaparte. And he might just have a chance. Have you noticed what the emperor has done? He's created a grand city for himself in the west and centre of Paris, but he's done nothing at all about the south and east.'

'Yes, sir, and that's precisely where the protestors seem to be based.'

'He's a shrewd man, Archer. He has sections of the National Guard eating out of his hand, and if the Paris mob is mobilized this coup d'état has every chance of succeeding.'

The following two weeks seemed to Keane to pass in an instant, such was the intensity of the work necessary to organize the planned coup. Archer sat for hours on end both in daylight and by candlelight working on the documents of Bonaparte's death and the necessary papers, until his eyes grew heavy and his head throbbed.

On the fifth day there was a report in the paper of the execution by firing squad of two royalist spies.

Morning came on the thirteenth day and, after a cup of strong coffee, taken with Archer in the front room of Macpherson's house, Keane was about to set off for his daily meeting with Fouché and Choiseul when there was a frantic banging at the front door. Both men sprang from their seats at the table and, opening the door cautiously, Keane was astonished to see the face of Colquhoun Grant.

'Let me in, man. I don't think I've been followed, but you never know.'

Keane pulled Grant through the entrance and closed and locked the door, turning to Archer. 'Keep a watch through the window. Major Grant may have been followed.' He looked at Grant. 'Good God, sir, what the devil are you doing here?'

'You'll find out soon enough. Is Macpherson here?'

'Yes, of course, sir, somewhere, here at any moment.'

'Good. We have a change of plan and he cannot know of it. Thank God I found you in time.'

The door opened and Macpherson entered.

'Captain Keane, what was that noise? Good heavens, Major Grant.'

'Macpherson. I know. This is against protocol. Highly dangerous and improper.'

'Major, your presence here endangers us all. You must go, sir, before we are all taken.'

'I am quite aware of that. I shall be quick. A matter of minutes, then I'll be gone. I need to speak with Captain Keane.'

'Very well, do so. But for heaven's sake hurry.'

Macpherson left the room and Grant began: 'Right, Keane. Here it is, as quick as I can. We must at all costs prevent General Malet from carrying out this coup d'état. At least it must certainly not succeed.'

'Wellington knows about this?'

'Yes, of course. I am here on his orders. He is absolutely adamant. We cannot support Malet's coup.'

'But why, sir? Surely this has a good chance of bringing down Bonaparte?'

'It might well do, but we cannot associate ourselves with it.'

'Why on earth not, sir?'

'It is republican, Keane. And we cannot possibly support a republican coup. Think about it. Think about America. My God, how many men did we lose in that war? In the name of England's sovereignty and monarchy? How can we possibly support a republican coup in France? Particularly at a time when the Americans are once again waging war against us.'

For the first time Keane was struck by the bigger picture.

'I do see, sir. It is absurd.'

'Good, Keane. It's just not part of the plan.'

Keane smiled. That was so like Grant. *Not part of the plan.* How good he was at saying so much in so very few words.

'James, you must be seen to proceed with the plan as it stands. Do whatever Macpherson and the others have in mind. Assist General Malet. But at the last moment I am relying on you to ensure that it fails. Wellington needs the war to continue in order that the French are completely defeated. We cannot finish it now.

'We most certainly cannot assassinate Napoleon. Nor can we bring down his government with such alacrity. That would plunge the country into anarchy and the way would be open for the republicans. That is what Talleyrand wants.'

He paused and his voice became lower as he spoke to both men.

'Macpherson is a fool. He was a good agent. Once. One of the best. But it's gone to his head. He's old Keane. Very, very old and he can see his power dwindling. He's no longer within the fold, James. He's slipped his leash, out of my control. We cannot allow the coup to succeed. It's up to you, James.

'The way that it stands, the situation is now so tenuously balanced that for the plot to succeed would be catastrophic to the future balance of power.'

Keane thought about that for a second. *The future balance of power.*

It occurred to him that everyone, the British and Spanish commanders in the Peninsula, Wellington, even the private soldiers, Grant himself, all presumed that Bonaparte would be defeated. And so, most assuredly, did he. But quite how long that would take he had no idea. And what of it when he was overthrown? What sort of world would they have then? It struck him that he had never really, properly thought about it. A world without the threat of Bonaparte? What on earth would it be like, and what would it mean for Britain and for him?

It threw him a little. He could almost, well, very nearly, imagine a world without the great monster of Europe. And then what? A return to the Europe of the Ancien Régime? A return to Europe before the Revolution? Before Robespierre and the terror? Before Madame la Guillotine and Boney the bogeyman? It was impossible that the world could ever return to such a state.

Grant spoke again. 'In fact we need to maintain Bonaparte's regime. It will be easier to defeat France with Bonaparte in power.'

Archer and Keane stared at him and Keane spoke. 'Keep him on the throne, sir? Surely that's madness. Surely the whole reason that I'm here, that I was sent here, was to establish a plot to get rid of Bonaparte?'

'Yes, absolute madness. But as you well know, James, we adapt to our circumstances. Hard as it might seem to you at this moment, we now have to keep Bonaparte in power. And now I should be gone.'

'Where will you go, sir?'

'Why, back to Spain. Did I tell you that Silver arrived in one piece, with his news. And what news it was. You did well with that. Wellington is enormously pleased. I see a promotion, James. I'm damn sure I do.'

Archer spoke. 'To Spain? Will you have to ride all the way, sir?'

'From Salamanca, with changes of horse. I had to come myself; I could not send a messenger. You had to hear this from my mouth to understand just how important a matter this really is.'

He moved to the door and before opening it turned back to them.

'Remember my words, James. Wellington is adamant. To stage and to be seen to support an insurrection is certainly a good thing. It will unsettle Napoleon's regime. But it cannot be allowed to unseat him. That will simply replace one form of dictatorship with another. When the emperor is defeated it must be on very specific terms. And those must be imposed by the allies and in particular by Wellington and his faction. You understand my meaning?'

'I have it exactly, sir.'

'Very well, James, Archer, until we meet again, wherever that may be, let there be no mistake about this: victory, when it comes, must come on the battlefield.'

12

General Malet had a plan and it was infallible. That at least was his opinion. To Keane, however, Malet appeared the least likely-looking conspirator he had ever seen. He was of small stature, had huge eyes set in a pale face, a feminine cupid's bow of a mouth and long sideburns. Keane knew that he had served with distinction in the early campaigns of the Revolution, but the place of their meeting said more about the man who was to lead the coup than any citations or medals ever could.

He had taken against Napoleon when he had proclaimed himself emperor and had resigned from the army. For the last two years, ever since he had been suspected of plotting against the emperor and being a member of an order of republican Masons, Malet had been in custody. More importantly, for the last four months, his residence had been a *maison de santé*, or asylum, in the Faubourg Saint-Antoine, to which he had been transferred at the intercession of his wife.

Ironically, thought Keane, it had been Savary, Fouché's inept successor as head of the police, who had agreed with her entreaties and so it was here in the early evening of 13th July that Keane and Archer found the disgraced hero, living among the demented, the erotomaniacs, the melancholics and the megalomaniacs of Paris.

As Keane approached Malet across the tree-shaded courtyard of the asylum, the general shot him a pleasant smile. 'Ah, Captain Williams, isn't it? I was informed that you were coming. How are the Irish today?'

'As well as might be expected, sir. It's an honour to meet you.'

Looking at his face Keane noticed that Malet's right eyebrow was twitching. It was an unfortunate stigma and not one which would have lent gravitas to any political or military leader. Watching him more closely as Malet began to talk to the director of the hospital, the renowned Doctor Pinel, and another of his visitors, Keane noticed too that the third finger of his right hand did not stop twitching. Looking around him at the other inmates, all of them preoccupied with their own imaginary worlds, Keane noticed that many of them demonstrated similar twitches and involuntary movements.

The other visitor, a captain of the National Guard named Rateau, who to his dismay had overnight been unexpectedly promoted from corporal, brought Malet across to Keane. 'Captain Williams, I have arranged for the release of General Malet. Will you kindly escort the general from here to the house near the Place Royale. You have the address?'

Keane nodded. 'Very well, sir. General, shall we go?'

Malet nodded and with Keane and Archer on either side began to march towards the entrance gate, which stood open. It cannot be this simple, thought Keane. But to his dismay, it was. Clearly Fouché's bribery, Talleyrand's influence or

Macpherson's trickery, or more probably a combination of the three, had done their work. The three men walked clear of the gates into the street and entered a carriage, which took off as soon as the door was shut.

They drove through the darkening streets to the address which lay just off the Place Royale at rue Saint-Gilles. It was curious, thought Keane, that they should be so close to his aunt's old house. To Keane's slight surprise the door was opened by a man wearing clerical garb, who spoke to him with a Spanish accent.

'You have our friend?'

Keane replied in Spanish. 'We have the package, father.'

'Excellent. General, sir, what an honour. Your uniform is in your portmanteau. Through there, sir.'

The priest directed them through to a small sitting room at the rear of the apartment, and within a few minutes Malet had swapped clothes, exchanging his everyday civilian dress for the splendid uniform of a general of the French army.

He turned to the priest. 'Now, father, we need some punch. You have some?'

The priest looked askance. 'No, general, I'm afraid not. I do have wine. Good Rhenish.'

Malet shrugged. 'That will have to do.' He turned to Keane. 'Captain, join me and I will explain my plan, after this sad news.'

'Sad news?'

'Why, the death of the emperor. Have you not been told? That is why I am here. I have just been informed. He is dead in Russia. Killed in action leading his men on 28th June. We must act.'

Keane shot Archer a glance that needed no explanation.

Malet was clearly insane. With large glasses of wine before them, he began.

From the portmanteau he produced the papers on which Archer had been working for the past fortnight. 'Here, gentlemen, are the papers. As you see, I have been appointed governor of Paris in the interim government. And here is a note for 100,000 francs to be drawn on the bank. And here is an order for the replacement of all Imperial bodies by bodies of the new government. It is all in order, is it not?'

Keane and Archer pretended to look and both nodded. 'Yes, of course it is, general.'

There was a knock on the door and Rateau, the young ex-corporal of the National Guard, appeared and with him another young man in his late twenties.

'General, you remember my friend André Boutreux, the poet. You may recall he's a student of law, from Rennes.'

'Yes, of course, the poet.'

Malet stood up and embraced Rateau. 'Dear friend, here, look, put on this.' From the portmanteau he produced another uniform, the light blue of an aide de camp to a general, and handed it to the astonished youth.

'General?'

'Rateau. You're as of this moment promoted to my aide de camp. Come on, put it on and then join us for wine, more wine.' To the other man he handed a tricolour sash. 'For you, monsieur poet, I have this. Put it round your waist.'

The poet tied the sash as directed. It gave him a look of a slightly tawdry but vaguely dignified local official. Like a law student or a failed poet, thought Keane, doing his best to look as much like a commissioner of police as he could.

Over the next four hours Malet expounded his plan and

motive with admirable clarity. This, thought Keane, was the true extent of madness. The ability to convince yourself, utterly, that you were right. All of those years languishing in prison had paid off. Malet had thought long and hard and had gone over every failing, every loophole. His own escape; the announcement of the emperor's death; the support of the generals; the perfect forgery of the documents of the death. Everything had been planned meticulously. He had drawn up minute-by-minute orders and knew where everyone was to be at the specified date and time.

Now even the damned royalists had come around to join him, and the word on the street and in the *maison de santé* had been that they had even gone so far as to scupper a plan of their own, sacrificing two agents in the process. For his part, Malet said, he had agreed to work with them and had agreed to take with him on his crusade some of their own men. He smiled at Keane and Archer.

'Welcome, gentlemen, to the future of France and the new provisional republican government. General Moreau, Lazare Carnot, Marshal Augerau, Count Frochot, myself of course, Vice-Admiral Truguet. I have also made provision for some of our royalist friends in the new council. The necessary forces for the coup will be found from the Gendarmerie of Paris and the 10th Cohort of the National Guard.' And so it continued.

It was almost one o' clock in the morning before the general finally left the priest's house. With the newly elevated Corporal Rateau by his side and Keane and Archer in front with the poet Boutreux, all of them armed with swords, the party walked back eastwards through the dark streets to the Popincourt barracks on the rue Popincourt in the Faubourg, close to the *maison de santé* where they had met Malet.

Arriving outside, Malet approached the sentry. 'Open the gates. I have business with the commanding officer.'

The captain of the guard, summoned from the guardhouse, spoke to Malet. 'I'm afraid that Colonel Soulier is unwell, general. He is not in his office. He is actually in bed with a fever.'

'No matter, let me in. I shall see him all the same.'

In due course the gates swung open and the five men entered the barracks. Malet, knowing the layout, headed for Soulier's bedroom, where the colonel, lying covered in sweat in bed, was taken entirely by surprise. He could though make out the figure of a French general and he sat up as straight as he could and straightened his sodden nightshirt.

'General, sir, what commands have you for me?'

'Has no one informed you, Soulier? We have had the most terrible misfortune to lose the emperor. In Russia on the twenty-eighth.'

With no warning, Soulier burst into tears. 'No, general, it can't be so. The emperor, dead?'

'Yes, it is true, man. Pull yourself together. We must act fast to preserve order.'

Malet handed Soulier a piece of paper and then went on, to Keane's astonishment, to pretend to be another general entirely. 'General Malet instructed me to give you this order, colonel. As you will see, it instructs you to muster your men under arms and place them under my direction.'

This was a brilliant twist, thought Keane, knowing the content of the papers in Soulier's hands which of course were all Archer's work. They stated additionally that Soulier should do everything as instructed by General Lamotte, and was signed by Malet. So in one moment Malet had passed himself off as

Lamotte. Soulier, seeing double as he attempted to climb out of bed, saluted Malet and began to call out his men.

Keane spoke quietly to Archer. 'Remind me what else those documents say.'

'That the 10th Cohort is to provide soldiers to arrest Savary, sir. And minister of war Clarke, and Cambacérès, and the commander of the Paris garrison General Hulin. Oh, and that Colonel Soulier is instantly to be promoted to the rank of *général de brigade* with a note made out to him for 100,000 francs.'

Malet waited for them on the parade ground and once all 1,200 men of the 10th Cohort of the Paris Guard were assembled, he read out his proclamation. Keane and Archer stood behind him and watched their reaction. There was the predictable shock at the reported death of Napoleon, and then what seemed to be relief as the men saw that, in Malet, one of their generals appeared to have taken charge.

Keane whispered to Archer, 'Good God, man. You don't suppose, do you, that this could actually work?'

Malet marched his men through the gates of the barracks and out into the streets, with Colonel Soulier at their head, now sweating out his fever into the thick serge of his uniform. Keane and Archer followed at the front, with Rateau and Boutreux, and the column began to make its way westwards through the very heart of Paris.

They passed by the Bastille, then along the rue Saint-Antoine. It had been planned well, thought Keane. This was a Friday, the weekly parade day for the Paris garrison, and now in the early morning the sound of marching feet and presence of a whole battalion did not excite any undue attention.

The column continued on its way, marching along the rue Saint-Antoine up to the gates of the prison of La Force. Here they halted and once again Malet himself took charge and called for the gates to be opened, which of course they were.

Entering the courtyard of the prison he found the captain of the guard, who failed to recognize him in his general's uniform. 'The prisoners Guidal and Lahorie – bring them to me.'

It didn't take long to find the two disgraced generals whose prison quarters he had shared for two years, and once they were with him outside the prison Malet ordered the guard to shut the gates again.

He embraced the two men. 'My friends, old friends, we have to act fast. The emperor is dead in Russia.' He produced the forged documents he had shown to Colonel Soulier.

'Do you see? The Senate has already reacted this very night. See the signatures – here and here.'

He was behaving, thought Keane, like an overexcited child. And now the frenzied commands began to pour out.

'General Lahorie, you will now take immediate command of this regiment, the 10th, and will personally take a company to arrest Chef de Police Savary. General Guidal, you will take another company of these men. Arrest Cambacérès and the minister of war, Clarke. I myself will need just fifty men. We're going to secure the prefecture.'

The two generals, who clearly had been forewarned of the plot and their parts in it during his incarceration, nodded to Malet, who turned and took control of his own detail of fifty men.

Keane watched Lahorie and Guidal take the remainder and was surprised to see that they did not separate their forces but left the barracks together. He thought that perhaps he should mention this to Malet, but the general was too preoccupied with his own force and Keane wondered what difference it might make. It was clear to him though that Malet was already losing control of the situation.

Things now began to move quickly. They marched up the newly built rue de Rivoli to the Hôtel de Ville.

Malet ordered the troops to take up battle positions across the Place de Grève and Keane watched bemused as the Parisians simply ignored them, as if this sort of event happened every day.

Malet turned to the commander of the detachment. 'Summon Prefect Frochot and have him prepare a room in the Hôtel de Ville for the new provisional government.'

As the man hurried off, Malet carried on towards the Place Vendôme and Keane and Archer, as instructed, went with him. The man was unstoppable, thought Keane. Single-minded in pursuit of this dream of so many years of planning. Fetching from Rateau two paper packets, Malet gave these to two junior officers of the 10th and ordered them to be taken to two other regiments of the Paris Guard. They contained, he told Keane, the same proclamation he had read out as well as specific instructions for each regiment.

'I have ordered one regiment to close the barriers of Paris; the other to occupy the bank, the treasury and all the ministries. Now it is our turn. Come on, captain, lieutenant.'

Following Malet and his fifty men with Rateau and Boutreux, Keane and Archer made their way along the rue du Faubourg Saint-Honoré past Macpherson's house and turned into the Place Vendôme.

Placing twenty-five men in order of battle in front of the

prefecture, Malet called over a young lieutenant and handed him another bundle. 'You, take these to General Doucet.'

Keane turned to him. 'May I ask, general, what that contained?'

'The proclamation of the emperor's death, as before, along with the commission of *général de brigade* for Doucet and a money order to him for 100,000 francs.'

Promotion and bribery, as before, thought Keane. The man was a professional. He wondered now how long he would have to let things run and began to think of means by which it could be brought swiftly to an end before it got out of hand.

The Place Vendôme began to fill with infantrymen – Lahorie and Guidal's cohort, the bulk of the regiment. Lahorie reported to Malet wearing a smile. 'We took Savary, sir. Found him still in his nightshirt and took him to La Force.'

'And the others?'

'We arrested the prefect of police, Pasquier, and we've turned the prefect of the Seine, Frochot. And also Desmarest, head of Savary's security division.' He looked pleased with himself.

Malet frowned. 'What of Cambacérès and Clarke? Did General Guidal not arrest them?'

'General Guidal came with me, sir. He said that he had a score to settle with Savary.'

Malet fumed. 'This is not the time to settle old scores. We are taking power, not squabbling in a playground. Order General Guidal to arrest those men now. And, Lahorie, you are of this moment the new minister of police.'

It was now around 8.30 in the morning and the streets were filling with Parisians, many of them now becoming more inquisitive at the actions being played out in their capital. It was clear that something was going on. One of them, a man in his thirties, approached one of the officers of the 10th Cohort. Keane could see him asking a question, which when answered brought an extraordinary reaction. The man threw his hands up in the air and stared wildly before running off towards a crowd of civilians. Even at this distance it was not hard to hear his words, '*L'empereur est mort. Napoléon est mort. Mort en Russe.*'

Instantly the crowd began to grow.

Keane turned to Archer. 'That's done it then. The news will spread like wildfire. All Paris will have it within the hour.'

He calculated that in the space of just a few hours the little force had incarcerated all the senior police officers of Paris. More worryingly, the news of the death of the emperor was steadily, moment by moment, gaining credibility throughout Paris. Now surely, he thought, must be the time for Archer and him to act. But still the opportunity had not presented itself. At that moment Malet walked across the Place Vendôme towards Keane and Archer, who were standing with Rateau and Boutreux.

As he approached them the newly promoted aide de camp spoke to Keane, a huge grin on his face. 'He is brilliant, isn't he? The general. He has worked everything out to perfection. You know an hour ago he even sent orders to Colonel Rabbe, the commander of the regiment of the Paris Guard. He's on his way here right now. Now we'll really have an army, won't we, captain?'

'Come with me, all of you. I have one more act before we take power.'

Keane and Archer followed close behind the general and

his aide. Keane moved forward, catching up with Malet. 'May I ask where we are heading, general? We are only five men.'

'This task will not take more than five men, captain. I intend to arrest General Hulin, the commander of the Paris garrison, to relieve him of his command and to acquire the official seal of the First Division.'

This then, thought Keane, was the final obstacle. With the commander of the city garrison in his power, Malet would effectively have control of the entire city and all its troops. Armed by Hulin with the necessary documents and seals to assume command of the First Division, once Colonel Rabbe's men appeared, Malet would assume control of all the military forces of Paris, and with them ensure the success of his coup. It would be a small army, but certainly big enough to defend the city against any immediate counter-attack. Of course Napoleon was not dead, but he was most certainly in Russia with his army. And who could say when he would return, even after word eventually reached him of Malet's coup? The fact that he was not actually dead would take weeks to reach Paris, and by that time Malet and his republican friends might be in control of France. Keane became worryingly aware that in this one moment the destiny of France, and with her the fate of Europe, hung on the actions of just two men. He looked at Malet and, noticing the pistol tucked into his belt, realized that somewhere along the way, sooner or later, the man was going to resort to violence. Clearly Malet was prepared for this, and now Keane was also aware of what would unfold. Timing would be everything.

It was nine o'clock in the morning by the time they arrived at Hulin's house in the rue Condorcet. Malet banged on the door and was admitted by the housekeeper. He turned to Rateau. 'Wait here. Admit no one.'

Pushing past the concierge, Malet ran up the wooden staircase, followed by the others, and went straight into General Hulin's office.

The general looked around and surveyed the curious group that had entered his room and disturbed his breakfast, his gaze darting from the two Irish soldiers to the bizarre, wild-eyed civilian with the sash around his waist. Finally his eyes settled on Malet. 'Good heavens, it's General Malet, isn't it? I thought you were inside. When did they let you out? And are you a general again? Since when? No one tells me anything.'

Malet didn't answer any of his questions. 'General Hulin, I have here a document announcing the death of the emperor. He has been killed, on campaign in Russia.'

'Good God, man. You can't be serious. Napoleon killed?'

Malet unfolded the declaration and Hulin took it, reading it with care.

'Yes, I see. This is very grave, if it is true.'

'It is quite true and very grave indeed, general, and as a consequence I am afraid that I now have to place you under arrest and ask for the seal of the First Division.'

Hulin put down the paper and at last removed the napkin from his collar where it had been tucked in. 'Under arrest? But why? I can still execute my orders, can't I? What's happening here, Malet? I don't understand. May I see the senatorial orders relieving me of command, and the arrest warrant?'

'There is no need for either of those. This is my authority.'

As Keane had expected, Malet at last showed a violent side, extracting a pistol from his belt and pointing it at Hulin.

'This is ridiculous, Malet. You don't intend to use that. And you clearly don't have the papers. I don't know what is going on here or what any of you are up to, but I smell a rat.'

Without another word, Malet raised the pistol and shot Hulin in the head. Luckily his aim was not good. The bullet passed through the general's cheek and Hulin fell to the floor, unconscious, blood seeping from the wound. Malet tucked the pistol back into his belt, moved across to the body and standing by it, reached over to the general's writing desk.

At the same time Keane signalled to Archer and the two men moved silently across the room towards Malet.

The deluded general was standing at the desk now, opening the drawers one by one till he eventually found what he wanted, the official seal of the First Division of the Paris garrison. He turned to the other four. 'Gentlemen, shall we go? I have all that I need.'

Keane shook his head. 'I'm afraid not. This has gone too far, Malet. You've achieved your aim so far, but now this is serious and it has to end. Here and now.'

'Captain? What do you suppose you're doing? You can't stop me. I'm the new government.'

Clutching the seal in his right hand, Malet reached again for the pistol, but realizing that it was now unloaded, reached for his sword. But before he could draw it from its scabbard, Keane flashed his blade across and cut Malet hard across the hand. The general gasped and grabbed at the bloody wound and at the same time Boutreux, who till now had been watching events unfold, moved towards Keane, his own sword held out before him. He lunged. But Archer was on him in an instant. His sword moved quickly and hit Boutreux in the upper arm.

The young man shrieked and dropped his own sword, looking aghast at the cut.

Archer put up his weapon and looked across to Keane, but as he did so, Boutreux's left hand went to his belt and drew out a pistol. As he cocked the weapon and began to aim it at Archer, Keane moved towards him and with a single, powerful lunge, drove the big blade of his cavalry sabre hard into Boutreux's chest. The hapless poet dropped the gun and looked down at the blade protruding from his body. He stared at Malet, then at Keane and then, as Keane withdrew the sword, slumped to the floor, lifeless.

Malet was staring wildly now, apparently in a state of shock, disarmed but still clutching on to the seal in his good hand, when there was a commotion on the staircase and seven men burst through the door, six of them with bayonet-tipped muskets which they pointed at the four men left alive in the room.

Their leader, Adjutant-Commander Colonel Jean Doucet, colonel of the Paris Guard, walked across slowly to Malet and looked at him carefully,

'I know you. You're Malet, aren't you? You've been locked up in an insane asylum for years. How the hell did you get out, and what the devil have you done?' He looked down at Hulin's body and called to his men, 'One of you, get a medic. The general's been shot.'

He looked back to Malet. 'You sent me a letter this morning telling me the emperor was dead and promoting me to *général de brigade* in the new government. I didn't believe any of it. Napoleon's not dead. Minister Clarke had a letter from him dated five days after the date you claim he was shot. And on the date you stamped the note from the Senate authorizing you to take control, I happen to know that the Senate did not meet at all. You're a mad old fool, Malet, and you're going before the firing squad. Along with all your co-conspirators.'

He pointed at Keane and Archer. 'Take them all.'

Keane spoke up. 'No, general. You don't understand, sir. It was we who stopped him. We were bringing him out to you.'

'Don't try to trick me, Irishman. Seize them. Seize them all.'

The five remaining guardsmen moved forward, two of them grabbing Malet, who, his spirit broken, made no attempt to struggle. As two more came for Keane, he made his move, punching one of the men firmly on the jaw and knocking him to the ground. Before the others could respond, Archer had smashed the hilt of his sword into the face of one of them, ripping open his mouth, and Keane had cut with his own blade across the arm of another.

Keane pushed hard into Doucet, using his body weight to knock him to the floor, while Archer did the same to another of the guards, sending him flying backwards out of the room and into the wooden post of the banister. Then the two men were out of the room and racing down the stairs. Behind them they could hear the noise of Doucet and his men struggling to get out of the room. But by the time the colonel and his guards reached the street door of Hulin's house, Keane and Archer had vanished from sight. An officer of Doucet's company approached him and watched as two of the guards emerged with Malet. Doucet spoke to him.

'Captain Lamballe, issue a proclamation. Any reports of the emperor's death are to be ignored. The emperor is alive and well and leading his army in Russia to certain victory. There has been an attempted coup in Paris today, but it was led by a madman who is now in custody and the danger is over. All that remains is to arrest the remaining conspirators, who will be brought swiftly to justice. *Vive l'empereur.*'

13

Keane and Archer had not stopped for the fifteen minutes since they had left the Place Vendôme. They had run only until they were clear of the square, in the rue des Capucines which was reached by a tiny alleyway. From there they walked at almost double pace, desperate but not wanting to appear to be running away. Neither man spoke, with Keane leading the way eastwards along the rue Casanova and the rue des Petits-Champs, until they were to the rear of the Palais-Royal.

There, without warning, Keane turned sharp right and instantly they found themselves in the grounds of the palace, among the arcades and the stalls, which, as the morning grew late and entertainment beckoned, were filling fast with the shoppers and promenaders, the dandies and groups of fashionable women. As their pace slowed, Archer spoke, catching his breath.

'We did it, sir. We stopped them, didn't we?'

'Yes, Archer, we certainly stopped them.' There was a note of irony in his voice. 'We should congratulate ourselves. We've kept Boney on his throne. And we almost got ourselves killed into the bargain. And now the whole of Paris is looking for us.'

He pushed his way deeper into the crowd, racking his brains for what to do next. Trying to think what might be the best way to lose themselves in the city. To become anonymous.

'The whole of Paris, sir?'

'Think about it. Colonel Doucet thinks that we were involved in shooting Hulin and believes that we're Malet's accomplices. And I shouldn't think that Malet will deny that, do you? Fouché will be after us too, to keep us quiet. The last thing he wants is for us to be captured by Savary's secret police and tortured into implicating him and Talleyrand, so he'll have his own men on to us. Even Macpherson will probably be after us, the moment he begins to suspect that we might have scuppered the plot. To be blunt, we're in a bit of a fix. We've got to keep on the alert for Fouché's thugs, the army, the Gendarmerie and the royalists. Add to that the fact that we failed to accomplish our original mission, and you have a fairly sound grasp of our position.' He laughed. 'Aside from that we're fine, Archer, and all we have to do is get out of this damned city and back to Spain. It's not really very much to ask, wouldn't you say?'

They had become nicely lost in the crowd now but Keane was still plotting their next move. His instinct was to head east, away from the centre of the action, but not as far as the barracks. For an hour they walked through the arcades and had begun to feel confident that the chase had gone cold. They took a seat at the Café Corazza, which lay under the arcades between numbers 7 and 12 of Galérie Montpensier, and Keane ordered them a pot of coffee.

'You know,' he said with a smile, 'this is the place where Boney used to come as a young man, when he was trying to get a name for himself. Macpherson told me. Apparently he still owes them for an unpaid bill.'

Archer laughed, and then as Keane watched his face darkened. 'Look, sir, over there.'

Turning slowly, Keane spotted a patrol of gendarmes across the gardens. He nodded to Archer. 'Well done. Time to go, I think. Come on.'

As the astonished waiter delivered their coffee, Keane pressed a hefty tip into his hand and both men stood up and walked calmly away through the arcades.

'That was close, too damn close. Keep walking.'

They crossed the gardens, losing themselves again in the crowds, and left by the rue de Valois, heading east once again, along a system of smaller streets that brought them quickly to the market place of Les Halles.

Here once again all was bustle as the market porters and traders went about their business and they were back in one of the poorest areas of the city, and right in its centre, on the rue Transnonain, one of the roughest areas of Paris. Keane felt more than a little uncomfortable as soldiers were not frequent visitors here and their dress was attracting attention.

He stopped a street vendor in the market and bought a broadsheet, so freshly printed that he could still smell the ink. It was now close to midday and no one in Paris was in any doubt that a planned plot had failed. The headline said it all:

'The Emperor Lives!'

He scanned the piece below. A royalist plot had been foiled. Several generals arrested. Rumours of the emperor's death were false. He was in Russia leading the Grande Armée to victory after victory. Most of the conspirators were in police hands, but two desperate men were still on the run. 'Two desperate men.'

Thankfully there was no description in the paper of either

him or Archer. But Keane knew that it would only be a matter of time before their details were posted on every wall in the city. There was no doubt in his mind that they had to lose themselves, quickly, and suddenly an idea came into his mind.

Something Macpherson had mentioned in the course of their conversation as they had walked through the city on that first day. Close to where they now were, in Les Halles, in the heart of the old district of central Paris, lay the Cemetery of the Saints-Innocents. He recalled Macpherson's words when probed further on the cemetery some days before: 'It stinks and thank God they're moving it. By night. Piece by piece. Putting the bones in the old quarries and tunnels around the city walls. Heaps of bones being moved through the city. During the day it is a meeting place for all sorts. Low types. And at night it's full of the same people. People you would not want to meet even in daylight. Whores, drunks, thieves and grave robbers are its inhabitants.'

Keane looked at Archer. 'You should feel at home where we're headed now, Archer. Naturally drawn to cemeteries, as I recollect, aren't you?'

Archer grimaced. 'Quite, sir. My natural habitat.'

'I thought as much. Come on.'

It was a short walk to the cemetery, and as they approached the stench of putrefaction became more intense. On sight it was clear that work was going on. Massive basket loads of soil stood about the field, which in the centre still contained a remnant of the original church along with a huge covered fountain, several monuments and massive tombs and what Keane took to be an ossuary. It was about the same size as the Place Vendôme, but instead of paving, the ground was a network of wooden causeways laid across bare earth and rock.

Astonishingly the place was full of people, walking across the wooden boards, chatting to one another. The difference between these Parisians and those at the Palais-Royal was that here the silks and satins were replaced by filthy cotton, and the scrubbed and made-up faces of the *palais* by toothless pock-marked wrecks.

Archer stopped in his tracks. 'Good Lord. What is this place, sir?'

'The Cemetery of the Holy Innocents. It's Paris's oldest graveyard and they're moving it, piece by ghastly piece, outside the city. Have been trying to at least for the last twenty years, so Macpherson told me. The thing is, people still keep dumping bodies here. Smells a bit, doesn't it?'

'It's vile. Why have we come here?'

'To lose ourselves. To throw off our pursuers. It's my guess that this is the last place they'll think to look for us. Any of them.'

'What do you suggest we do, sir?'

Keane pointed to the line of roofed arches which lined one side of the site. 'I think we take refuge in there, Archer. Follow me.'

They stepped out across the mud and slime, both wondering on quite what it was they might be walking and trying to avoid contact with their fellow living inhabitants of this place of death.

'What are all the people doing here, sir?'

'Who knows. Macpherson told me that traditionally magicians would come here at night and take body parts to use in their experiments. There was mass-scale grave robbing too. That should amuse you.'

'But these just seem like a lot of poor people, sir.'

'Which is probably what they are. We should feel at home. Look, there are a few tarts out to turn a trick. There's a pick-pocket, if I ever saw one. As for the others, who knows? The occasional lunatic or perhaps a general. Macpherson reckoned that there might even be people who come here searching for their loved ones. You know that during the Revolution every night baskets of severed heads or headless bodies were just left here, and some say some of them are still here. Perhaps those are relatives trying to find some of the disappeared.'

They had made it across to the *charniers* now, the arches which had once been piled high with bones and rotting bodies and which smelt as if they still were. Although the bodies had been cleared, nameless fragments still clung to the brickwork, and murals of the Danse Macabre, dating back to the sixteenth century, still decorated the walls, with Death wielding his scythe as he cavorted around the figures of the doomed.

'Right,' said Keane, 'in here. Safest place in Paris, I reckon.'

They stepped inside one of the arches and instantly both reached for their handkerchiefs, which they tied around their mouths and noses. Then, sliding into the shadows at the back of one of the *charniers*, they tried to get some rest.

Keane awoke as the sun was going down, its dying rays casting an eerie orange glow around the walls and monuments of the old cemetery.

The crowd of visitors did not seem to have thinned out a great deal, although on closer inspection he could see that the proportion of whores to thieves had increased. Scanning the perimeter with military precision, at length, in the distance by the northernmost wall, Keane glimpsed a small patrol of gendarmes. There was no way they could possibly make it out of the cemetery grounds without being spotted. He woke Archer. 'We need to take cover. How are you with graves?'

Together, trying to stay as close to the wall as they could, the two men moved from their position. Ahead of them Keane could see an area where the ground had been disturbed and it was towards this that he was heading. He expected to hear at any moment a cry from the gendarmes, but nothing came and it was with huge relief that he threw himself down into one of the holes, conscious that Archer would do the same. Keane landed with a thump that jarred his back. The hole was three inches deep in water and mud. You could not describe it as a grave, although that certainly was how it had started out. Now it was just a hole. And along its sides in the dying light Keane began to make out curious forms. Tree roots, he thought. But if that were so, then where were the trees above? It was only when he reached out to touch one of the forms that he realized what they were. He was surrounded by bones. Human bones.

He could hear voices up above them now, but this far down, eight feet in the ground, it was hard to understand them properly. They came closer, male voices now, more distinct. He heard a question and made out a few words: 'criminals . . . soldiers . . . Irish.'

The Gendarmerie were searching for them, and it seemed had even extended their probings to this place. Keane held his breath, tried to press himself into the side of the hole; to blend into the soil in case anyone should choose to look down. But no one did. Who, they asked themselves, other than a madman, would choose to hide themselves down there, among the stinking, rotting dead?

After a few minutes the voices drifted away. Keane and Archer lay motionless for a further half an hour, during which time the moon came out, casting a pale light across the Cemetery of the Holy Innocents. It seemed to both of them like an eternity. It struck Keane that this must surely be the worst situation in which he had ever had the misfortune to find himself. Having to cohabit with the dead in a filthy, stagnant pit while above them not one but three sets of enemies hunted them down, determined to take them in dead or alive.

At length Keane opened his eyes and brushed the dirt from his hair and his clothes. Archer, in his hole, followed suit and then to his horror found himself looking into the ghastly cadaver of a dead woman. She had been young, not more than thirty, and could only have been dead a week. But her flesh was beginning to rot and her eyeballs hung down upon her cheeks above an open mouth outlined by bloodless lips. It was all that he could do to stifle a scream, and in doing so, he almost wretched. Keane scrambled up out of the hole, by using the protruding body parts as supports, denying his knowledge of what they were, and called down to Archer to do the same. The man needed no second telling.

'Christ, sir, let's get out of this place. You're quite right. They're still dumping bodies here.'

'Yes, let's. But be careful. They may have left someone to stand guard.'

Together they began to make their way, crouched in the darkness along the border of the graveyard. Eventually they came to the east gate and emerged into the rue Berger.

Keane turned to Archer. 'We should make for my aunt's old house. There are cellars there where we should be able to hide safely for the night. We might even stay longer. Go to ground.

Places that no one else ever really knew but me and Sophie. Come on. It's this way.'

They moved silently and in the shadows past the old gothic church of Saint-Merri, but it was not until they were walking down the easternmost section of the rue de la Bretonnerie that Keane realized they were being followed.

This was home ground to Keane now, familiar from his boyhood, the old Jewish quarter of the Marais, with its twisting streets and dead ends. Keane moved fast to the left, taking Archer with him down an alleyway off the rue du Vieille Temple. Then he doubled back along the tiny rue du Trésor and into the rue des Écouffes and the rue des Rosiers. It was a route that only a native of the area would know. A young boy, having stolen a *tarte* from a patisserie on a dare from a friend, running for his life and the honour of his aunt.

At the corner they stopped. Keane pushed Archer into a doorway and, wrapping his cloak around himself, waited in the shadows. After five minutes nothing had happened and he wondered whether he might have been mistaken. But a few seconds later a figure moved at the end of the street and began to walk towards them.

It was a man, but Keane was unable to make out the features. For a few seconds the pursuer paused in the moonlight at the opposite corner of the street and waited as if searching, almost sniffing out something. Then he was off again, eastwards, in the direction of the Place Royale.

Keane slowly emerged from the shadows and the two men now began to follow their pursuer, turning the tables on him.

They walked at a discreet distance along the street, ducking to take cover at every chance they could, using every niche and bulwark so that the man would have no inkling of his being followed. The man appeared to be at a loss now, and as they entered the square he stopped and looked about. They were beneath one of Fouché's celebratedly rare street lights when Keane saw him. His hand went to the hilt of his sword and he began to draw it from the scabbard.

Chef-Inspecteur Jadot stepped out of the shadows.

'Captain Williams. No need for your sword, I hope.'

'Jadot, how did you find us?'

'You forget I know something of your past. It was a hunch that you would come here.'

'You were right. Well, now you have found us. What next? Do you intend to take us in?'

'Macpherson was furious when he found out what had happened. Still is. He blames you and you alone for ruining the operation.'

'I guessed that he would. Presumably he wants our heads. What about you?' His hand went back to his sword hilt.

Jadot shook his head. 'Macpherson is deluded, captain. His idea of backing Malet was wrong. There must still be a royalist network maintained in this city, until Bonaparte is defeated, but Macpherson will not be its head. That honour now falls to me.'

'You're taking over? By force?'

'If needs be. I have the power.'

'By whose authority, I wonder.'

'Since you ask, it is your Major Grant's. He came to see me directly after visiting you. But that's not important. It's worse than that. Macpherson's betrayed you.'

'What?'

'To Fouché.'

'Christ, we're finished.'

'You need to leave Paris, obviously. And you've no time to hide where you're heading.'

'You know about the old house?'

'From Macpherson. And you won't be safe there. Fouché's men will be here before you know it.'

Keane nodded. 'Yes, you're right. But seeing you just now, in the shadows, something worse has occurred to me.'

Archer spoke. 'Sir?'

'That my aunt's house is now lived in by my cousin.'

'But you said yourself you didn't know who owned it?'

'Seeing the inspector here reminded me of our encounter with Harrison on these streets. Something he said to me then. Almost in passing. That night when he followed us. Something about knowing who his father's killer might be and that a woman in Paris might have the answer. He said that he knew where to find her. Don't you see? It's Sophie. The woman he meant. She's here, in Paris, and Harrison has discovered who she is and where she is. And I'm willing to bet that she's in the old house.'

He stopped for a moment. 'And now Macpherson's told Fouché who I really am. Harrison will have Sophie, and if she knows anything of the truth the bastard will have got it out of her. He may well know that it was my father who killed his own in battle. He's a clever man, Jadot, isn't he?'

'Harrison? One of the most brilliant spies I have ever met.'

Keane was thinking fast. 'I don't know what she knows. She certainly doesn't know who I am now. But if she has told Harrison what he wants to know about her family, about my father, he might have worked out enough to put two and two together. He's certainly clever enough to do that. And he'll know that when I realize what he's done that I'll come to the

old house; that I must save Sophie. But he will assume that
for the present I'm occupied with Malet's plot. He'll think he
has all the time in the world. The last thing he'll expect is for
us to turn up so soon. Come on. We haven't a second to lose.
Inspector?'

Jadot nodded and together the three of them ran down the
street towards the Place des Vosges.

Entering the square, Keane was surprised to find it little
changed from his memories of it as a boy.

The gardens in the centre were in fine condition. Re-made,
he guessed, after having been ruined during the Revolution.
But the grand hotels on all four sides were as he recollected
them, if somewhat neglected, the slates of their roofs in the
moonlight showing great gaps, like missing teeth. His aunt's
house stood on the north side and they made directly for it.
Keane could not see any lights in the windows, but given the
time of night that proved little. Instead of going to the front
door, Keane led the way to the left and through a low service
entrance which led to an alleyway down the side of the house.
The place seemed well kept and he could only presume that it
was being lived in. About halfway along the wall of the house
he stopped and began to search around in the gravel under
their feet. After a few minutes he looked up at Archer with a
grin of satisfaction. 'Here it is. Look.'

Below them in the gravel and loose soil Archer saw a weath-
ered iron ring. Keane pulled at it and at first nothing happened.
'It's stuck. That's good. Means they don't know about it.'

He pulled again and this time felt movement. One more tug
and the ring began to give and with it came a square wooden
trapdoor.

'Thank God,' said Keane, opening the hatch fully and peering inside. The cellar smelt of must and damp. 'Come on.' He went in first, lowering himself until his feet found the steps he knew must be there. Then he climbed down and Archer and Jadot followed quickly. 'Close the trapdoor behind you. Come on.'

They were in a pitch-black cellar, but gradually their eyes became accustomed to the gloom and, as they looked, a vaulted ceiling began to appear. Keane at once recalled the layout of the vaults.

'We used to play here as children,' he said softly. 'I know every square foot of them. Follow me.'

He walked in silence, checking every footfall in case it might be on a piece of wood or broken glass that would give them away. After going several yards he stopped. By his reckoning they were now directly beneath the old drawing room of the house. Sure enough he was right, for above they suddenly heard voices.

There were two men and then a woman speaking, high, agitated, but the words were unintelligible. No more than noises. Keane led the others further into the cellars until ahead of them they could see the first few steps of a staircase which appeared to lead upwards directly into the ceiling.

He turned and spoke in a barely audible whisper. 'You had better draw your weapons.' Then without hesitation he began to climb the stairs until his head was touching the ceiling. Reaching up, he fumbled around until his fingers alighted upon a catch. He clicked it and released another trapdoor, which fell down this time, swinging loose. Keane continued to climb the stairs and gradually his body disappeared out of sight. The other two followed, first Archer then Jadot, until at last all three of them were standing in a small room. It was almost as dark as the cellar had at first been, although a small amount of illumination was provided by a line of light in the outline of a square, which penetrated through the wall before them. It was clearly a secret door, and as they watched, Keane put his head close to it and flipped something on the wall. He stood there for some moments before turning to them and speaking in the softest voice he could manage.

'There's a spyhole here. There are four of them and one of them is a girl. I wonder what she is doing here. We can take them, but we must use our surprise well.'

Jadot whispered, 'Who are they? Do you know them?'

Keane nodded. 'Harrison and more of Fouché's men. Fouché's not there. I have a plan. Wait for my signal, then burst in and take whoever you can. Try to push the girl clear to the floor.'

Putting his eye back to the hole in the wall, Keane watched and waited. Some minutes later, as one of the men crossed the floor, he saw his chance. With a great heave he threw his weight at the secret door and it flew open, crashing into the man who had been standing directly in front of it and throwing him across the room and to the floor. Their surprise was complete and perfectly executed.

Keane was first through the gap and running across the room he grabbed the girl by the arm and flung her as far as he could before turning on her captor and plunging his sword through the man's lower chest. Withdrawing it, he turned and saw that the other two were already engaged. Keane looked to the fourth man, who was Harrison himself, and saw him racing across to where the girl had landed and was now attempting to get to her feet. Just as Harrison was reaching her, Keane slashed at him, catching him a glancing blow on the calf, which made him turn. Harrison had his sword drawn and was facing Keane now, half crouched, ready to defend himself against attack.

The American hissed at him. 'You. Fouché was right. You stopped Malet.'

Keane shook his head. 'Malet stopped himself. He was never up to it, Harrison. The man's insane. Deluded.'

'How very British of you. The man's a republican. He must clearly be insane.'

It was clear from the noise of steel on steel that Jadot and Archer were still both in the thick of their own fights. Harrison made a jab at Keane, who sidestepped it and replied, but his thrust also missed its mark. He answered Harrison's jibe.

'That bloody plot never had a chance. I was merely the agent of its failure.'

'You're very eloquent for a British bastard, Captain Keane. I'm right, aren't I? You're Keane. I know all about you, and your father. She talked. Eventually.'

Keane swore and, casting a glance at the girl, recognized Sophie instantly. And at the same time saw the bruises and the blood on her face.

He shouted at Harrison, 'You bastard.'

Keane's sword shone in the candlelight as he edged towards the American.

The girl gasped as Harrison lunged and caught Keane on the arm, cutting into his forearm. He winced and riposted with a lunge that took Harrison in the shoulder, making him reel backwards.

'Why should you be angry? I'm the one who suffered. Your father took my father from me. This moment was meant to be,

Keane. This is fate.' He lunged at Keane again, but the attack
was wild and with no proper aim.

Keane parried easily, cutting to the left and pushing
Harrison's sword away. Then he pushed through and cut at
Harrison's head. The sword made contact and took away the
lower part of Harrison's ear. The American fell back, groping
at the wound.

He attacked again and this time his fury won through and
his wild slash caught Keane across the abdomen. The pain was
intense, but Keane was aware that the wound was not serious.
Despite the blood, he came en garde again and for an instant
was aware that one of the two fights in the room had ended.
Archer was standing, breathing heavily and clutching his side,
while Jadot continued to fight the other man. He watched
Archer flash across the room and help the Frenchman, just as
Harrison made another attack.

'This is for my father.'

The sword cut an arc through the air above Keane's head.
Instantly Keane saw it and raised his blade. The great cavalry
sabre struck the American's lesser blade with a deafening
clamour and deflected the blow. And then Keane was on him,
slashing and hacking in a fury born of frustration.

And quite suddenly a cut took the American deep across
the chest and the blade ran on into his upper arm. Harrison
stopped in mid-stroke and clutched at his chest, which was
running crimson with blood.

Keane lowered his blade and watched the American sink to
the floor. He walked across and, kneeling, cradled the dying
man's shoulders. Archer and Jadot, who together had dealt
with the fourth man, walked towards them.

Harrison smiled at him. 'Thank you, Keane. I doubt if your father did the same for mine.' He gasped for breath.

Keane looked him in the eyes. 'My father, Harrison, was no traitor like yours. And I'm sure he did what he had to do: his duty.'

Harrison looked back at him. 'Maybe. We all live with the legacy of our fathers. Those of us who know who they were.'

'You know who he was, don't you? My father. Tell me. Who was he? You have to tell me.'

Harrison smiled at him. 'I don't have to tell you anything at all. That would be too easy. But I will tell you something. You won't like what you learn. But you'll have to live with it, Keane. You'd be better off dead.' He grimaced with pain.

He looked into Keane's eyes and then suddenly his own became curiously glassy, almost grey. It was a look that Keane recognized and he held Harrison harder. The American relaxed and gave out a quiet hiss as the life ebbed out of him.

Keane held tight, imploring the corpse. 'No. No, wait. My father, tell me his name. His name, Harrison.'

But Harrison was gone.

Keane let him fall to the floor and, getting up, shook his head in despair. Then he looked around and found the girl. She was standing in the corner where she had run for shelter. Keane walked towards her. 'Sophie, it is you. I knew it. It's me, James.'

'Yes, I know, they told me.' She paused. 'Who were these men?'

She was as pretty as he had remembered her. Her lip was cut and her dress torn.

'I can't explain it all now and I'm so very sorry that you

were involved. We need to get away from here. More of them will be coming. We need to take you with us.'

Archer spoke. 'Where can we go, sir? Where is safe now? How do we get out of the city?'

'All of the barriers and gates will be warned to look out for us,' Keane added.

Jadot nodded. 'Yes, you're right. But I have an idea.'

14

They left the old house by the same route they had entered, through the secret passage and out via the trapdoor. Keane and Archer reconnoitred the front and rear of the house and were satisfied that none of Fouché's men had yet arrived and within a matter of minutes they were all clear of the Place des Vosges and walking fast through the darkness to the rue des Tournelles.

For once Keane was thankful for Fouché's appalling track record with the street lighting. They raced north-east, along the rue du Chemin Vert, with Jadot leading the way, stopping from time to time to allow Sophie to catch up, with Keane helping her.

They paused to catch their breath and Jadot told them of a way to escape from the city without leaving a trace.

'Smugglers, of wine mostly, have a network of tunnels beneath the city wall which come up outside. My men are continually searching for them and blocking them up. But there is one near here which I know we haven't yet secured. That's where we're going. That's your way out.'

Keane nodded. 'And then on to Orléans. Back to Madame

Duplessis. From there we'll aim for Bayonne, if we can. I hope to God that Major Grant made it through.' He had no idea where they were now. Jadot, however, appeared to have a good knowledge of these nameless streets. At length he could make out a large walled area over to their right. He asked Jadot, 'What's that? Is that where we're going?'

'You could say that. It's where we're all headed, in the end. It's the new cemetery. Père Lachaise. It's on our route.'

They stopped near the cemetery, in the rue des Partants, about three hundred yards away from the city wall.

Jadot turned to Keane. 'This is where I leave you, Captain Keane.'

Keane looked at him. 'You know my name.'

'I heard Harrison say it. But I had guessed it long before. As far as I'm aware, Fouché does not know. Nor will he from me. You must go through this door and down into the tunnel. It will take you out beyond the city wall. From there you're on your own. But it should not be hard to get where you want to go. I'm sure that you've managed harder things, captain. I can help with one thing. Make your way to the Bassin de la Villette, north by the canal. I will have three horses ready for you. Good luck. It's been a pleasure to have known you.'

'James, I'm frightened. Stay close to me, please.'

Keane took Sophie's hand in his and together, with Archer following, they made their way along the tunnel. It was damp and airless and the only light came from the intermittent air vents which had been drilled by the smugglers up through the tunnel roof. Their feet slithered along the floor of the passage, ankle deep in liquid.

Suddenly Keane came up against a solid wall which he realized was a door and was aware of a void off to his left and another to his right. For a moment he hesitated. 'Archer, did Jadot say anything about turning off?'

'No, sir. We keep going straight, I believe.'

But that didn't seem to be an option. Although he was unable to see Sophie, he felt her presence beside him and it was curiously comforting. As if, after a long absence, he had found something wholly familiar. There was so much to say after so many years, but Keane was as aware as she was that this was hardly the time or the place.

Keane wondered if Jadot had tricked them. Was the door locked? He tried it and found that it was. Would Fouché's men, or Doucet's, suddenly appear behind them or were they waiting in silence behind the door, biding their time? But no one appeared and after a few minutes Keane tried again. But there was still no response.

Archer approached him. 'Jadot didn't say anything about this, sir. But it strikes me that we're dealing with tunnels made by smugglers. These men are no fools, sir. They have to think one pace ahead of the game, if you see what I mean. It's my betting that there's some sort of mechanism that operates the door so that you can't get in and you can't get out. All we have to do is discover what it is.'

'Nicely put, Archer. Any ideas?'

Archer thought for a moment and then, feeling his way along the top of the wooden door, he stopped as his fingers alighted on a piece of protruding metal. He pushed down hard, and with a creak the door swung open.

'Archer, you're a bloody marvel.'

'Thank you, sir. A little knowledge picked up in my former career. Common way to secure a robber-proof coffin.'

They emerged, blinking, from the tunnel and saw before

them the Bassin de la Villette, Bonaparte's great waterworks which brought fresh water to the people of Paris. It was a long rectangular reservoir, flanked on either side by rows of poplar trees and at one end by a large neo-classical structure with the appearance of a temple.

As they approached the building, Keane saw two men in civilian clothes standing beside it. Tethered to the iron railings that formed the perimeter stood three horses, all saddled and equipped with blanket rolls and portmanteaux. Jadot, it seemed, had been as good as his word.

The first day's riding, with breaks for rest, brought them along the Loire past Blois and Tours before turning south to Poitiers. Sophie was a good horsewoman and quite capable of keeping pace with Keane and Archer.

They halted above the city in the evening sunlight, gazing down across the river at the spires of the churches and the cathedral. The inns in the centre of the city were tempting, but Keane knew better than to chance it. His intelligence had been for some time that the place was fast growing as a garrison town and he had no wish to encounter inquisitive French officers who would certainly wonder why two officers of the Irish Legion might be this far from their unit and travelling in the wrong direction.

Instead the three travellers took the road that led to the east around the city and further south, and only when they had Poitiers behind them did Keane call a halt.

They made camp away from the road, halfway up a hillside at a spot that Keane could see at once had a commanding view of the surrounding country.

Jadot had looked after them well, and inside the valises they found a skinned rabbit, a chicken, some sausage, bread, hard biscuit and cheese as well as three bottles of red wine and a canteen of brandy.

They exchanged few words as Archer cooked the rabbit over a low fire, suspending it on two cleft sticks. It was simple food, but to the three of them it tasted as if it might have come from the smartest of restaurants in the Palais-Royal. Keane watched Sophie as she ate, noting how naturally she took to life on campaign. She tore at the meat and wiped her fingers on the silk brocade of her yellow dress, then, seeing his stare, smiled at him. Keane smiled back and looked away. He was surprised about the way he felt for her. It was not the desperate ardour that he had felt for Henriette, but something closer to the love that he had once had for Kitty Blackwood, in what now seemed an age ago. And it was a feeling which he hoped would continue.

As they ate, Archer broke the silence. 'How long do you reckon, sir? Till we get to Bayonne.'

'Two more days, I'd say, judging by our journey north.' He turned to Sophie. 'Think you can manage that, cousin?'

She laughed. 'Why should I not be able to manage something that you can, James? Don't you recall the games we used to play? I always won. Don't you remember?'

Archer smiled. 'Really, sir?'

Keane shook his head. 'You're exaggerating. In any case, I was younger than you. Things have changed.'

'I think you'll find that you are still younger than me and that I can still beat you at most things.'

'Really?'

'Really.'

Keane laughed. 'You certainly haven't lost your spirit.

Remember that time you locked me in the cellars of the old house?'

'Of course. You were terrified.'

Archer laughed.

'Nonsense. It just gave me time to explore them. Which as it turns out was rather lucky, wasn't it?'

She smiled and Keane thought that he saw a melancholy look in her eye. He had been intending to ask her how she had managed to escape the Revolution and what had become of her mother. But he decided that now was not the right time.

Archer took the first watch and Keane relieved him halfway through the night. But aside from a lone wildcat that Keane saw off with a well-aimed stone, nothing disturbed them.

The next day brought more hard riding and Keane was again impressed by Sophie's ability in the saddle. The roads were fairly clear of travellers, apart from the usual civilians, and no one took notice of them. The only event was Keane's sighting of a regiment of infantry south of Angoulême, en route, he presumed, for Poitiers. The three of them took evasive action, riding off the main road and into a wood where they waited until the soldiers had passed.

By evening Bordeaux stood ahead of them. Keane reined in his horse and patted her neck. 'One more day and we'll be in Bayonne. We have friends there. We'll be safe.'

He prayed that he was right. That Madame Duplessis had not been discovered and that other royalists aside from her might receive them favourably and offer their help. For after Paris he was certain of nothing now.

They made camp as before, away from the city, and finished the last of Jadot's rations, cooking the chicken as they had the rabbit. This time Keane could not resist asking his cousin a few probing questions.

'It must have been terrifying for you – the Revolution. I managed to get away just in time.'

'Yes. It was terrible. Poor Papa. My mother almost went mad from grief.'

'She escaped though?'

'Yes, I presumed that you knew. She went back home. To England. To my grandparents' house.'

'Your grandparents? Our grandparents? I had thought that they were dead. That's what I was told by my mother.'

Sophie stared at him. 'You didn't know anything of them?'

'Not until recently. I never met them.'

She said nothing for a moment, then, 'You are right. They are dead. I am so sorry. I had no idea. How terrible.'

'What did you do? Where did you go after the Revolution?'

'I went with Maman. We had a little cottage. On the big estate. It was a quiet time. No one ever came to see us. And then when she died—'

He cut her short. 'Your mother's dead?'

'Yes. Five years ago. It was sudden. Unexpected. Influenza. That's when I decided to come back here. I'd heard everything had changed, under the emperor.'

'I'm so sorry.'

Keane's mind was filled with regret and anger. His grandparents had been alive and in England all the time he had been growing up and he had never been allowed to see them. Sophie too. Had his mother had any say in the matter? He knew that it had been their doing. The words of Patrick Curtis about his mother came back to him. 'They cut her off. Someone told me they were nobility.'

'Yes, of course.'

'But you never mentioned that.'

'Why should I?'

'As I recall you just called them grandfather and grand-mother. No one used a name. What were their names?'

'Mountjoy. The Earls of Newport.'

'Good God.' Curtis had been right. His mother's parents were from a noble line. And so were Sophie and himself. His grandparents had been too scandalized to ever meet their grandson. Had his father really been so scurrilous a person?

'So you know nothing about my father?'

'No. Nothing. I was told that he had been killed in battle. That was all. You were told that too, weren't you?'

'Yes. It seems as if someone was determined to cover any trace of whoever he might have been. Might still be.'

'You think your father's alive?'

'I have some reason to think so. I can only hope.'

'At least you have that hope. I know for certain that my father is dead. I saw them do it.'

'You saw your own father's death?'

She nodded. 'Yes, on the guillotine. It was hideous, but he went to it with great bravery. I was hiding in the crowd. Maman and I had managed to escape from the house and hid in the coach-house until they had gone. The mob. There was no trial. They just took him. Put him in La Force for a week and then cut off his head.'

Keane said nothing. There was nothing to say. He put his hand around her shoulders and drew her to him and knew in that moment that he would never lose her again.

*

Archer kept his own counsel but then, as Sophie slept, in the minutes when they changed their watch, he whispered, 'She's quite something, sir. Your cousin. You seem very close.'

'Yes, Archer, we are. At least, we were. And we will be so again.'

The final day of their journey took them away from Bordeaux through a grey dawn drizzle across the Leyre and into the sodden heathland and forest of Landes.

There were fewer than ever travellers on the road here, although twice they saw shepherds, walking on stilts through the wetlands as they herded their flocks. They passed through the deer forests of Lesperon and at Magescq took the even quieter road to the west. At Labenne they halted, within sight of the sea.

Sophie gasped. 'It's magnificent. So vast.'

'Yes, and what's more it means that we're almost home. Back in Spain.'

'You consider Spain to be your home?'

Keane nodded. 'Yes, I suppose I do. More than anywhere else on earth. I've been there for the last four years. I suppose I have a claim to call it home.'

Riding into Bayonne, it did not take Keane long to retrace their steps to the inn where just two months before, almost to the day, they had boarded the Paris diligence. This time there was no sign of the army. Nevertheless they did not stop, but rode through the streets towards the Duplessis house on the south bank of the city.

Keane had retained the sketch map and with it they now found their way back to the house. It did not appear to have changed at all. It stood quiet and with an air of tranquillity in its shady courtyard while the fountain babbled away and the scent of mimosa filled their nostrils. Keane dismounted as did the others and together they led their horses across to the far corner of the courtyard.

Keane drew his sword and went to try the door. It was impossible, he surmised, for Fouché's men to have beaten them to Bayonne or even to have sent word of their escape so quickly. Something though was not right here. The door stood slightly ajar and he nodded to Archer, who pushed Sophie gently back behind the horses and drew a pistol from his belt. Keane did the same and slowly he pushed open the door.

The room looked just as it had done when they had left. Nothing seemed out of place and yet there was no sign of life. They climbed the stairs to the bedroom where two months earlier they had left their belongings. Nothing had changed and there in the armoire were the neat bundles of their uniforms. Silver's of course had gone, but the other two were just as they had been.

They entered every room of the house and its small outbuilding, but of Madame Duplessis there was not a trace. It wasn't right. She was not the sort of woman to be away from her home. Keane knew instinctively that something was wrong and he prayed it would not be his worst fears.

He signed to Sophie to come into the house and then, with the two packages safely tucked inside their valises, they left the little courtyard, Keane leading the way.

'I don't suppose for one minute that Major Grant will be awaiting our arrival, do you, Archer?'

'No, sir, it would seem unlikely. Although if he were to be here, I would have supposed that he might have been in this house, sir.'

'No, I think that would have been too obvious and too dangerous. He's probably gone back to Spain.' He paused. 'But you know, Archer. If I were Grant – if I had risked two of my agents behind enemy lines – I would want to make damn sure that I personally got them back. Wouldn't you? I have an idea.'

He reached into his pocket and drew out the scrap of paper on which was written Madame Duplessis's address. Underneath it Curtis had added another address, and Keane read it and understood.

'Come on. I think I know where to find him.'

The little church of Saint Zenobius stood at the confluence of four streets in a small square. It was a modest building, typical of the area, with a single flat-roofed bell tower. The only distinguishing features were two Corinthian columns in the porch which had obviously once been part of an earlier Roman structure.

Keane and the others entered the square, where a small market was taking place. But strangely, save for several abandoned stalls and tables, the place was deserted. It was as if all the inhabitants had been removed, leaving behind all their goods. Keane walked over to a fruit stall and picked up a half-drunk glass of wine. Another was sitting close by and on another table someone had left a hat and a pair of spectacles. He turned to Archer.

'On your guard. Sophie, get behind me.'

'Give me a sword, James, or a gun. Anything.'

Keane reached into his belt, drew out his pistol and gave it to her before turning back to the church. According to his directions, this was meant to be the rendezvous for any meeting with Grant. But what had happened?

Without warning the two church doors opened to reveal four men. They wore the blue of the French infantry and their muskets were levelled and pointing directly at Keane. From their rear an officer appeared.

'Captain Keane, I presume. Or is it Captain Williams?'

Keane nodded. 'Keane will do nicely, thank you. And you are?'

'Major Leflaive, 105th infantry. I would advise you not to think of running, captain. My men are very good shots. I would be obliged to you for your weapons.'

Keane knew that he had no alternative but to comply. A good gambler always recognized the moment when his luck ran out, and for Keane clearly that moment had arrived.

Drawing his sword, he walked across and held it by the blade to present it to the major, who took it. Archer and Sophie followed suit and within a few minutes the space between the major and the church had filled with half of the company.

The major turned to them. 'Captain Martel, one platoon to guard the prisoners while we form up. Oh, and bring out the other prisoner.'

As Keane watched the French formed a line and presented their muskets at the three prisoners, and as they did, another man emerged from the church, flanked by two Frenchmen. Grant looked at Keane and smiled. 'James, I knew you would come. But perhaps not so soon. Thank you.'

Keane shook his head. 'I told them, sir. That you would be here. But I hadn't expected this.'

Major Leflaive walked across to them. 'Your friend, Captain Keane. An extra gift for the emperor. I smell promotion.'

Keane looked at him. 'What will you do with us? Back to Paris?'

The major nodded. 'Of course. And then, who knows what? Though your pretty friend we might keep here for our return. I'm sure she'd make entertaining company.'

Keane stopped himself from giving the looked-for reaction. Sophie looked at him. 'James?'

'Don't worry, you are not going anywhere that I'm not.'

Leflaive shook his head and smiled. 'We should get ready to move though. I want to get you back to the capital as quickly as possible. I've no room for any mistakes. While we keep you, we merely endanger ourselves.'

Keane, who was now standing in between Archer and Grant, with Sophie close behind him, looked from the French major towards his men and as he did so something caught his eye, a face in the line. He paused and looked again. Just to make certain. But there was no mistaking the man. Sergeant O'Gara, a familiar face from the charnel house of Badajoz, last seen attempting to rape the colonel's wife. O'Gara smiled back at Keane and he knew that the recognition was mutual. And then, to Keane's surprise, O'Gara spoke, directly to Major Leflaive.

'Sir, why do we need to take them back? Keep the girl, of course. But I think we should just shoot the others here and now. They're spies, sir. Bloody spies. And spies are shot, sir. Ain't that right? Whatever happens. And you said so yourself, sir, while they're alive they put us all in danger. I say we shoot them, sir.'

There were cries from the other infantrymen of 'Shoot them' and 'Shoot the spies'.

Keane stared at O'Gara and was rewarded with another smile. To his further horror, the French major appeared to be considering O'Gara's request.

'It is most irregular. We should take him back to the colonel. That is the protocol.' He seemed to be weighing it up, calculating as to whether producing Keane, Grant and Archer alive or dead would further enhance his chance of promotion.

O'Gara spoke, seeming to read the officer's mind. 'Won't affect your promotion, sir. Dead or alive they're wanted. That's what we was told. All of them. Dead or alive. Price on their heads. That's what it is. They're dirty spies. British bloody officers.' He spat. 'They're why I joined your army, sir. God save Ireland. I say we shoot them.'

O'Gara levelled his musket and aimed it at Keane's head. To Keane's alarm, he was followed by eight other men in the line. The major wavered and said nothing. Instead he motioned to two men to take Sophie away from the three men. Struggling, she was pushed across the square behind the major. Keane was sweating now. He whispered to Grant, 'Looks bad, sir. I'm sorry, my fault. Bloody Irishman.'

He looked around the square for one last time, desperate to find some hidden means of escape, some magic trick worthy of the Church's miracle-working saint. As if in answer his eye was caught by a glint of sunlight in one of the crenellations of a balustrade on an opposite rooftop. Sun on metal. The gleam of a musket barrel. He whispered again, first to Archer, 'Get ready to drop', then to Grant, 'Sir, do exactly what I say and do. This might hurt.'

Keane looked back at Leflaive, whose hand was now raised in the air, and judged that his moment had come. As Leflaive's mouth opened to give the command to fire, Keane shoved hard at Grant's back and also at that of Archer, sending both man and officer crashing to the ground and, an instant later, he followed them. At that moment Leflaive dropped his hand, but just as eight fingers squeezed the triggers of eight French muskets, the square exploded in noise and the crash of gunfire as a series of shots rang out from the rooftops. One of them hit the major in the hand and the others hit every one of the soldiers in the line of the guard who fell, two dead and the others wounded, onto the dusty ground.

Keane looked up and saw smoke curling up from the balustrade and at the windows of houses on two sides of the square and then the space was suddenly filled with horsemen.

Most of them wore civilian clothes, but all carried weapons, and Keane noticed at once that every one of them wore in his hat a white cockade. Royalists.

The French, caught off guard, were helpless. Keane stood up and, helped by Archer, got Grant to his feet. 'Thank you, dear boy. I wasn't expecting that.'

'My apologies, major. It was all I could do. I saw the muskets on the roof.'

Leaving Grant to dust himself off, Keane walked across to the French major and, bending down, recovered his sword where the officer had dropped it, as the royalists disarmed the remaining French infantry in the square and encircled the entrance to the church.

'How many, major? How many more men do you have in the church?'

'A half company. Thirty men.'

'Well, I suggest that you and your men out here go and join them.'

He turned to find the leader of his rescuers and spotted a man with a sword, close to the entrance. Seeing Keane, the man walked towards him.

'Captain Keane?'

'Colonel Hulot. What a pleasant surprise to see you. Badajoz seems an eternity away.'

'So it does, my dear Captain Keane. Always nice to be able to repay a favour. You know Major Grant, and Lieutenant Archer?'

Grant nodded. 'Thank you, colonel. I thought it was all over for us.'

'It very nearly was. Might still be, unless we move quickly. Can I suggest that we leave as soon as we can, gentlemen, we've a few miles to ride.'

'Before we do, colonel, I've some business to attend to.'

Keane walked across to the line of French soldiers who had formed his guard. But of O'Gara there was no sign. He turned to Hulot. 'Colonel, did you see anyone get away?'

The colonel shook his head and, on turning back, Keane noticed behind one of the buttresses of the church what looked like the tail of a blue coat. Walking across to it, he found the uniform of a French infantryman and beneath it the dead body of what he presumed must be one of Hulot's men. He called Hulot over.

'Yes, he's one of mine. A pity.'

Walking back, Keane found Sophie, Archer and Grant together.

'That was close, sir.'

'Close as we've ever been, James.'

Sophie looked at Keane. 'You've done this before?'

Grant laughed. 'Madame, you must understand that Major Keane is one of the Duke's most valued soldiers.'

Keane stopped him, 'Major Keane?'

'Didn't I tell you? You're promoted. Brevet of course, but it'll only be a matter of time. Oh and Archer, almost forgot. A field commission for you, young man. Well done.'

They mounted up and Hulot led the column through the back streets of the city and out through a breach in the wall into the open countryside.

Hulot drove them hard and Keane was pleased to see that Sophie was, as she had said, able to match them for speed. They rode along the cliffs above the ocean, leaving the city behind them. After some five miles Hulot called a halt and walked the horses down a narrow path that led to a sandy beach. It was as secluded a spot as any, thought Keane, as he rode up to join him.

'May I ask where we're going, colonel? I presumed that we were on our way to rejoin Wellington's army.'

Hulot shook his head. 'I'm afraid not, captain. At least not immediately. You have another army to meet first.'

Hulot pointed towards a cave cut into the bottom of the cliff and as Keane rode across, followed by Archer, Sophie and Grant, he was met by a line of familiar faces.

'Martin, Silver, Ross, all of you! Are you all here?'

Sergeant Ross replied, 'Yes, sir. We couldn't wait you see. We've missed you that much. Besides – I thought they could do with a little jaunt. They've been sitting on their asses since you left.'

Silver spoke. 'Hardly, sir, you've had us run ragged.'

'Not exactly, Silver, but you have been kept busy.'

Keane and the others dismounted and the two men undressed and swapped the Irish coats in which they had lived so long for the red that felt like home.

Keane smiled. 'By God, that's better. I'd had quite enough of that green rag.'

'Yes, sir, you look better in red.'

'You too, Archer.'

Fastening his tunic, he turned to Grant. 'How did they know about this? The French. And about us?'

'Macpherson gave up the Zenobius code to Fouché.'

'Yes, I heard that he'd betrayed us.'

'He realized after my visit to you that his position was being usurped. I didn't think he'd go so far, though, as to expose the whole group. Luckily Father Curtis managed to escape before they came for him. Fouché sent word by courier. It arrived yesterday.'

'And what happened to Madame Duplessis, sir? There was no one at her house, but no sign of anything amiss. Our uniforms were exactly where we had left them.'

Grant shook his head. 'It's a tragic story. The old lady took her own life. Just a week ago.'

'She killed herself?'

'Hanged herself in the house. I found her, with Silver, when we arrived to wait for you.'

'But why? Her son?'

Grant shook his head. 'No, I don't think so. She had lived with his loss for years. But perhaps coming on top of that . . . ?'

'What? What happened?'

'One of the royalist spies. The ones in Paris whom you delivered to Fouché. Rochambeau. He was her brother.'

Keane shook his head. It was unthinkable. He had unwittingly caused the death of a sad old woman who might have lived out her days.

'It's my fault, sir. I killed her.'

Grant shook his head. 'No, James. The war killed her. It was almost bound to happen. One way or another, her time had come.'

Keane looked around at his men. Silver, Garland, Martin, Heredia . . . the old guard and the newcomers too.

'I seem to have been away rather a long time. It is good to see you. All of you. And looking so well. What have they been feeding you, Martin? They haven't been working you hard enough.'

'We thought you might have started talking French, sir.'

Ross spoke. 'You do look a bit, well, Frenchified, sir.'

'Thank you, Sarn't Ross. Let's hope it isn't lasting.'

Grant saw the joy on his face. 'I did my best, James, to keep them all together. Cavanagh would have dispersed them to other regiments. But I stopped him. Took them away myself and hid them. One by one, didn't I, lads?'

Martin answered for all of them. 'Major Grant was a bloody marvel, sir. The minute papers came for one of us, he would just spirit us away.'

'And now you're back with me, thank God. Thank you, sir.'

Grant clapped him on the back. 'It's good to have you back, James. Let's get you back to Spain and sanity.'

'You'd best tell me what's going on first, sir.'

'Wellington's got Marshal Marmont where he wants him. Outside Salamanca. He anticipates a victory.'

'I wish I could report the same. I wonder how the commander will take it.'

'Take it? How other than as a success? He can only be delighted. As I said, James, promotion. The coup was never meant to work.

'Sir?'

'We couldn't tell you that, of course. It might have compromised the entire operation. But don't you see? We've succeeded in our aim. We meant to sow seeds of doubt among the French high command. And that's exactly what we have done. Savary's arrest has left an indelible stain upon his record. Think about it. How did he react in the coup? He panicked. His position was not only embarrassing but it was dangerous. How on earth could it happen that the empire's new chief of secret police could himself be arrested in his bed, by a certified lunatic, accompanied by a few unfit National Guardsmen?

'Better than all that though, James, we have made Bonaparte doubt his own greatness. This Russian adventure may well be a disaster for him. His generals have been advising him, telling him not to invade. He should have looked at history, at Charles XII of Sweden. What happened to him will happen to Bonaparte. It wasn't the Russian army that beat Karl. It was winter. "General Winter", the Russians call it. Their invincible commander. Their secret weapon. Mark my words, James, by October Bonaparte will be in trouble. And if he stays there longer than that, his army will begin to die in its thousands, then in its hundreds of thousands. He doesn't have a hope.'

Keane nodded. He saw it all quite clearly. Grant was right. The Russians would defeat Boney in the field, using their own country as a weapon.

He spoke. 'Yes, of course. And in time Wellington will do the same to them in Spain. The French will be driven from the Peninsula and chased through their own country.'

Grant nodded. 'Yes, that will be Wellington's victory. But we, James – you and I – we have already defeated him in a far more subtle way. We have done what no one else has ever done, James. We've got inside the emperor's mind. We've sown a seed of self-doubt and it's that seed that's going to bring him down.'

Keane smiled and nodded. 'Yes, of course. So we have done

what we were sent to do, sir, haven't we? We've undermined
the empire from within. But not just inside the state, inside
Bonaparte's own mind. And once Boney thinks that we can
second-guess him, that with everything he plans we're one
step ahead, he'll begin to doubt his every move. And when that
starts to happen, that will really be the beginning of the end.'

Historical Note

The siege of Badajoz was one of the bloodiest episodes in the entire Peninsular War. It began on 17 March 1812 and lasted until 7 April.

Close on 5,000 British and Portuguese soldiers were killed during the storming and in consequence, when the city fell, the enraged British soldiers broke into liquor stores and inns and, fuelled by alcohol, went on the rampage. Ignoring their officers and even, by accounts, killing several, they murdered some 4,000 Spanish civilians, butchered many of the French defenders and indulged in mass rape and looting.

Having, uncharacteristically, allowed his men to assuage their fury for around eighteen hours, Wellington finally gave the command to bring the army to account. However, it apparently took around another seventy-two hours before order was completely restored. A good number of British rank and file were flogged as punishment and a gallows was erected, although no one was hanged.

Fitzroy Somerset was, according to some accounts, the first man on top of the parapet and did in fact lead a party to secure the surrender of the city from the Governor. The episode with the Governor's wife and the captive ladies is largely of my invention. Colonel Hulot is also fictional, although he is intended to stand as an example of certain of Napoleon's officers who nurtured sentiments against the Emperor.

Bonaparte had always of course had his enemies at home and the plots against him in 1800 and 1804 were very real.

The plot of the rue Saint-Nicaise, also known as the 'plot of the Machine Infernale', took place in Paris on 24 December 1800. The work of seven Breton royalist Chouans, it involved the crude device of a barrel of gunpowder tied to a cart which was exploded near the Tuileries. Napoleon, passing in his carriage, was shaken but unhurt, although 52 other passers-by were killed and wounded.

Keane's mission to Paris is largely based on similar events which befell the real Colquhoun Grant in 1812. Grant, as always, wearing his British uniform, was captured by French dragoons in April 1812 and his servant Leon was shot. Sent to Marshal Marmont and, something of a celebrity prisoner, Grant was invited to dine with the marshal, who hoped to find out more about Wellington, but was angered by Grant's unwillingness. In prison Grant, aided by Father Patrick Curtis, sent and received secret messages. Ultimately Marmont offered Grant parole but encouraged by his second in command, de la Martinière, he appears to have ordered Grant's execution.

Marmont sent Grant to Paris. But seeing a copy of Marmont's letter to the Parisian authorities, Grant became aware that his death had been arranged. Consequently, he felt no compunction in breaking his parole and contrived to escape.

Aided by Macpherson, Grant passed himself off as an American officer, and infiltrated the salons of Paris, sending intelligence reports to Wellington. He then escaped to England, rejoining the army in Spain in early 1814.

Morillo and Sanchez were genuine guerrilla leaders (see my note in book 1) who established a close relationship with Wellington and his spy network.

Father Patrick Curtis, known also as Don Patrizio Cortes, who was aged 72 in 1812, was indeed a professor at the University of Salamanca and one of Wellington's chief spies in the Peninsula. After the war he was granted a state pension and was appointed Archbishop of Armagh in 1819. He died of cholera in 1832.

The Irish Legion was originally formed as a single battalion intended to lead an invasion of Ireland in 1803 and later expanded to a four-battalion regiment. From 1807 the 2nd battalion served in Spain. It fought with honour at the siege of Astorga and at Fuentes de Onoro.

The 1st battalion fought in the Low Countries at the battle of Flushing in 1809 and the regiment fought against the Russians in the German campaign of 1813.

Macpherson is based on a real character, an aged Jacobite of the same surname, employed by Wellington as a spy, but, in the absence of factual information, I have taken a few liberties with his character and situation.

Fouché was Napoleon's Chief of Police and once again I have tried to tie his character in the book to the truth as depicted by his biographers. He was known to be addicted to gambling and it seems reasonable to assume that he might have attended the gaming houses in the infamous Palais Royal. Although by this time he had fallen from favour with the Emperor and was no longer officially employed as Chief of Police, it was well known that his network of spies and informers was still very much in existence and active in serving his interest.

The essence of Malet's plot is entirely based on truth.

Napoleon's stepson, Eugene de Beauharnais accused Malet of conspiring against the Emperor and the general was imprisoned in France. In 1812, following his wife's entreaties, he was allowed to retire to a sanatorium where he met a number of royalist agents. Although it appears Malet was a republican, rather than a royalist, he was quite prepared to work with the royalists to bring down the Emperor.

Napoleon's absence with the Grande Armée afforded Malet the opportunity to make his move.

At 4 a.m. on 23 October, 1812, Malet escaped from the sanatorium in a general's uniform. He approached Colonel Gabriel Soulier, commandeer of the 10th Cohort of the Garde Nationale and told him that Napoleon had died while on active service in Russia, supporting this claim with forged documents. Soulier, instantly 'promoted' to general by Malet, called out his men and went with Malet to the prison of La Force where they liberated the two disgraced generals Lahorie and Guidal. Malet then sent Lahorie to arrest the Minister of Police; and Guidal, he sent to seize the Minister of War, Henri Clarke, Duc de Feltre, and the Arch-Chancellor, Jean-Jacques de Cambacérès.

The two generals went together to take the latter and placed him in La Force, but in a cataclysmic lack of judgment, they failed to arrest the others.

Lahorie was now created Minister of General Police. At the same time, Malet confronted General Hulin, the commander of the Paris garrison, in his house. The general demanded to see the official papers authorizing his surrender of the seal of office and Malet shot him in the jaw.

Malet then entered the military headquarters opposite Hulin's house and attempted to command Colonel Doucet to join him in the new government. But Doucet was suspicious, however, having seen letters written by Napoleon after the supposed date of his death as announced in Malet's forged papers.

He also thought that he recognized Malet and, once alone with the general, overpowered him. Doucet then ordered the National Guard to return to barracks, released Cambacérès and informed Clarke of the coup.

Malet, Lahorie, and Guidal were tried before a council of war and executed by firing squad on 29 October. Others, including the hapless Colonel Soulier, were shot two days later. Colonel Jean-François Rabbe, commander of the Paris Guard, who had also been tricked, was spared execution.

Paris – the city of light – was, as I have portrayed it, a place of jaw-dropping wonder for most strangers. Napoleon had worked hard on its outward appearance, seeking to transform the old city into a fitting capital for his empire. Much of it though, such as the part-completed Arc de Triomphe with its canvas fakeries, was merely a façade.

The cemeteries of Paris had become horribly overcrowded by the late eighteenth century and that of the Innocents was by far the worst. After a particularly rainy period in the spring of 1780, the cemetery was finally closed as the earth literally began to fall apart. Bodies began to be exhumed and bones moved to the catacombs from 1786.

The church was destroyed in 1787 and the cemetery was scheduled to be replaced by a vegetable market. However, the Revolution intervened and the place was not fully cleared until the end of the empire. During this period it became the refuge of the most dangerous and criminal classes of the city.

The *Fountain of the Nymphs*, erected in 1549 next to the church, was dismantled and rebuilt in what became the new market. Today known as the *Fountain of the Innocents* it stands on what is now the place Joachim-du-Bellay.

The smugglers' tunnels were also real although many of them were made into catacombs and some blocked up. It is a well-documented fact that 185 miles of tunnels still exist today beneath the modern city.